TALK SHOW

MELISSA HARTMAN

Acknowledgments

Special thanks are due:
To Lyn Woodward, for making the book work—to say nothing of the marriage.
To ReBecca Béguin, for editorial direction, exceptional kindness, and relentless advocacy.
To Katherine V. Forrest, for her insight, diligence, and friendship.
To my father and stepmother, Robert and Elisabeth Hartman, and my friend, Judy Wayne-Sigman, for astute revision suggestions and daily infusions of courage.
To Dr. James Ragan, poet, playwright, teacher, and friend, and the faculty and staff of U.S.C.'s professional Writing Program.
To Beth Dingman and Claudia Lamperti, for this opportunity.

TALK SHOW

A novel by

MELISSA HARTMAN

NEW VICTORIA PUBLISHERS
NORWICH, VERMONT

Published by New Victoria Publishers Inc., PO Box 27 Norwich, VT.
05055
A Feminist Literary and Cultural Organization founded in 1976.

1 2 3 4 5   1999 2000 2001 2002 2004
Printed and Bound in Canada

Library of Congress Cataloging-in-Publication Data

Hartman, Melissa, 1961-
    Talk show : a novel / by Melissa Hartman.
      p. cm.
    ISBN 1-892281-04-X
    I. Title.
PS3558. A7126T35   1999
813'.54--dc21   99-25692
                                                       CIP

For Lyn, Best Friend and Most Severe Critic

And in memory of my mother

ONE

Alone at the mahogany conference table I sorted through the memorabilia of my mother's long career, shivering in my thin polo shirt and well-washed jeans. The room had been closed off all night with the air conditioning blasting. Record promos, publicity photos, concert reviews, articles: I handled them tentatively at first, my fingers stiff with cold. I hadn't looked at the stuff since sealing it up more than a year ago. This morning I'd loaded the three cardboard file boxes labeled MOM into the car, dreading the work ahead of me.

I lingered now over every word, studied each photo—both fascinated and repelled by the varieties of expression my mother had invented for the public. Accentuating the addict-chic vulnerability that came so naturally to her, bruised eyes simulated by heavy make-up. Smirking at anyone who dared respond to her invitation to violate her privacy. A wholesome California girl, a back-alley bitch, a menacingly raspy voice unleashing the subconscious of every adolescent wannabe sexual predator.

Before long I was drained, though I felt obliged to look busy: my aunt Jane might pop in at any moment. She'd told me to report for my first day's work on *The Jane Wilde Show* at eight sharp—with the boxes—so we could spend the hour before the production meeting together. In typical star fashion she was running late.

The best is always worth waiting for...so they never mind waiting for me—my mother's credo. I leafed through a concert program. She was your basic rockstar poseur: a leather dominatrix wrenching the strings of her phallic guitar to jerk off the crowd, diving thoughtlessly into the roiling mosh pit, riding transcendent on a cherry-picker above the upswept faces...

I pressed on. A photo shoot of the last tour. The opening band

5

scattering backstage at the Astrodome, taking cover from a hail of garbage and insults. My body pulsates with the audience's rhythmic chant: Gi-na! Gi-na! Gi-na! Their need nauseates me. They crave a shot of self-destruction, vicarious access to a basic impulse they're too afraid to seek in themselves. Because she doesn't share that fear—and always pays the price for her lack of self-preservation—she makes them wait. Ten minutes, twenty, forty. She sips a Perrier and vocalizes softly to herself. Her face, in three-quarters' profile, keeps something from me that only the spotlight will reveal.

The crowd's anticipation breaks in deafening waves of sound, halted abruptly by a collective gasp when the arena goes completely dark. Seconds crawl by.

The announcer's voice booms over the PA, "Ladies and gentlemen, the moment you have all been waiting for!" He pauses. Gratifying screams, spine-chilling cheers. Hollis, her drummer and occasional fuckbuddy, begins a roll that quickly picks up speed and volume. "And now...Houston, Texas...give a big Lone Star welcome...to Capitol Records' recording artist...MISS GEE-NAH WILDE!"

Dressed in black leather from her oversized Stetson to fringed vest and chaps, my mother blows me a kiss, whispers "Be good while I'm gone, Nita," and races past me to work the crowd. No backward glance. She's on. Eighty thousand strangers quiet. The band smashes into the thundering chords of "Rush," her trademark opening number:

> You tell yourself you do it!
> To prove you hardly need it!
> Or because it makes sex better!
> Or it's just a lousy habit!

By the second line, the audience is singing along with her. She lets them finish the last chorus by themselves:

> You never let yourself believe
> It's the rush you're after
> The high means more than love
> Or pride or hope or laughter...

The drummer hits the end beat; the stage goes dark again. My mother's miked voice blazes across the black: "Good evening Houston Texas!" The lights come back up and she takes a deep bow, her blonde hair falling forward. She stands, radiating satisfaction, and I turn away, heading for her dressing room, where I'll curl up on the couch, watch TV, and wait it out.

Her triumph, I know, goes beyond a mastery of the audience's response. She's sober. Being onstage is the one inviolable time, a reward for the crowd. Shows start with 'Rush' because it's her personal favorite. Written in the hospital while she recovered from an O.D., the song's immense popularity was a sign for her that although sobriety ultimately might be out of reach, honesty counted for something. And I guess it did, with people who never knew her, who now think she's even more glamorous because drugs and alcohol took her life—

The conference room's heavy door slammed back against the wall as my aunt Jane burst in. A small woman whose intensity lends her a good deal of stature, she always makes an entrance. Her golden hair, expressive eyes, and delicate bone structure come together in a face made for the camera, and right now her tendency to behave as though she were perpetually in front of one annoyed me. Something about my expression made her eyes narrow. "How's my favorite niece this morning?"

Her tone was commanding, adoring. I managed to recite my routine response to this tag she had assigned me long ago: "I'm your only niece."

She held out her arms and I went to her, let myself feel the comfort of her embrace. "You're ice cold, baby!" Rubbing my hands between hers, she called through the open door to her long-time secretary, "Victoria, turn off the damn air! It's a friggin' morgue in here. And bring us some coffee." She tossed her purse onto the table. "Please!" came as an afterthought. I cringed at her imperiousness, even though I knew her people were used to it.

We sat side-by-side. "So, Nita, how far did you get?"

Jane had never made it clear what exactly we were supposed to be doing with all these mementos, but it didn't seem wise to mention this now. "Not too far."

She glanced down at the open concert program: my mother lying onstage on her back, neck arched, looking ready to give the microphone she held to her lips a blow job. "Hmm…I can see how one could get sidetracked." She sounded disapproving, and when my eyes met hers she gave a shudder of distaste, snapping shut the program. It made me giggle. "Well, it takes all kinds, Nita, not just our kind. Any-hoo, let's get some of this crap into chronological order so we can see what we can use for the show."

Crap? Didn't she realize this was pretty much all I had left of my mother? I convinced myself I was being too sensitive. This project would be difficult enough without going nuts about little things.

We'd scarcely begun to separate the items when the phone rang and Victoria's Boston accent breezed over the intercom. "Line four, Jane, PFLAG co-chair wants you to emcee their annual bash. Will you pick up?"

Jane reached for the receiver. "Hey Harriet, can it be meet-the-queer night again already?"

I remembered how three years ago, at the age of eighteen, I had come out to my openly-gay aunt. Actually, she was the one who had noticed my sudden interest in a friend of my mother's, twice my age, and correctly interpreted it as romantic. Jane had taken me to lunch at Masa Sushi, my favorite restaurant, and, after stuffing me full of spicy tuna rolls and yellowtail and salmon, made me drop my chopsticks when she leaned across the littered table, arched an eyebrow, and popped the big question, "Now what's all the frou-frou over Julia?"

While she carried on her phone conversation, I separated maga-zine and newspaper articles from photos and promo materials. What brilliant publicist had got my mother on the cover of *People*—"At Home with Gina Wilde: Off Drugs and Back on Track?" Heck, the magazine could've saved a bundle by running that one a couple of times a year. Most of the articles I'd collected were reviews of her albums and live performances—but then I picked up one I had absolutely no recall of clipping: "Rocker Gina Wilde Found Dead by Distraught Daughter." That night when reporters caught up to me and Jane—and Julia—at the hospital's private exit as we tried to elude them, I'd felt like a hunted animal.

I glanced at my aunt still on the phone, crumpled the page, and slipped it into my jeans pocket. I didn't want her staff to see it. Terrified that something else exposing me at my worst hour might be lurking there, I tore through the rest of the articles. A cursory flip through perhaps fifty pages yielded nothing, and I began to calm down. Victoria appeared at the doorway, the smile on her face serving to prop up her lips.

Jane banged down the receiver. "Hold all other calls, Vic, even if it's God the sponsor herself." The woman set down the steaming cups and turned to go. "And thank you!"

I glanced up at the wall clock. Only a few minutes before the start of the meeting at nine.

Jane followed my gaze. "Nita, I'm sorry I'm late. I planned to be here early to make sure you're okay with these shows on your mother, but one of the assistant directors managed to catch me at home on the phone, and by the time I left...well, you know. I meant to call you from the car to tell you I was running late, but he called me back as soon as I got on the road."

Whatever.

The pictures on the table in front of me slowly kaleidoscoped in my vision, fragmenting into meaningless, though pretty, colors and patterns. A hand came down heavily on my shoulder. I refocused. "Sweetie, there's still time to say no—right now, right this very minute. Or tomorrow. Anytime."

She'd assured me of this enough times that I was ready to believe her, but also realized each passing moment tacitly sealed my approval. She looked at me expectantly.

"I appreciate that," was all I said, while inside me a disgusting, panicky voice whimpered, She should know it's not okay, but she doesn't!

Jane continued, "I hate the negative publicity surrounding her death, and I've waited a respectable eighteen months to go ahead with this project. Your mother worked too long and too hard—and had too much talent—just to provide grist for the rumor mill." She paused, gave me a look, then focused again on the papers in front of us. "And I do think you'll get something out of working on it with me. It'll help you put closure on this, to heal."

It was a nice idea, anyway. Even after we'd talked it into the ground, I wasn't certain we were doing the right thing—televising an inquiry into my mother's death.

Jane's motivations were sure to be misunderstood, and the tabloids would have a field day: "Jane Wilde's No-Holds-Barred Ratings Bid," "Singer's Suicide Crowns Jane Sleaze Queen," "Plea by Sister's Ghost to Gay Talk Show Host: Get Back in the Closet!"

One thing I know about my aunt, when she gets an idea in her head there's no stopping her. I'm not willing to have the project go forward without me, so I have no choice but to get on board.

The clock struck nine. Jane's top guns began to file in, four women and one man whose banter and body language made them a seemingly impenetrable unit. Jane gave me a wink and a thumb's-up, which I returned lamely, not meaning it.

Did I really want to work here for a whole year?

When everyone had been seated, Jane began rapid-fire, "As usual, we're short on time, so let's get straight to it. The season opener—one week, five shows. First segment, hook our audience, make them care. We start with my sister's career highlights, the Gina the audience knew, then move on to the one they didn't. We'll cover the last tour, the new album. And then," she went on in a more moderate tone, "her final days. The circumstances of her death. The police investigation, pathology report. What her passing did to our family. Why we don't buy the idea of suicide—why an O.D. makes more sense, even if barely. Now the audience knows Gina as a person, and they'll mourn her loss on that level. Next, phase two. The media character assassination. We pick up on some features and nail them on their inconsistencies."

Again I was offended, listening to Jane cast her own sister's story in terms of selling it to an audience—and, worse, to sponsors. Privately, she'd come at it from a different angle: stopping the rumors and clearing the air. How using our frustration to fight back might make us both feel better. Her all-business approach now was an eye-opener.

She glanced at me, and I wondered whether she had any idea of the impact of her words. "You'll recall from my memo last week that my niece, Nita, has joined our staff as a production assistant." She paused, and to my embarrassment, everyone applauded—three quick claps, to be exact—but then I realized from their expressions this was something they did routinely to show the requisite approval, no big deal.

Jane continued in a formal tone, "Together we've discussed the feasibility of this project, its potential benefit to us and to our audience, and we've decided to green-light it despite the personal challenges that lie ahead. Of course Nita's insight into her mother's private life and struggles will be invaluable as we build our series of shows."

Even after all her assurances, the idea of sharing any personal information with this group seemed distasteful, somehow compromising. Conscious of the balled-up newspaper article in my pocket, I tried to convince myself that once I got to know them, it might not be so bad. I stared at my hands, steepled them, watched my fingers collapse and intertwine. I was having a hard time believing me. When I looked up, people glanced nervously away.

"We have two goals." Jane jabbed the tabletop with her pen for emphasis. "One, find out what really happened to Gina Wilde. Two, take a shot at the tabloids. There's a growing campaign against what's been called the 'media-ocracy' and we belong in the fight." She paused and glanced around the table. "In case you're thinking otherwise, I have no illusions. The person in line at the checkout will still plunk down a dollar twenty-nine to be entertained while sitting on the can." She turned to her executive producer. "So what do you say, General?"

Tonia Talbot, deep in thought, snapped to full attention. "I got lost in the beauty of the image." Everyone snickered. One of a handful of African-American women to break through the industry's glass ceiling, she had met Jane more than ten years ago on a network news soundstage in Manhattan. Tonia had a take-charge attitude I found reassuring, no doubt a result of that crank-it-out Big-Apple production experience. She nodded at the senior associate producer, the beads on her long, delicate braids clicking softly together. "Linda, your people will dig up everything on the major tabloids—appeal, market, especially methods." The diminutive, stylishly-dressed woman began scribbling notes. Her nails were impeccably polished, yet I noticed that her fingers were tobacco-stained. "Get to their fact-checkers and the people in charge. This will be very time-consuming, very expensive. Run what you plan to use by me—"

Several people finished the sentence for her. "For budget." They laughed.

Tonia made a face. "Good, after five years you finally know the drill." She turned to another associate producer, a balding man with a ponytail, wispy mustache and goatee, who had relaxed comfortably into his conference chair, seemingly ready to hit whatever was pitched to him. "Bob, get your staff out on the street. Ask people who read this junk to tell you how much of it they believe. Draft a survey for our studio audience."

He snapped his fingers and pointed to her. "Not a problem, Tone."

Oh, gak!

Tonia continued down the line to a woman who looked a little older than me, with a lavish sweep of chestnut hair that turned her into a Miss Clairol candidate, and lively, intelligent eyes that hinted she'd be overqualified for the job. "Allie, be our bloodhound. Find us our tabloid tales. Bring me the whole bunch of bananas, I'll kick a couple back to you to outline for the show."

"Do I tend toward the garden variety misrepresentation or the shameless whopper?"

Jane grinned. "Paint the spectrum, Ms. Glass. No matter what we do, the media dogs are going to bite back. Just keep in mind we can't afford to be dragged through litigation, of course. Everything we go with must have Sammy's okay."

Samantha Diaz, my aunt's lover, is an entertainment lawyer, the show's legal consultant, which mainly entails playing Border Collie to Jane's mad sheep act.

To the remaining assistant, a woman with a scowl etched so deeply into her face that I doubted surgery could have removed it, Tonia directed, "Karen, your staff will produce Gina's bio and background. Do highlights, a chronology."

Ms. Congeniality glared at Tonia. I thought she was going to object or something, but all she said was, "Sure."

Jane ran a hand over the materials in front of her. "Thanks to Nita, undoubtedly her mom's biggest fan—"

I could have strangled her.

"—here are some photos and promos you'll find useful. I can also get you old home movies and maybe letters, but proceed with caution! We're going to do reality TV like it's never been done before. If it comes crashing down, it'll be on my head. Understand I'm going to have my say about what goes for this—and especially what doesn't go. I'm expecting Nita to be a real help in this area." She sent me a look, and I nodded, hopefully disguising my outrage. She could go right ahead and turn over her letters if she wanted to, but fuck if I was giving up anything that personal of mine.

Then Tonia asked what I'd been wondering. "Speaking of Nita, do you have a permanent place for her in mind, Janie, or is she going to rotate through the A.P.'s?"

A.P.'s are associate or assistant producers. They're also referred to, not nicely, as 'ass prods.' There's some truth in that as a job description.

"Since she'll help Karen in preparing the bio…"

The scowl kicked up a few notches, and I sensed anything but an eagerness to Babysit The Niece.

Just then one of the others—Allie—caught my eye with a look I couldn't quite place. "May I make a suggestion? Lend Nita to Karen on a consulting basis, but let her work with me on my assignment. She'll get a sense of what research is about, and, no disrespect intended, I think I've been sans staff long enough."

Maybe she was only asking for her own purposes, but being wanted, for whatever reason, was preferable to being tolerated. When Jane agreed to the idea, Allie gave me an encouraging wink that put me on the defensive. How badly might this chick want the big inside pooper-scoop on Gina Wilde, winning my confidence and walking away?

I'd had enough of that, the kids who'd wanted to hang out at my house so they could brag about it later. Mom's business manager, Carly—after ten years of invitations to Disneyland and Magic Mountain with her own daughters, Christmas shopping and baking holiday cookies together, I really believed her when she said, "You're part of the family, Nita." At the funeral… "Remember, I'm your second mom." Then she wouldn't take my calls.

Tonia adjourned the meeting, and I followed Allie out.

"Let's go to my broom closet—I mean office," she said. "It's so small, we'll have to take turns breathing."

The room was tiny, and windowless, but she had added a few touches to personalize it, including a Japanese print of a cresting tsunami. I went over to get a closer look.

"That's symbolic of the way they throw the work at you." Allie smiled, patting the folding chair next to her. "This will have to do for now. We'll track down a desk for you later."

13

Resisting an impulse to remain standing, I took the seat she offered. What the hell, it gave me a chance to check her out. There was a lot I'd missed at first glance: the slight upsweep of her chestnut hair before it cascaded to her shoulders, the fragile hollows at her temples, the set of her finely drawn nose, the line of her jaw. My gaze traveled from her delicate neck to her collarbone, to her knit blouse, the stripes of white and pistachio sheltering the gentle swell of her breasts—

I thanked her for seeking out my assistance, to see what her response would be.

Her expression was open and friendly. "You're quite welcome, but understand I did it for me."

She was playing with my expectations, but why?

She continued, "I need the help."

Help with exactly what? She had to know right away that I wasn't just an easy touch. "I don't know very much about the business, I'm not sure how helpful I can be."

"Are you trying to talk your way out of the job?" She cocked her head to one side. The pose suited her.

"No, just being honest. Maybe that's why Karen didn't want my help."

Allie grimaced, her lips turning up at one corner as she slowly shook her head. "Hey, don't you know Karen is an Eskimo word for ice? The woman doesn't like anybody. I'm sure she'll make some sort of backstabbing remark about how I took you from her, but, after all, being backstabbed is a genuine measure of success in L.A.," she said blithely.

I considered her sarcasm for a moment. She seemed more tolerant of the Hollywood crapola than I expected from someone of her intelligence. "Despite that, L.A.'s your place?"

She shrugged. "Can you control what makes you happy?"

I caught her drift.

Leaning back in her chair, she asked, "So, if this isn't your idea of a good time, what is? Knowing how your aunt feels about you, she'd want you to enjoy what you're doing."

I didn't feel like getting into the issue too deeply, and certainly not with this stranger. "I thought I'd work for a year before going on to graduate school, but I had nothing in particular lined up. She offered me the job. I took it."

"Well, that sounds right."

I knew she wanted more, though I wasn't obliged to give it. Checking my impulse to be snippy, I replied with as much sincerity as I could muster, "When this project was proposed, I wasn't too thrilled. But I'm beginning to understand why it should be done. Jane thinks if I'm in on it, I'll feel better."

"Okay, how do you feel now?" She glanced at her watch. "You've been in on it officially for half an hour."

I felt a sudden flash of annoyance. It takes more than a butter knife to cut through my bullshit. Who did she think she was? "What's your point?"

She sat up, leaned closer to me. I caught a whiff of Nina Ricci, my mother's favorite scent, and drew back. "My point is, do things for yourself, not for anyone else. Be here because you want to, because you can learn something—about your mom, about yourself. Otherwise there's no reason to do it."

The truth of what she'd said dissolved my resentment. "That's a good point." I rubbed an imaginary spot on the desk in front of me.

She continued, "Jane wants you to be comfortable here. She wouldn't do anything to make you feel otherwise."

I debated for an instant whether to reveal the terms of the understanding I had with my aunt, but figured Allie should know. And maybe if I said it out loud, there was some chance I really would begin to believe it. I tried to sound unassuming. "Jane and Tonia promised to kill the project if I'm not happy with it."

Allie's eyes widened in surprise. I wondered what she was thinking—how naive I was to believe that the executive producer, by profession a tightwad, would sink an enormous bundle into the enterprise and then merrily agree to my veto. Or maybe that it was incredibly inappropriate to have given me this authority, something I might act on if my coffee was brought to me cold, or I had P.M.S. But instead what Allie said was completely unexpected and oddly reassuring, given what I suspected might be the underlying nature of her character.

"It's none of my business really—but that sounds right to me."

TWO

At eight that evening, I approached the cavernous glass and white marble lobby of the Wilshire Park Terrace. The middle-aged doorman suspiciously eyed me and the bunch of flowers I carried. Before he could point to the delivery entrance, I gave my name and asked him to call apartment 20-D. His manner changed. "Ms. Reynolds said to send you right up."

I proceeded to the elevator bank, past potted palms and birds-of-paradise forever captive in this fortress, feeling ill-at-ease as the elevator doors closed me in. The vestige of an anxiety-filled day. Calling Julia had been instinctual. I didn't expect her to calm me down, but the familiarity of her brand of crazy seemed as comforting as the old Nikes I'd worn throughout college.

When the elevator opened on the twentieth floor, Julia was standing in the doorway of her apartment. She wore tight black pants and a black silk shirt, unbuttoned to the top of her breasts. Her features were the same perfect sculpture, her shoulder-length hair just a shade darker than the last time I'd seen her. Cranberry-colored lipstick accentuated the fullness of her lips, set now in a smile that widened as our eyes met. She closed the door behind us. I exhaled slowly, then drew what felt like the first real breath of the day.

The living room, with its white carpet and white Italian leather sofa, was softly illuminated by ceiling track lights; one wall was consumed by a picture window that looked out over Westwood and the U.C.L.A. campus. Opposite, above the sofa, was the Andy Warhol lithograph of Julia herself, in shades of yellow, lime green, and fuchsia; on either side, a gold record—her own. But Julia Reynolds' brush with fame had all but faded. As lead singer of the popular but short-lived early-eighties punk band Diva, she'd been unable to make the transition after the fad's heyday, and her career died. Thanks to judicious investments she didn't have to work. Her days were spent at the gym, doing volunteer work, shopping. Evenings were for charity events, concerts. Or someone like me.

I had six cream-colored roses for her, her favorite, and she lifted the bouquet to her face. "It's been a long time since you brought me flowers." She studied me for a moment. "Come to think of it, Neet, it's been a while since you brought me you."

"It's good to see you, too, Julia."

Her tone was theatrical. "Then what is the point of standing even an inch apart from me, darling? Or have you forgotten how to kiss?"

I went to her, because that's what I was there for, but I wished she'd drop the needy and demanding routine. Julia has seen me through so many crises—my mother's DUI's, checking her in and out of Betty Ford, the night she died—I owe her more than I can ever repay. That aside, when she's not saving the day, she can be hell to deal with.

I put my hand in the softness of her hair. Her lips were both familiar and exciting, and I enjoyed her in my arms again.

When we broke the kiss, the self-assured, understanding Julia had returned. "Why don't we take care of a few civilized matters first, like putting these flowers in water and having a glass of wine?" My eye fell on the bar counter, where a bottle was kept chilled in a silver ice bucket.

I followed her into the kitchen. Taller by several inches, I could more easily reach a vase from the cabinet above the refrigerator. Not the best place to keep crystal in earthquake country, but denial, for Julia, is a prerequisite to existence.

In the living room, she opened the wine, poured two glasses, and joined me on the couch. "So what are you doing with yourself this summer, Ms. U.C.L.A. graduate-with-honors?"

I wondered what she would say when I told her. Jane and Julia had been acquainted for years, but they had never been friends. Starfly that she was, Julia went out of her way to be cordial to Jane at any occasion of their meeting, but my aunt kept her distance. She tolerated Julia because of the kindness she had shown me, but it was plain the eighteen years Julia had on me rankled my aunt to the core.

17

"I'm working for Jane."

Julia did a double-take. "You're what? Don't tell me you finally got bitten by the 'biz bug."

"No, I just didn't know what to do with myself. I had a lot of nervous energy to use up after school ended."

She grinned. "That's when you come see Julia, darling."

I took her hand. "And so I did."

"Tell me about this new endeavor of yours, then, before we take care of your nervous energy."

As I described the project, she tensed. "Your aunt's taking a real risk. Breaking the rules by dragging her life in front of the camera. Your life, too."

Her tone was emotional, but I discounted it, knowing her propensity for melodrama. "You don't think it's worthwhile?"

She played with my fingers, stroking them, interlacing them with her own. "If it works—maybe. If it doesn't..." Her eyes met mine. "You could get hurt either way. Nita, your mother was a lovely and talented woman, but in the last few years—her problems came like a torpedo straight at you. It took all your strength simply to get out of the way. Why go back in the water now?"

"There's too much I don't understand about her death. Remember that book I told you about? *Making Sense of Suicide?* There's always a sign, always. She didn't give us one single clue. Why commit suicide when everything was going right—including being sober? She wasn't using, I could tell. One hello on the telephone, I'd know."

Growing up, I'd felt a sense of pride being such a good detective. Now I understood the extent to which I'd been caught up in her addiction, and I resented having developed those skills for day-to-day survival.

"I could tell, too, or so I thought." Julia shook her head musingly before continuing, "I knew your mother eighteen years. I hate to say this, but the only certain thing about her was her inconsistency. She could start using again like that." She snapped her fingers. "Of course, this time she was clean almost a year. That's why it's so hard to believe she relapsed."

"So you think she probably just wanted to get high, that she didn't try to kill herself?"

Julia tossed her head impatiently, as if my idea of her as some kind of authority on self-destruction was a lasso she had to slip off before it got too tight. "Nita, I prefer to think your mother just wanted to get high, but who knows?"

"Well, you were there from the beginning. You saw her using more and more. She didn't hide from you like she did from Jane. You were friends."

"True, I was there, but remember I never did drugs. I wasn't privy to precisely what she was doing when and with whom."

"What if I just don't want to believe she could kill herself?" This possibility had been bothering me ever since my analyst, Joseph, mentioned it during last Thursday's session. After today, I was afraid someone at the studio might confront me with the idea—Allie, maybe. "Am I being egotistical to think she wouldn't have done this to me on purpose?"

Julia frowned. "Not egotistical, but it's wrong to think your presence in her life might have prevented her suicide. All that matters to someone so ill is herself. I've said this before, and I won't let up until you get it through that thick head of yours, but unless there's a scalpel or a gun in your hand, you can't make a person live, and you can't make her die."

I looked away, concentrating on the bottle of wine sweating in the bucket of ice. I pointed my index finger toward it, cocked an imaginary hammer, and pulled the trigger. "Bang."

Julia leaned closer. "Finding out whether it was suicide or not won't bring her back. Of course you miss her, despite all she put you through." She sighed. "I haven't forgiven her."

"I'm the one who has to do that." I sat up straight.

"Right you are," she said softly. "And as for the tabloids, I'm a great believer in 'words will never hurt me.'"

I drained my wine in a few swallows. "Jules, I want to know what really happened. Then maybe I can stop thinking about it." I went to the bar, refilled my glass. In my head I heard a refrain of Allie's words earlier: Do things for yourself, not anyone else. Something can be learned—about your mom, yourself.

Julia stood and crossed the room. She laid a hand on my shoulder. "Find yourself some peace of mind, Nita. At the very least, everyone deserves that."

Several hours later, I lay wide awake, Julia a dead weight in my arms. Sex has a soporific effect on me as well, but tonight sleep seemed out of the question.

There really was no escaping the sense of uneasiness chasing me. Being with Julia again was a temporary comfort. It reminded me of the times I'd lain in this bed, staring out into the night sky at the few stars not obliterated by the lights of the city, content as I never was elsewhere, with this beautiful, entertaining woman beside me.

The first time I had been to Julia's was a few weeks after my seventeenth birthday. My mother had O.D.ed and been taken by ambulance to U.C.L.A. Medical Center. Although this wasn't the first time she'd been carted away to the emergency room, I was still scared out of my mind. I'd driven there with her current boyfriend, but shortly after we arrived he'd taken off. Jane and Sam were on vacation somewhere, so I called the person who lived closest to the hospital: my mother's friend Julia.

She arrived in minutes, looked briefly at the patient out cold in the hospital bed, and took me to get a bite to eat. I had been told by this time that my mother would recover, and my relief had slowly boiled into anger. Julia sensed my reluctance to go home, inviting me back to her place with, "How does a mindless movie and a pint of Häagen-Dazs sound?"

My immediate problems faded as the elevator ascended to the twentieth floor. We watched videos until two or three in the morning, when my eyes began to close, and she gave me a pair of pajamas to change into, small for me, but I made do.

As she offered me the guest bedroom, a wave of loneliness overwhelmed me—no, more than that, a sense of being utterly alone. Evidently my expression betrayed me, because without another word she put an arm around me and we went to her room.

After the lights were out she moved close, and I fell asleep with my head on her shoulder, a solid, dreamless slumber. I woke to her welcoming smile, the sun streaming in through the window, and a feeling of well-being that made the previous night's events not seem quite so dismal.

I've been aware of my attraction to women since the age of four or five. My identity is apparent to those who have a stake in knowing, and Julia's sexual orientation hadn't been a secret in our household. We'd never discussed the common thread running through both our lives, and there was no need to during the week I stayed with her.

We slipped into a daily routine that was, for me, very reassuring. She drove me to school, picked me up when it was over, asked about my day, filled me in about hers. I did my homework at her dining table. We went out for meals or had food delivered. After an evening of watching videos or reading, we slept together in her bed, my head on her shoulder. She expressed no romantic interest whatsoever, nor made any advances—contrary to what my aunt will go to her grave believing. Julia was simply a friend when I needed one.

When my mother was released, chastened, we went back home to Brentwood. She would take time off work, we would travel, she would make it up to me. Of course there was no way to 'make up' the week she had caused us to lose. She just didn't get it. I waited a few days for an acknowledgement that the extent of her problem now warranted some plan of action, but none came. At least she stayed sober, which was a major deal, since she'd been using daily for years.

One evening as I went into the kitchen for something to fortify me for a grueling stretch of calculus, I met her coming out, wearing only an oversized man-tailored shirt buttoned wrong, Bud Lite in hand. I was incredulous.

"What?" she said.

I went back to Julia's. It was the middle of the night and I was mindful she might have someone there with her—someone who may have been kept away on my account. I realized I should call, but instead got in my Wrangler and drove directly to her building. It's too easy to be reasoned with over the telephone, to be diverted from your purpose.

Gorgeous in jade silk pajamas, Julia appeared surprised to see me, but nevertheless welcomed me in. When I told her my mother was drinking, she said I could stay, but only if I called to report my whereabouts, something I submitted to after an unforgettable display of petulance: Why should I, when she doesn't care enough to make me not worry about her!

My mother was defensive, claiming that had been her first drink. She swore she'd put it back in the refrigerator after seeing how upset it made me. She did sound sober.

"Oh Mom, what do you mean, it's only beer? Jesus Effing Christ, how could you start drinking again after what you put us through? You're not supposed to put it back—dump it down the drain! You're just too stupid to get it, and maybe you never will!"

I slammed down the receiver. I wanted to trust her, and believed her word was likely good for that night. But not in the long run: I had to face it. For the first time in my life I actually believed things would never get better.

Julia offered to go back with me to the house to confront her and try to get her into treatment, but I was too angry. It was something we did later, several times over the years, but not that night.

We watched a movie. I composed myself. As it ended, a resolve stole over me. From now on my life would not be merely a function of my mother's. Screw her and her drinking and my worries. Going to Julia's was not so much an escape from my problems, but a move toward something I'd waited a lifetime to experience.

I turned to Julia and kissed her on the lips.

It took her a moment to respond, but when she did—take it from someone who had spent an entire adolescence fantasizing how it would feel to kiss a woman for the first time—it was exciting beyond anything I had ever imagined.

Her lips were at first soft and full, and then they slid to a wet tautness across my mouth. Her tongue stroked and tugged at mine, sensations I also experienced at my groin. When she breathed into my mouth, I slowly released my breath, realizing I'd been holding it far too long.

Then she broke the kiss, pushing me away.

"Oh my God, what just happened?" She jumped up and stood there quivering, wiped her mouth with the back of her hand. Shocked, I remained where I was, the tremors of my excitement dying away. "Nita, I'm sorry, oh my God! Things got way, way out of hand. Please—your mother! You have to promise, don't tell! Oh God!"

She was so hysterical, I said whatever I could think of to calm her. "I kissed you, and you kissed me back. There's nothing wrong. I liked it, you liked it. You liked it, I could tell." I got up, approached her.

She backed away, her eyes wide. "Stop! You—stay there! Like it!

I did not! You just took me by surprise, is all. And it's been a couple of months since—oh my God, why am I telling you this?"

I took a step closer, bold with the irrefutable evidence of her passionate kiss. "You're saying whatever comes to mind, and none of it is true, except maybe you haven't been with anybody in a while." She kind of winced. "I kissed you, Julia, and you liked it, admit it—"

"Stop saying that! Jesus!"

"Kiss me again."

She looked indignant. "I will not."

"Kiss me again," I leaned closer, got right up in her face. "Or I'll tell!"

"You won't!" She was almost shouting.

"How can you be so sure?"

"Because you're too fucking nice to tell on anybody!"

Glaring at each other, faces inches apart—we burst out laughing. For maybe a minute I laughed, until tears came to my eyes.

"This is—so absurd!" she gasped. "Like a...scene from...a Neil...Simon play!"

As soon as she got her breath, I kissed her. She resisted briefly, then responded even more fervently than before. "N-N-Nita! Stop this!" Again she pushed me away. "Right now, that's enough! This isn't funny anymore, I'm afraid I'm going to have to ask you to—"

We both cracked up again.

"Whew!" she huffed, rubbing her eyes. "I'm really going to need therapy after this!"

Not really conscious of what I was about to do, I took her hand, then dropped to one knee before her. Startled, she opened her mouth, then shut it without saying a word. Looking up, I said, "I think you're the most beautiful woman I've ever met, and one of the nicest. Whatever you tell me to do, I'll do."

She blinked a couple of times, then closed her eyes, took a deep breath. Heart pounding, I waited to hear my fate.

When she regarded me again, I couldn't read her expression. "Get up," she said, and holding me by the hand, started to lead me—to the bedroom.

I had slept there for a week, in a kind of haze of safety and comfort, but now felt I was seeing it for the first time: the massive bed topped by a white satin spread that spilled onto the floor, the fabric gathered into plump, shiny scallops that just barely reached the thick black carpeting. Fat cut-glass perfume bottles filled with amber liquid on top of a white-painted chiffonier. Above it, the oval mirror reflect-ed...our embrace.

"This is my first time," I said, so she would understand my awk-wardness.

Julia brought a finger to my lips. She dimmed the lights, and the city beneath us shimmered in the windows. The satin spread was cool against my skin, a contrast to the warm fullness of her body in my arms. Kissing me, she opened her silk top and guided my hands to her breasts, heavy and soft, nipples tensing at my touch. My instinct was to have her breasts against mine, and I was contemplating exactly how to remove my shirt without taking my hands from her, when she drew it over my head, sighing as our bodies met.

Minutes later, completely nude, I snaked a thigh between hers, and she rode sinuously. I waited until I felt a gentle brush of wetness, and then I put my hand on her, searching for the exact boundary of inti-macy, where one skin ended and the other began.

She pressed against my fingers, her movements both guided by mine and guiding mine. Within moments her breathing changed sub-tly, growing rapid and shallow, her grip tightening on my shoulder.

When she drew all her breath inside herself and held it, I under-stood what would happen next: she shuddered, and waves of pleasure washed over her face. I almost came, too.

She smiled through half-closed eyes, and reached for me immedi-ately, willing me to open my thighs, touching me confidently with her long, slender fingers. There was nothing I could do except open myself fully, give myself fully to the gratification she offered. Her initial gen-tleness was deceptive, her true nature quickly asserting itself: she was ruthless, relentless, bent on her goal. She created cravings, extin-guished them, brought them to life once more, driving the threshold of my pleasure higher and higher.

I arched against her, and she held me tight and kissed me. When I finally opened my eyes, she smiled and smoothed my hair over my forehead. "Did you like that, lover?"

Lover. I turned the word over in my mind. Lover! Look at me. I finally joined the human race...

When Julia woke me the next morning, she was fully dressed in a skirt and halter top. I sat up, holding the blanket to my breasts. My first thought was that my mother had landed in the hospital again, or God forbid—"What's wrong?"

"Nita, about last night..." She wouldn't meet my gaze. "It should never have happened. I'm sorry."

Not this again. "But—"

"I may have been out of my mind last night, but this morning I'm stark raving sane!"

I started to say something more, but she held up a hand. "Don't even try. There's nothing you can say, absolutely nothing will change the way I feel now."

The words tore through me, sounding so final I knew she wouldn't listen no matter what I said. I turned away from her, my heart pounding. I thought I would choke, afraid I might cry and she'd see.

"You were upset and you came to me for help. I betrayed your trust. I'm more disappointed in myself than I can say."

Who was this Girl Scout? What possibly could have brought on such a radical change of heart?

"I'm very sorry. I hope you'll forgive me."

Forgive her? Okay, for her no big deal, but for me... "It's not fair!" My voice broke, and I cursed myself for not being able to hold back my tears.

"Nita—" I felt her hand on my shoulder and I jerked away. "Oh, hell." She moved closer, sending me to the edge of the bed, and then put an arm around me, tried to reel me in. "Please, darling, please don't cry."

I wanted to block the scent of her skin, her hair, the rose-scented soap, the slight acridity of hairspray. "Why are you doing this?" I whispered.

"People make mistakes... Big ones. I hope you'll accept my apology, and we can stay friends."

Not that line. I was beside myself. "That's it? You made a mistake?" I started to get angry. "You'll never catch me making such big mistakes!"

She sighed. "My mistakes seem to get bigger as I get older."

Patting my back, she sat up, her breasts pressing against me as she left my side. "Why don't you get dressed now? We can get some breakfast if you'd like."

She went out and shut the door. I grabbed my clothes and headed for the bathroom, feeling like a gutted fish. I stared at my face in the bathroom mirror, still slightly steamy from her shower. Typical butch, L.A.-style: blonde hair layered short, slightly hooked nose, dimpled chin, a smattering of freckles across my face. I still looked like me, but behind those eyes was a whole different person. In the past twelve hours I had known such happiness that its loss was unendurably cruel. I had made love—had sex—with a gorgeous, desirable woman whom I now loathed.

The counter beside the sink was cluttered with tubes of lipstick, bottles of nail polish, and jars of makeup. I felt like smashing them. The hairdryer, curling irons of every shape and size, hot rollers, hairbrushes—all begged to be swept to the floor. Her things insinuated the intimacy I'd so briefly had access to. I splashed water on my face, passed a hand through my hair, threw on my clothes without showering.

She looked up from the couch when I came out. "That was fast." She stood. "I'll just grab my purse, and we'll go."

Fuck if I'd spend another second in her presence. I was already halfway to the vestibule when she started toward the bedroom. I let myself out of the apartment, quietly closed the door, and bolted for the stairs.

I ran down the entire twenty floors like a prisoner on a breakout. Winded, legs shaking, I hit the garage, started my car, and peeled out onto Wilshire Boulevard, heading back to Brentwood.

I'll never understand, I thought bitterly, why every single person I care about flips out on me. I swore I wouldn't ever fuck with anybody like this.

I was so royally sick of saying, 'This must have happened so I can learn to do better.'

Yet a part of me was damn glad last night had happened. My first time, and with an attractive, experienced, older woman. No one could take the memory from me. Her scent was still on my fingers. She had wanted me, even if only for one night.

Now, home to my same old life, same old mom, sober or sky-high.

Well, she—and Julia—could go to hell.

When I pulled up to the house, all the cars were parked in the driveway, so she was home—or out riding shotgun on some drug mission. Disgusted, I let myself in.

"Nita, is that you?" Her voice, gravelly from what I guessed had been a sleepless, chainsmoking night, came from the kitchen.

Shit. In no mood to face her—or the inevitable attempts to redeem herself with meaningless small talk—I proceeded through the living room as noiselessly as possible, trying to get to the stairs without being seen.

She caught me. I couldn't help but think her conservative cream-colored slacks and cashmere sweater were meant to counter my image of her the night before, beer in hand.

"Hey, baby, did you have a good time? Julia can be a lot of fun. I'll bet you laughed a lot. I'm so glad you're home, I really missed you." She paused to give me time to reply, but when I said nothing, she continued, "So, would you like to have lunch together later? Why don't we splurge and go back to Citrus? Oh, that incredible triple chocolate torte!"

I was in no mood to be bribed. Her light brown eyes, flecked with green and gold, swept mine like a searchlight, desperate for empathy, for forgiveness. I didn't react. A look of hopelessness washed over her face.

"I'm sorry, Neet," she whispered, approaching me suddenly and trapping me in an embrace. A wave of Nina Ricci and tobacco breath overcame me.

You're my mother—a fuckup—and that's all. You drove me from the house last night, but it's fine; I got what I wanted.

"You're always sorry," I said, shaking with anger, and pushed past her. I took the stairs two at a time, raced to my room, locked the door behind me.

After last night you don't mean that much to me. You have nothing to do with the most important part of my life. You can't come in and screw with it.

Julia had already left a message on my machine, saying she trusted I got home safely and apologizing again. I ignored a whole bunch of messages she left during the next few days.

I managed to hold my mother off until the end of the week, when she was so upset I still wasn't talking to her she agreed to try a new outpatient program in Beverly Hills. Big whoop, but it was better than nothing.

And the following Saturday night as usual there was a party going full swing downstairs. She'd promised not to drink or use, but I'd had it with playing booze police to make sure she kept her word.

I was holed up in my room with a six pack of Cokes and a bag of Doritos, blocking out the noise with MTV when I heard a knock at the door. It wasn't the typical frantic banging of an inebriated celebrant about to piss himself, but I called out anyway, "The bathroom's to your right, at the end of the hall!"

When I heard, "Nita, it's Julia," I damn near fell off the bed. My heart began to pound. Jesus, what did she want from me now?

"What's up?" I asked, trying to sound casual.

"Will you please open the door?"

Despite my apprehensiveness, I felt kind of flattered, her scheming to see me after I hadn't returned her calls. These days she didn't usually attend my mother's parties.

Dressed all in black, from her denim shirt and jeans to the pointy toes of her boots, she looked so good I was speechless.

"Mind if I come in?"

I shrugged. "What choice do I have?"

She stayed where she was. "It's your room, darling. You have a choice."

I toyed with the idea of telling her to shove off, but curiosity had got the better of me. "Whatever." I walked away, knowing she would follow.

She closed the door and sat at my desk. Screams of laughter came up from the first floor. "It's a nice room," she said, looking around. "And the housekeeper seems able to keep it neat. The rest of the house, I imagine, presents more of a challenge." She was right—the house was always trashed, my mother's bedroom often the worst.

"I do my own room. I hate people touching my stuff."

Julia'd been fingering the margin of a textbook; she took her hand away. "Sorry."

"That's not why I said that." I sat on the edge of my bed, picked

28

up the bag of chips and rolled the top closed.

"And that's not what I came to say sorry about." Her eyes met mine. "I'd like you to accept my apology for the other night." When I said nothing, she continued, "I wish I hadn't gone from someone you could trust to just another asshole who betrays you. I crossed lines that shouldn't have been crossed."

Hearing her call herself an asshole surprised me. Interesting, she realized what she was. Apparently, however, it wasn't enough to change her behavior. "You know damn well we didn't have sex because I was upset and you felt sorry for me!"

She glanced around nervously. "Hush, darling, the house is full of people."

"It's full of people too stoned to know what's going on. Anyway, you're the one who decided to come up here and have this conversation with me now. Maybe you're stoned, too."

She shook her head. "I don't do drugs."

"Congratulations!"

She sighed. "If only you didn't have to worry every second about her doing something dumb. That's no way to live."

"I don't worry." I didn't need her pity. "I'm fine."

"Oh, Nita, what a bad liar you are! Perhaps that's why I have to be honest with you." She drew a deep breath. "All right, I'm not sorry we—were together."

That was more like it. "What made you say so, then?"

She rolled her eyes. "Because it was wrong! You're half my age, the daughter of a close friend, someone I watched grow up. You came to me for help, and by some miracle I think I was truly helpful. For once I was there when someone needed me."

"Yes, you were there for me," I admitted.

"Now screw that to hell, right? Well, it really meant something to me. In case you don't realize, not a lot of people have much use for me, Nita. It's been a long time since I felt useful to someone." Her voice caught.

I thought she was being sincere, but I had to make sure. "So why did you do it if it was wrong? I was such a cute baby butch when I got down on my knees you couldn't control yourself?"

She snorted. "After thinking about it all week, I came to the conclusion that going to bed with you means something about me and the mess I've made of my life. A couple of weeks ago, I saw a vanity plate—HASBEEN. How dare someone else have it, I'm the original one-hit wonder!"

Her whining about her own disappointment while we were engaged in a much more important discussion was exasperating. "Well, why did you give up your career if it's so all-fired important to you? Giving up is so stupid."

"Give up!" She smacked the desktop. "You have no idea what you're talking about."

"I may not understand the exact circumstances, but I know you have loads of talent, you're very smart, you could still go back and do something—"

"Keep talking, you sound younger and younger," she interrupted viciously. Then she hung her head, covered her face with her hands. "Oh God, failure really has affected my judgment. I'm so desperate for reinforcement I slept with a kid who thinks I'm some kind of prize."

She sounded so melodramatic, I wanted to shake her—and I resented her characterization of me. "First of all, I may be seventeen, but I'm no kid. I'm more mature than a lot of people I know, I don't care what age. Second, I wouldn't describe you as a prize, exactly. What's that expression? Oh, yeah, piece of work."

She giggled, her breath blowing a few strands of hair away from her face. The pattern we'd established the other night—it was starting again. I relaxed, realizing I was handling the situation just right, gaining the confidence I needed to keep going. "It's too bad HASBEEN is taken, but there are lots of words to describe you that can fit onto a license plate." Several others popped into my head. "Why not try SCREWUP...or DIMWIT...or DUMBASS?" She laughed outright.

I went for the clincher. "Do you want me to tell you why you really slept with me?" She raised her head. "Aside, of course, from needing a fan club to make you feel like you still have a career going..."

She smiled.

"Because I'm a nice person, too fucking nice, if I remember your words correctly. When I stayed at your apartment, we connected— maybe only because helping me made you feel like a nice person, I don't know. But when you picked me up after school, we talked. When we watched movies, we laughed at the same places, thought the same things were well done or really lame. You liked having someone around, you liked being...useful." I took a chance. "And you liked me sleeping in your bed, even if you believed you were only doing me a favor. You didn't feel so all alone."

She looked away. Maybe fifteen seconds passed before she spoke. "Okay, so we thought about the same things this week."

"Wrong!" Did she look surprised. I continued, "All this occurred to me just now. I spent the week hating your guts."

She giggled again.

"Do you think you've corrupted me, Julia? All the years you've known me, it never occurred to you I might be gay?"

She looked me in the eye. "I always knew you were going to be gay. I just never imagined I was going to be gay with you."

Her words were like an intimate touch, and without wanting to, I got excited. When I looked at her, I knew she could tell.

She gave me a quick kiss, then took me back to her apartment.

I cautiously extricated my arm, now completely numb, from under Julia's head, trying not to disturb her sleep. I sat up. Still wide awake, I couldn't lie there any longer.

For the first few months of our four years as lovers, I'd actually believed Julia and I could live together happily ever after. When I got to college, she encouraged me to go out with girls my own age, and I did, but somehow kept finding my way back to her bed. As for her hot pursuits, they invariably ended in a fiery crash. She'd regale me with the continuing installments of her dyke drama, poignant because humor couldn't quite cover up the injuries. Through it all, she remained my valued friend, the first person to see me as an adult—through completely sober eyes.

But that first night together—how naive I'd been to think my silently-declared independence from my mother signified actually breaking away from her influence. At least the thought had given me the courage to reach out to another person, but here it was four years later, and I felt more closely tied to my mother than ever before. After all, wasn't I in therapy every two weeks because of her, not even able to make up my own mind about how she died? Hadn't I this very day started a job focused entirely on her? Her story was the season opener. For the next several months, she was my job.

Even in her death she succeeded in tightening my leash.

Tonight I'd sought out Julia because the day at the studio had really rattled me, the 'project' threatening to crash down on my head like the tsunami in Allie's poster. But this time what Julia had to offer wasn't enough; I couldn't stay.

She stirred in a dream, her brow wrinkling over some shadowy concern, her hair spreading across the pillow. I tucked the thick comforter over her breasts. Not a lot of acquaintances had good things to say about this woman; she led what many considered a frivolous life, and she had an arrogance that put people off. But she had been kind to me.

Did it mean anything that I now felt beyond her care?

On the rare occasions when I've said, "Julia, I love you," I've meant it. I whispered it now, as I carefully slipped from beneath the covers. I wrote it in cranberry lipstick on the bathroom mirror. Then I threw on my clothes, took the elevator down to my car, and drove out into the dark cool of the Southern California night.

THREE

"Field trip!" Allie announced cheerfully as I appeared in the doorway of what was now 'our' office, at eight-thirty the next morning, a cup of coffee in each hand. She wore a loose-fitting tunic tucked into a skirt that quit midthigh, both in a shade of apricot that brought out the richness of her tan. Next to her, I was distinctly unspectacular in a polo shirt and jeans.

I smiled, contemplating her enthusiasm as I handed her one of the cups. "Where to?"

She took a sip. "Tonia's sending us on a fabulous, once-in-a-lifetime, all-day, all-expenses-paid trip to...the public library! Your aunt will stop by in a minute with the details."

Indulging her cheerfulness—even though I didn't share it—I snickered, "You must not get out too often."

"True, I'm afraid." With a thumbnail she etched a design into the Styrofoam of her cup.

I tried to stifle a yawn, covering my mouth with my hand.

She regarded me for an instant. "But I assume that's not the case for everyone."

An image of Julia and me, arms and legs entwined, flashed through my head. I dismissed my suspicion that Allie could see it, too. "A social life can be a mixed blessing."

After leaving Julia's, I had driven down Wilshire to an all-night Jack-in-the-Box for a Coke and fries, then back to my studio apartment in West L.A., where I finally fell asleep at about three a.m. The phone had rung at six. Julia had not been pleased to wake up alone.

Allie's sly smile briefly caused my suspicion to return. "I guess it's a while since I've been...blessed."

I laughed out loud at the intimation, and she blushed from her fore-head down the front of her neck, a sight I found appealing. I couldn't resist saying, "Well, bless you, then."

"If only it were that easy—"

"Hey, girlfriends!" Dressed in a pale-blue pantsuit with a slightly metallic sheen, Jane swooped into the room like a full-throttle starship that instantly zapped our little flirting game. I rose from my chair to kiss the cheek she offered me. "I hope you two are anxious to get out of the starting gate this morning. Allie, did you bring Nita up to speed about what I need from the library?"

"Not exactly. No one's brought me up to speed about what you need." Allie's celebrity-conscious phrasing seemed to come naturally, and my aunt ate it up.

"Okay, here goes. I want to find out what the average person read about Gina's death when it happened. So I'm sending you to the library to experience the mainstream print media's coverage in all its biased glory. What sources set you up to believe suicide? Who wants you to buy the O.D.?" She flashed an ingratiating smile. "Of course, Ms. Glass, as my investigative reporter in no way are you average!"

Allie beamed back. "I'm glad you cleared that up."

It goes with the territory in Hollywood, but all the brown-nosing and empty praise still sticks in my craw.

The banter with Allie stopped abruptly, Jane all of a sudden decid-ing now was the time to baby me. "Sweetie, there's no reason to go along if it'll only bring you down. I can dig up some work right here for you. And we're due for our weekly aunt-niece mental health luncheon, so it's cool if you stay here."

I knew she was only trying to be nice, but I resented her making allowances. Already she was violating our deal that I would be treated like any other employee. We both recognized the improbability of the arrangement, but I had expected more of an effort on her part to keep up appearances—especially in front of Allie, who was supposed to be my supervisor. "Thanks, but I'll be fine. Maybe I can learn a thing or two from your investigative reporter."

Seeming pleased, Allie pretended to chide my aunt. "Imagine try-ing to take away my staff after only one day."

Jane, shrugging, acquiesced good naturedly. "Okay, suit yourselves!"

I followed Allie out to the parking lot, shaking off a tiny suspicion that Jane's concern might possibly be legitimate. It seemed more important to prove to Allie—and myself—that I could do whatever the job required.

We took her Miata to the library, and as we drove through Hollywood, she revealed a little about herself. Now twenty-seven, she'd earned a degree in broadcast journalism from Cal State Northridge, then interned for a season on the show before being hired. She lived in Burbank near the Warner Brothers Studios with Lana, who was, it pleased me to learn, a Persian cat. Allie had fallen in love with television at an early age.

"My mom was watching some old rerun, and I heard her say, 'Hello, Mr. Television,' right before the announcer came on and said, 'Hello out there in television land.' So I started dressing up whenever the TV was on because I believed it could see me."

When I asked to know more about her family, she hesitated; I sensed I'd touched a sore spot. I said, "I didn't mean to pry."

"You're not," she answered, yet she sounded defensive. "My parents are Orthodox Jews. Primarily a positive influence on me until the day it dawned on them my college roommate was more like my wife. Then they sat shiva for me." She threw me a sidelong glance. "Do you know what that means?" Except for her tone, I might've thought it was a good thing. I shook my head. "It's a ritual to mourn the dead."

I didn't know what to say. "I'm not one to criticize anyone's religion, but it sounds extreme. You don't see them?"

"Haven't for the past two years. Actually they don't see me. I'm considered to be dead—literally. The last time I came knocking, my father opened the door, said, 'There's no one here' to my mother, then shut it in my face." Her grip tightened on the steering wheel.

I was astonished. Is everyone's family so fucked up, not just mine? "That really is nuts."

She shrugged. "I accept their decision."

Her equanimity was beyond my understanding; I doubt I could have found it, in her situation. I sometimes silently chanted the stages of grief, as my analyst Joseph had named them for me, like a mantra: denial, anger, negotiating, sorrow, acceptance. Intellectually I understood each one, but Allie apparently had realized them emotionally.

Suddenly feeling hopeless, I glanced out the window, taking in the passing scene on Hollywood Boulevard. Transients camped outside abandoned buildings. Taggers engulfed by their baggy shorts, tears tattooed at the corners of their eyes. They'd kill for the glory of throwing their tag up on a wall, the only way of making a name for themselves. For that they were willing to risk their lives. Was it really so different from what my mother had done? She'd lived on the edge to make her name a household word, and paid the ultimate price. For that matter, what was the difference between her and the kid hustlers prancing over to slowing cars, maimed by the gold rings and studs piercing their eyebrows, noses, lips, tongues? The voice that was hers to prostitute—by the luck of the draw—brought money beyond anything they could ever hope for. Without it, what would have kept her off the streets?

Although I had lived most of my years with someone who thrived on disorder and danger, I knew I never could conduct my life that way…

We passed my mother's star a few blocks before the Capitol Records Tower on Vine. An image of her during the dedication ceremony five years ago came to mind: skintight black minidress, spike heels, her mouth a gash of blood-red lipstick. I had been there, coerced by her publicist to wear a dress (non-mini) and heels (non-spike) and carry a purse, as though in drag. The last time, thank goddess, for that.

"To all my fans… Thank you… You're the reason I'm here today… And to everyone else… Is there something wrong with you, or what?"

My thoughts returned to Allie, how her parents treated her like a ghost. I couldn't imagine that kind of rejection…

The sound of her voice startled me. "Well, that was a real conversation-stopper. Serves me right for bringing religion into a perfectly nice discussion. It's partly your fault, for being so easy to talk to."

I knew she was simply being friendly, but her words switched on a red-alert. The barest hint of flattery raises my hackles, my impulse to be supportive forced instinctively into check. "Am I really so easy to talk to? Why is that?" I sounded hostile, and instantly regretted my words.

"Well, yes, I find you to be—until now. Does being complimented always provoke this reaction?"

I realized I had sounded paranoid. "Until I know the person," I said in all honesty.

"What more do you care to know about me, Nita?" I didn't like her tone, and thought it wise to keep silent. "Don't assume everyone wants to use you as a rung on their ladder. Some of us are capable of making it on our own, without your help—and a few wouldn't have it any other way."

I was stung by her response. "I'm sorry. That hasn't always been the case."

When she spoke again, she sounded more controlled. "I can see where you're coming from, but when I say you're easy to talk to, that's all I mean, okay?"

I nodded, considering whether to explain myself, my background, why I trusted almost no one—but there was no reason to. It was time for the conversation to recapture level ground. "On the outside chance you do decide to say something nice about me again, I promise just to say thank you."

Her smile was conciliatory. "I'll hold you to your word."

At the library, we hogged the InfoTrak computer for quite a while, then hit the microfilm room to take a look at the articles we'd found— "Singer's Death a Mystery—Gina Wilde Dead at 42."

LOS ANGELES January 26—The partially-clad body of five-time Grammy Award Winner, Gina Wilde, was discovered sprawled in the master bedroom of her lavish Brentwood estate late Sunday afternoon. Despite attempted resuscitation by paramedics, Wilde was pronounced dead at 8:01 P.M. at U.C.L.A. Medical Center. An autopsy has been scheduled to determine the exact cause of death.

Was it only yesterday when I'd vowed not to share the worst event of my life with Jane's staff? When she had offered me an out, why hadn't I taken it? Why endure the humiliating experience of going over in agonizing detail how my mother had died, and with a woman I hardly knew?

The pop singer, an admitted alcoholic and abuser of both illegal and prescription drugs, had been hospitalized numerous times at U.C.L.A. Medical Center for drug overdose. Wilde had only recently completed a stint at the Betty Ford Clinic in the affluent desert community of Rancho Mirage, renowned for its celebrity clientele, where she repeatedly sought treatment at the desperate urging of family and friends. At the time of her death, Wilde, remembered for her aggressive vocals and compelling lyrics that captured the essence of a tortured existence in the Hollywood limelight, was recording her ninth album *Everything to Everyone* for Capitol Records.

I gave in to a silent urge to make line-by-line corrections to the article. Jeans and a Garfield tee shirt that said 'Let's Work Out...Tomorrow' is not partially-clad. Not sprawled—lying peacefully on top of the covers. A stay in rehab is not a 'stint.'

Wilde is survived by a daughter, Anita, 20, reportedly fathered by NASCAR Champion Brian Crane, killed tragically at Daytona ten months after the child's birth when his car flipped over a guard rail and burst into flames, and one sister, avowed lesbian talk show host, Jane Wilde, 45, whose publicist declined to issue a statement.

This mass-consumption version of the truth brought on a sense of unreality. I tried to imagine how Allie might envision the scene, a half-naked body draped across a rumpled bed, like something out of a made-for-TV movie. I resented her the luxury of filtering the details of her life, holding back whatever she wished. In her world you could throw out your trash without someone combing through it for stuff to sell to the tabloids.

Private services are scheduled at 10:00 A.M. on Friday, at Our Lady of Hope Chapel in Bel Air, followed by interment at Forest Lawn, Hollywood Hills. A public memorial is to be held at a future unspecified date. In lieu of flowers, the family requests donations be made to the Gina Wilde Foundation, to aid economically-disadvantaged youngsters interested in a career in the arts.

When I found my mother, I shook her and got no response. I wasn't particularly concerned at first. Then I remembered, What the fuck is this? She isn't doing drugs anymore!

Her mouth, her nose—no breath. Her wrist, her throat—no pulse! Cigarette butts in a glass of water on the nightstand. How many times have I said gross, disgusting? Dump it! With the fuckin' cigarette butts, fuck'em anyway!

Water splashing on her face pooling in the hollow of her throat, spilling in dirty rivulets onto the pink satin pillowcase where her head—

Move Goddammit! She doesn't!

Her cheek, slap! Nothing! Slap-slap-slap!

9! 1! 1!

Pulse? I can't find one. No, not breathing. Yes, the singer. Yes, a history. Daughter, Nita, twenty. CPR, yes, training—but I can't remember now!

Pinch her nose closed. Cover your mouth with hers. And breathe, rest! Breathe, rest!

Please, breathe, breathe, breathe! Oh God, no!

Don't panic! Ah! Nita! A unit is on the way!

Please, oh, please, please breathe!

Stay with it! Doing great, Nita! Just hang in there! Doing fine!

My mouth forcing air into your lungs, filling your chest with air from my lungs, into your chest from my lungs, into your chest from my lungs, into your chest—

No!

Oh God, somebody, she can't be gone!

"This junk is unbelievable," Allie remarked.

Did she realize how outrageous the published account was? "Some of the facts have been creatively rearranged." Not that I was about to tell her the true story of what happened that night.

"Unfortunately that's what sells newspapers. One reason I decided against becoming a reporter."

"For example, she was dressed when I found her."

"It's none of my business," she replied softly. Then, "I'm sorry you were the one."

I persisted, possessed by a need I couldn't explain. "Everyone thinks it was an overdose. The coroner said she committed suicide. I'm not sure."

Allie stared straight ahead at the microfilm screen. "Isn't that why we're here?"

"And Brian Crane was my father. Not reportedly. They just weren't married." The guy next to us jerked to attention.

"The sad thing is that you grew up without him." She rotated the dial of the machine; the film whirred by.

"Three thousand people crashed the funeral..." I realized I was losing control.

"These media bastards have stolen enough from you, Nita, don't you think? Now it's time to get some back."

She stopped the film, found the next piece. Comforted, I started to read.

The mood lightened a little as we unearthed a ridiculous store of speculations about the cause of death: a massive heart attack brought on by an injection of pure heroin, alcohol poisoning, even a self-inflicted gunshot wound. Taking any of it seriously began to seem absurd. It was amazing how many times my aunt was referred to as an 'avowed' lesbian.

Traffic was heavy on the way back to the studio. I felt totally tapped out. To distract myself, I scanned the radio for songs I especially liked. As soon as one ended, I would look for another. Life's too short to listen to music you don't love. As I searched, I was aware my mother's voice might be lurking out there somewhere. I preferred not to hear it.

This particular brand of channel-surfing is a habit most people find annoying, so when Allie snapped, "Must you do that?" I didn't take offense.

"Sorry."

A moment later we stopped at a red light, and she said, "It didn't really bother me."

"Either it did, or something else did."

"Something else." She wouldn't meet my gaze. "I've never spent the day reading the obituaries of the mother of the person beside me."

"I've never spent the day reading my mother's obits either."

She turned to me. The sun caught her eyes. She blinked, but didn't look away. "What I'm trying to say is that as we proceed with this project I may have to fake a little insensitivity." The light changed, but she didn't move.

I'd had enough of the preprinted sentiment of sympathy cards and awkward, platitudinous conversations to last a lifetime. Her condolence, however oblique, seemed more sincere.

Someone honked; she gave the car gas. We drove the rest of the way back to the studio without talking, while I played with the radio.

FOUR

After a few weeks of working on the show, I woke up one Friday morning actually looking forward to the day's events. The feeling caught me off guard, but I decided to just go with it. In the shower, I adjusted the temperature and the angle of spray to its most invigorating, anticipating the sense of renewal that cleanliness brings. I chose my clothes carefully, then inspected my image in the mirror, the memory of once finding myself on campus with a white Nike on one foot and a sheepskin slipper on the other still vivid. On the way to the studio, I stopped for a quick breakfast, truly appreciating the dense chew of my bagel, and realized that everything had finally stopped tasting like raw potato.

A half hour before the workday officially began, I settled at my desk, content. The so-called news items I'd collected did their best to destroy my mother's name and make her look like just another hopeless Hollywood fuck-up whose main talent was recuperating from orgiastic self-medication. Nevertheless, I pored over them with a sense of satisfaction: ultimately their pretense at legitimacy would be exposed.

Not surprisingly, very few called her death a suicide. The ones that did invariably added a dimension to the story that simply wasn't true, publishing what was purported to be the text of the suicide note, when none was ever found. Most unforgettable was the story claiming the suicide fulfilled my parents' pact to reunite in the afterlife. Presumably to rekindle the flames of their lost romance in the fires of hell.

By far most accounts linked my mother's death to her legendary history of drug and alcohol abuse, declaring she had died "searching for that last high." One clever writer even accused police and the coroner

42

of colluding to rule the overdose a suicide, in order to "protect the identity of the high-profile companion who fled the death scene after supplying the music star with a lethal dose of barbiturates."

The only articles that really bothered me were those insisting my mother was still alive. A witness, usually in a suburban outpost, saw her shopping at the local Wal-Mart or Food King, or getting cash at an ATM. One account made my mother an important government witness in a drug case, claiming she had been given a new identity by the Federal Witness Protection Program. Another, "I Gave Gina Wilde a New Lease on Life," was told by a P.I. who swore she hired him to spirit her off to a secret hideaway in an unspecified Mexican seaside resort to escape the limelight.

These disturbed me because they launched a direct attack on a part of my brain that stupidly persisted in denying the incontrovertible reality of my mother's death. They played on a desperate longing I couldn't shake—to have my mother come walking back into my life. Even if most people I knew thought me better off without her.

Taking steps toward finding the actual cause of death wasn't as scary as I'd imagined. It was a relief to finally begin facing whatever truth lay ahead. And Allie made it easier.

Her cheerfulness and sly sense of humor were things I grew to depend on. She made me laugh whenever she could, shared my outrage at offensive reports, and disregarded my mother's very public indiscretions.

Sometimes hours passed without a word between us, but I was reassured simply by her proximity. I liked the way her lips parted ever so slightly when she was concentrating, how she pushed back the few strands of hair that fell across her face.

Things that might have annoyed me had someone else done them I endured in Allie with no trouble. She had a knack for losing her personal belongings, her keys, sunglasses, earrings she removed when she took a call, the scraps of paper she used for phone numbers and messages. I have a natural sense of where things are likely to end up, so when I'd hear that wail of frustration I could usually point her to the wayward item. A neat freak by nature, I didn't mind her taking the stacks of papers I organized at night before we left and spreading them all around her every morning. She looked so content that way, like a bird in a nest, I would pick them up again later without a word.

I had never felt this way about other women; Julia's habits were exasperating. And once, on a date with a volleyball player, I grew so tired of sentences liberally sprinkled with 'you know,' the gum snapping, the toxic strawberry lip gloss, that I went home early, giving the not entirely false excuse of a headache. So why was everything Allie did endearing?

Time is a healer, but a woman's presence can make the clock run faster.

We met with Jane and Tonia later in the morning to share our findings and learn our next assignment. I wasn't surprised to see my aunt's lover, Samantha, join us at the conference table. All three seemed pleased by our work, although as they listened to lie after outrageous lie, Jane's indignation surged. "Sammy, what makes these people think they can get away with this?"

"Hon, believing they're actually capable of thought is assuming a lot," Sam said coolly, gazing over the top of her reading glasses at my aunt before returning her attention to a clipping we'd given her.

It was easy to see why Jane found Sam attractive, apart from her intelligence and kind nature. She had deep brown eyes, accentuated by thick dark lashes that curled abruptly back, an easy smile evidenced by fine laugh lines etched into the bronze of her skin. Her hair, touched by gray, was layered short. Now in her early fifties, Sam, when asked about her upbringing, would paraphrase Sancho Panza: "'Not every woman was born with a silver spoon in her mouth,'" adding, "Mine was plastic." The daughter of Mexican immigrants, she had earned a place at U.S.C. School of Law at a time when, as she recalled, "I was the only Chicana in the dining room not busing tables."

She and Jane had been together for twelve years, and were still very much in love. I considered Sam to be my aunt as well, and cherished the example of their relationship in my life.

Jane tossed aside the article she was reading. "I can't look at this stuff anymore. Where to now?"

Tonia leaned back in her chair, folding her hands behind her head. "Why don't we hear from our young friends?"

Allie didn't hesitate. "There are a couple of aspects I think we should investigate further. One, the conspiracy theory behind the autopsy ruling. Two, those so-called sightings."

It amazed me to hear her choices matched mine exactly. Then she turned to me, a questioning look in her eyes. In a moment I understood. She was asking for confirmation that she had guessed what I wanted. I nodded, overwhelmed.

A glance passed from Jane to Sam; I could've placed it if I cared to.

Jane said, "Sounds good to me. General?"

The executive producer, looking a little dreamy, suddenly sat upright. "Get on it."

Later that day, I was going to have the distinct displeasure of being interviewed by Karen, the A.P. with the perpetual frown, to give her some background for my mother's bio. Jane was supposed to be there for moral support. Maybe she'd smooth some of Karen's rough edges.

When I got to the studio, Vince, the audio engineer, was fiddling with the mixing board in his soundproofed booth, while Karen shuffled through index cards in the control room. I hovered outside the door, not anxious to spend more time than necessary in her company.

Karen was long-legged and lanky; she didn't so much sit in a chair as drape her limbs across it. Her blonde hair hung limply and drifted often across the sallow landscape of her face; I resisted the urge to push her hair back and tell her to sit up straight. She looked up suddenly. "Come on in already!"

I slunk miserably nearer and took the hot-seat beside her.

She burbled on, "I'm all set on the public Gina. I've got concert footage, music, you name it. What I need from you is the behind-the-scenes stuff."

"Let me know what I can do." After three weeks, Karen hadn't proved to be at all likeable, but I was determined to be helpful. I mentally prepared for battle, not with Karen, but with the personal details of life with my mother.

"Sorry I'm late!" Jane rushed into the room looking flushed, her hair out-of-place. "Sponsors love to hear their own voices, you just can't shut them up! Even worse than talk show hosts." She smiled brightly at Vince through the glass partition, speaking to him over the mike. "Ready to go, my man?"

My man! Cringe.

The audio tech pushed his thick glasses further up on the bridge of his sweaty, pudgy nose, and nodded. "It's a go, J.W."

J.W.! Gak!

Jane patted my shoulder. "I'll be in the booth with Vincent, let me know if you need me to jump in." Since I had no idea what 'jumping in' meant, I just nodded like a dumbass. She extended an arm like Ed Sullivan presenting a troupe of plate-spinning unicyclists. "Karen, she's all yours."

Great, I was at the total mercy of this grinch.

Vince put on his headphones, then held up both hands, fingers extended, giving the ten-second signal. He folded them in one by one, finishing the count-down by pointing at Karen.

"Okay, Nita, complete this sentence for me." She glanced down at an index card. "If there's one thing I want the world to know about my mom, it's…" She swung the mike under my nose.

The abruptness of the question startled me, and my silent answer, That she loved me too much to have committed suicide, shocked me even more. I can't say that, it's pathetic!

Suddenly feeling hot, I looked at Jane, who smiled encouragingly. I turned to my tormentor. "Would you mind giving me a moment to think?"

"Cut!" She sneered, "If you have to think, your answer is bullshit. Say what you feel off the top of your head. That's the real answer, that's what I want. Just now, didn't you come up with something, only you don't want me to know what it was?"

She made my flesh crawl. "Maybe you could try another interviewing technique?"

"No, trust me, this works well."

"It really does," my aunt chimed in over the PA

Karen's brow furrowed. "Here, let's go for another one." Vince cued another start. "My mom was the kind of mom who…"

Attended parent-teacher conferences stoned out of her mind. Again I hesitated.

Now Karen was glaring. "You did it again! Cut, damn it!"

Fuck you, dweeb! "Sorry." Stay calm, be tactful.

Vince cued us again. She cleared her throat; was she going to spit? "All right, Nita. My favorite memory of my mom is…"

"Writing a song for my fifth birthday called "You Can't Tell A Gift When to Come!"" I leaned in a little too close to the mike; Vince grimaced, lifting his headphones from his ears. Backing off, I continued, "She sang it every year for me."

Karen looked kind of smug. "She wrote that for you? Sing it for me now."

Huh? "Oh crap, no way." Not only have I inherited nothing of my mother's vocal ability, but the song, for many reasons, is extremely personal to me. It started to play in my head:

> When you appeared, the time wasn't right
> They said you'd kill my career
> Keep me up all night
> A singer's sense of timing's good
> But yours is so much wiser
> You showed me what I never understood
> The unexpected present's nicer
> Baby you proved, when all's said and done
> Life is a plan of eternity
> But you can't tell a gift when to come...

"Oh, come on, Nita, loosen up. Sing!"

It occurred to me this chick wasn't only insensitive, but possibly insane. "If you'd like to ask another question, go ahead, but I will not sing!"

Through the glass partition, I saw Jane laugh—as if she were laughing at me. When our eyes met she sobered immediately, realizing, I guess, she'd hurt my feelings. Her voice came over the PA "Whoa, that's enough. Vincent, cut the mike."

Relieved, I rose from my chair and headed for the door. Fuck resolving to just go with whatever was happening and not ask for special treatment. "Yeah, I think I need more time to prepare for this interview."

Karen looked irate. "But—"

She and Jane exchanged a glance. Then Jane got up, motioning me to the hallway outside.

As we met up, she looped an arm around my shoulders. I resisted the impulse to shrug it off, at least until we had walked out of sight of the others. "Sorry." She put her hands behind her back and leaned against the wall in a pose I perceived as studied casualness. "I could tell you were having a little difficulty in there, but your favorite memory was excellent. Now, what can we do to keep the momentum going?"

I didn't know what disturbed me more, her critiquing my short-comings as an interviewee or expecting the whole thing to proceed no matter how uncomfortable it made me. "I won't continue if she's going to throw personal questions at me and demand I answer them without thinking. That's the difficulty."

Jane nodded, then squinted up at the acoustic ceiling tiles as though they held the explanation she was searching for, or maybe, the key to her patience. "At times, Karen's direct approach may be inap-propriate, but she always comes back with the story I send her to get, and that's what counts."

Was there something wrong with me for not reacting favorably to Karen? I didn't appreciate the insinuation, and couldn't help resorting to sarcasm. "Well, maybe I'm a different story altogether."

She looked into my eyes, and then quickly away. "Oh, Nita, I cer-tainly didn't mean to suggest…" She sighed, regarding me quizzically. "You're as sensitive as your mom, you know that?"

I resented the comparison, her tendency to see me through Gina-colored glasses. My personality is not simply a variation of my moth-er's. Something occurred to me I should have asked a long time ago. "Just how is my interview going to be worked into the bio?"

She looked away again. "As part of the voice-over narration."

You have gotta be fuckin' kidding. "I'm supposed to help you nar-rate this? You want to tape my answers to the questions she's asking me, like what I want people to know about my mom, so you can put them on the air?" My voice cracked.

She flinched, then gave an all-out fingernails-on-a-blackboard gri-mace. "That's the general idea, but we can come up with something else if you don't like it."

I didn't like it. Worse, I didn't like that she would put this plan into motion without asking my opinion—no, my permission. Obviously Karen and Vince had been privy to the idea; why had Jane waited until I asked to tell me? What happened to the two of us being a team?

"Even on tape, I wouldn't be comfortable talking about Mom to millions of people."

"What would you feel comfortable doing, then?"

That put me on the spot. "I'm not sure. But using my voice...never occurred to me."

She brightened immediately. "Would you like some time to think about it, then?"

Her tone told me she really was hell-bent on going ahead—maybe she hadn't considered my feelings at all, or didn't care to. Tears came to my eyes. "Aunt Jane, I'd like to do what you want, but must I give up my privacy to prove it?"

Her distress was so immediate I could tell she hadn't anticipated my reaction. "I'm sorry, I never meant to pressure you." Her apology seemed sincere. She added fervently, "Don't give it another thought. When you are ready, you'll let me know. If you're ready." She spoke quickly, like someone who has only a few seconds to defuse a bomb. "If not, fine."

I willed myself to believe her, to disregard that part of my brain that whispered she was entirely self-serving.

It's not the same between us, now that we're working together on this project. I feel like I don't know her anymore. I high-tailed it the hell out of there.

I spent the next hour or so writing out potential responses to the questions I'd been asked, so I'd be ready if and when the time came. People should know my mother regretted not being able to maintain her sobriety. That she never took her talent for granted. Of all her accomplishments, she said being my mom made her happiest...

That afternoon, from behind the closed door of the staff kitchen, I heard a voice in the hallway: "The jaws of life couldn't have pried a response from our dear Ms. Niece." Karen.

Worse, it was Allie who replied. "I think it takes her a while to open up." At least her comment showed understanding.

"Well, you should know all about opening her up. You two are spending a lot of time locked in that teeny, tiny office together. Bet she doesn't mind one teeny, tiny bit."

I was torn between outrage and a real curiosity to hear Allie's reply.

"Right. She has a thing for cramped, airless spaces."

Bad choice of words.

"What she has a thing for, Ms. Alice Glass, is you. It doesn't take a genius to know what a baby butch might see in you."

"Or you, Kar."

"Don't even go there! Butches make me gag."

"Maybe you make them gag."

I might've laughed, had I not been incensed.

"Very funny." Karen continued, "Anyhow, never hurts to do the boss's relative. And she's wanting some so bad, wouldn't be much work at all."

"Oh, I generally enjoy more of a challenge, but if I land a promotion, you'll know why."

Footsteps faded down the hallway. I leaned against the counter. Karen was too lame for words, but what I really couldn't comprehend was Allie letting her get away with such bullshit. A sense of betrayal clamped down like a vise.

It was trivial, I knew, but still it hurt me. Allie had seemed ready to defend me at first, but then she'd wormed her way out of the conversation.

I was considering my next move when the door swung open and Jane entered, giving me a once-over. "What's the matter with you, girl? You look like you've seen a ghost." She took a Diet Pepsi from the refrigerator.

"No. I'm. Fine." I stammered, before excusing myself and leaving the room.

Working with Allie the rest of the afternoon was difficult. What she'd actually said—or hadn't said—didn't bother me. I just couldn't get over how easily she slipped into Karen's mentality and talked on her level. Did she do the same with me? Her friendliness, her sincerity— was it all an act, as I had originally suspected?

Eventually she asked why I was so quiet, and I lied, saying I was tired. I could tell she didn't buy it, but she just shrugged and went back to work. The nonchalance with which she turned away provoked me. I felt compelled to confront her.

Closing the door to the office, I stood with my back against it. She was tapping away at the computer keyboard; she seemed fixated on the monitor's glowing screen. I said, "Okay, I'm not tired."

She typed a few more keystrokes with a staccato that suggested annoyance, and swiveled in her chair. "No kidding," she said dryly, leaning back and crossing her feet at the ankles, and looked up at me expectantly.

"I heard you talking to Karen earlier," I continued.

"Unfortunately, that's something we all have to do occasionally."

I thought she knew what I was referring to, but was stalling. Her coolness really started to make me angry. "You were discussing me."

"Were we? It was rather forgettable." She inspected her nails.

So it hadn't meant much to her. "Well, let me refresh your memory. Karen said some well-engineered interest in me might do wonders for your career. You assured her you would keep her updated on your progress. Do you remember now?"

Allie sat up straight. "I can't believe you would take anything Karen says seriously." The color rose in her face; at last she was losing her maddening self-control. "Or anything I said because I was put on the spot."

She was right, but that only angered me further. "No, but I take seriously your comeback—I'd be easy to 'do,' only you prefer a challenge."

She shot a glance at the door, then back at me. Her eyes were imploring, though her voice was firm. "This isn't the place to discuss it."

"Why not? After all, there's at least the same privacy behind this closed door as there was in the public hallway."

"Karen cornered me, and I wanted to shut her up." She bit her lip, and continued with a regret that seemed feigned, "If I offended you, I apologize. I assure you none of it was true."

Her highhandedness put me off. "Are you in the habit of lying, or was this a one-time special?"

Allie lowered her voice. "I can understand how you feel."

"Like hell you can." I yanked my jacket from the back of my chair, and turned to go.

She caught my arm; her fingers were cold. "I really am sorry about this. Why don't we take a short drive so we can talk?"

"I couldn't make you understand if I tried."

She trailed me down the hallway. "Try," she said.

We drove off the lot in my car, parking several blocks away on a residential street. The old lady watching over some kids playing in the dirt from the sagging porch of a rundown bungalow...had she once been like Allie, ambitious and self-assured, tossing off whatever it took to get her way?

Allie unbuckled her seat belt and played with the catch, snapping it with her fingers. "Um, I'm sorry you had to hear our conversation. I simply think, with a small-minded personality like Karen's, the less conflict, the better. She was out of line, but she's ahead of me in the pecking order."

"Why you think you have to play that game is beyond me." What I couldn't understand was that for all her sensitivity, her integrity, Allie could belong to this unscrupulous, mean-spirited, kiss-ass world, could want to belong to it.

"Of course it's beyond you, and I doubt you can see why. I have one chance to do something important to me, and if I have to take some crap for it every now and then, fine." Her eyes flashed with defensiveness.

So there I had it: yet one more person who would do anything to make it in the business. What an idiot I'd been, getting caught up in her, thinking she was helping me feel better.

I turned the ignition, but before I could give the car gas, she put her hand on the steering wheel. Our eyes met, and I looked away.

"Here's the thing, Nita. You're a nice person. I think we could be friends, given time. But anything more, I get the feeling it's just not a reality—don't you agree?"

I raced the engine a little. Obviously she knew I liked her—and the attraction wasn't mutual. If that was the case, why mention it at all? Did she think after today I still cared?

I pulled out into traffic, narrowly missed an oncoming car, and was rewarded by the sharp blast of a horn.

"This is nothing to get us killed over," she said snidely.

I drove back to the lot, pulled up in front of the bungalow.

She remained for a moment, gripping the door handle. "I'm sorry. I wish this hadn't happened."

I was glad it had. I needed to be reminded what kind of person I was dealing with. I sat poised, waiting for her to leave, so I could drive away. Get out, get out, get out, I ordered her silently.

"It's not that I don't like you. I do." She sounded exactly like someone scared to death of losing her job.

Right, I thought. Now get the fuck out.

Finally she obliged.

FIVE

Facing the Friday evening freeway traffic would've sent me completely over the edge right then, so I went home on the surface streets. It would take longer, but the slow-and-steady of the streets seemed preferable to the stop-and-go of the freeway: at least I'd have the sense of getting somewhere. I drove down Sunset Boulevard through Beverly Hills, then skirted the U.C.L.A. campus, comforted by sight of the buttery stucco and red brick buildings set amidst their dense shelter of evergreens. When a wave of nostalgia hit me, I shook it off. I was enjoying life a whole lot more since my graduation two months ago—except for today.

Throughout college I'd followed a reassuring routine: going to class, studying my ass off, and partying all weekend. Gratefully I'd slipped right back into it after my mother's death in January of my junior year, and was rewarded by steadily improving grades through the spring quarter and both summer sessions. Hey, I was no wuss; I probably could have become a justified basketcase right then, but that wasn't my style.

There was, however, one person who seemed to be priming me for entry into The Prozac Zone: Jane. When she proposed the idea of a therapist, I was less than enthusiastic. Just because I'd lost my mother didn't mean I'd lost my mind!

In the nicest way of course, Jane told me I was being ridiculous. No one had insinuated I was going crazy. She and Sam had been going to see Dr. Joseph Gallagher for years. Both claimed their relationship was better for it, and they were more easily able to deal with the stress caused by their careers. She pointed out the benefit of talking with him just as a safeguard. Why not take advantage of something that might help me through what was a rough time? But I brushed her suggestion aside, instinctively suspicious of 'mental health professionals'—they were a fixture in my mother's life, not mine.

I was fine until fall midterms.

The first exam was in a class I truly enjoyed, the history of medieval and renaissance science. Professor Plavic was a young guy with frizzy hair that seemed ready for imminent liftoff from the launchpad of his skull, and an enthusiasm for his subject that made me regret never having the opportunity to personally know Kepler, Copernicus, or Galileo. The morning of the test I took my seat in the classroom with confidence, feeling an 'A' coming on. I opened my exam booklet and read the instructions. And reread them in astonishment, as my mind rearranged the words into meaningless groupings:

YO UH AVE ON EH OUR TOW RITE THI SEX AM I NATION.
PLEA SET
URN IT IN WI THY OUR NAME ONT HE COVER. GOO DLUCK!

Something is wrong! With my eyes! How can I take a test! I can't read!

I broke out into a cold sweat. Scanned the page. The exam questions. More of the same:

PAR TONE MAT CHING. PARTT WOSH OR TIDENT IF I CATION.

Maybe this is a stroke! Something in my brain!

My watch—ten minutes gone. My pulse—hammer-hammer-hammer, hammer-hammer-hammer. Everyone else, writing away! Position your pen. Close your eyes. Draw lines from Column A to Column B. Nothing will match—it doesn't matter. At least you're doing something. Skip the identifications, fuck'em for now. Go to the essay questions. Choose one, choose one, choose one, okay, okay, okay! The medieval roots of Galileo's contributions to science. Calm down! You studied this. You can do it! You'll still have time to go back and correct the first part of the test.

But I couldn't remember what I had known so well only minutes before, as though I'd locked the information away somewhere and no longer had access to it.

Write something! Anything! Galileo was an extremely innovative man. He is a great inspiration to all scientists. Today there are many scientific associations, probably none of which would exist without Galileo's memory.

This is bullshit!

I tore out the sheet, began over: When one thinks of the Middle Ages, one thinks of a backward time where people acted largely without thought, and if they did think about why they were out there jousting or raping or pillaging, it was because of superstition or blind allegiance to a lord. Today we are supposed to get a sense of what the Middle Ages was like by buying a ticket to the Medieval Times Dinner Theater in Buena Park and sitting in the audience munching on a roast turkey drumstick while stuntmen unhorse each other with lances. Well, I think those same audience members would be surprised to learn how many scientific advances were made by Medieval thinkers, and how much the Italian physicist and astronomer Galileo was influenced by their findings.

That was it. I put my pen down. I couldn't tell whether this was more bullshit, or there was a potential for an amusing introduction, albeit with retarded overtones. My hands were shaking so much my handwriting was barely legible. I had to stop.

'Professor Plavic, I carefully prepared for your midterm but something is very wrong. I had trouble reading the test and then I panicked. Everything I studied seems to have gone right out of my head. Of course I have heard about test anxiety, and I think I must be experiencing a very severe form of it. I'm not trying to make excuses or ask for special consideration, only explain why I failed this test. I enjoy your class and wish I could've done better.'

Sweaty, I stood, the first one to get up, and walked to the desk, trying to ignore the way people's eyes lifted in meanspirited stares, before smugly returning to their own exams. I placed my booklet in front of Plavic. He looked up puzzled, almost hurt. My eyes filled unexpectedly with tears.

I mouthed, "Sorry," and walked out.

As I started down the hall, the door to the classroom opened. "Ms. Wilde, wait!"

I stopped and turned, willing my tears back.

He had my test in his hand, and gestured toward me with it. "This—uh—can happen to anyone." He smiled encouragingly. "You've been conscientious all term. Assuming nothing else goes awry, we'll figure out a way for you to make up the points."

I sincerely could've hugged him. "Thank you, thank you very much," I repeated over and over.

He seemed almost embarrassed. "Try not to let this worry you. I'm sure you've had enough stress this year, what with your mother." He looked away and cleared his throat, continuing immediately, "See you Wednesday, Ms. Wilde. Don't forget to read Chapter Eleven, on the Alchemical World View. No doubt you'll be called on to give your perceptive take on the subject."

Blown away by his compassion—and the compliment—I walked aimlessly out into the quad. The test had really freaked me, but because of his kindness I now felt calm. He'd mentioned my mom with no trace of prurient interest, just recognized how hard her dying must have been for me. He made me feel like a normal human being.

I tried to think what to do next, and remembered from an orientation at the Learning Center that counselors were available to discuss all kinds of learning problems, including test anxiety. Tomorrow's midterm was in my most difficult class, Milton, so I thought maybe it would be a good idea to haul my butt over there. By the time I reached the lobby, though, I felt a different sort of apprehension. The lady at the desk was beefy and her manner intense, her round black-rimmed glasses fogged over by an all-too-apparent desire To Be Of Help. The thought of confessing to a total stranger that I had so royally fucked up seemed to make the experience too traumatic. So I left. I could just go home and surf the Net for test-taking strategies.

As I passed Rolfe Hall, where the English Department offices were, I thought of stopping by to see Jane's college roommate, Katherine Hanlon, now assistant professor of journalism. Kathy was gay, a Southerner with a great sense of humor, and we got along so well that she often took me to lunch in Westwood Village just to shoot the breeze. I could tell her what happened; she'd know what to do.

But she wasn't in. I left a note, saying I needed advice and would call her later, then went home to study Milton. I'd barely opened my books when she called.

After listening to my story, she said I wasn't going crazy, didn't have a brain tumor. "What you need are some relaxation techniques, like deep breathing. Try them with me over the phone."

I practiced a couple of times, my tension diverted into laughter when she accused me of sounding like an obscene phone caller. She assured me everything would go fine tomorrow, and invited me to come by after the exam to grab lunch.

Not only was Milton my most difficult subject, but the professor, Cameron Rennet, was my least favorite. A middle-aged dilapidated-looking Australian who came to class reeking of the pipe he smoked surreptitiously in his office, he delivered lectures in a monotone, half mumble, half drone, only compounding the difficulty of the material. I had studied my ass off for the test, and went to class that morning feeling nervous, but determined not to let yesterday's scene get to me.

Rennet was late.

Three minutes, four minutes, five, six, seven! Stabs of pain! Behind my right eye! Count my pulse, shit one hundred, shit one hundred and ten, shit one hundred and twenty! Eight, nine minutes! Fuck Kathy's deep breathing, I'll throw up! Choke on my own vomit! How many rockers get drunk and die like that! Hendrix! Led Zeppelin's drummer, John Bonham! That guy whatshisface who was supposed to open for Mom that time in Portland—

Ten minutes. Here's the jerk. Not even a fuckin' apology. Fuck oh fuck, passing out the exam booklets in alphabetical order—I'll be last, I'll be last, I'll be last!

I'm last. I turn over the sheets of paper, don't even read what's there. Get up, go out to the hallway, into the bathroom. Slap cold water on my face, drink a little from the tap.

Better, no not really.

Mirror—don't look, fuckup is there!

When was Milton born; when did he die? How soon hath time did but prompt the age and avenge o lord thy slaughter'd saints of man's first disobedience and the fruit, fruit, fruit, of that Fuckin' Tree whose mortal taste brought death into the world and Somehow! Nothing makes any fuckin' sense—Mom! Not now! Not now, Goddamn it! I have to go, get out, back to class. Take the test.

You won't take the test, you fuckin' wuss, you can't, you'll just pack up your stuff and go.

Fine! Watch this wuss pack up and go. And run the gauntlet of eyes that follow your retreat! You'll completely freak! I see you bursting into wussy tears! Screaming at the top of your lungs! It happened to your mother, now it's happening to you! Isn't that interesting. Now it's happening to you!

I went and locked myself in a stall, knowing that it was the only confine of my sanity...

Oh, God, somebody, please stop these thoughts. There's an enemy in my head that wants me to humiliate myself, that wants me to ruin three years of hard work in two days, that's screaming at me like my mother screamed at me only without stopping for a drink or a pill. God, somebody, please help me stop these thoughts. If they're supposed to teach me what it's like to go crazy, that you can't stop yourself, that I never understood my mother because I thought she could help herself, I've learned my lesson, and I'm sorry. If I could go back and change things I would. Oh, God, somebody, I'm sorry. I really am.

I willed my heart to slow, my breathing to return to normal, and eventually, miraculously, they did. I opened my eyes, unconscious of how much time might have passed. I glanced at my watch—a few minutes past the hour. I released myself from my place of refuge, and headed back to the classroom.

Just tell him the truth, he'll understand. Plavic had. He'd said this could happen to anyone. I'll make up the work, do whatever it takes. I've been a good student in this class, too, never missed a session, raised my hand all the time.

Rennet was stuffing exams into his mangy briefcase. He looked up as I entered. "You didn't bother to stay for the test, I noticed. Pressing social engagement?" He gave a cutting smile, revealing tobacco-stained teeth.

Such incredible disdain set my heart pounding. "I got really anxious, waiting for you—"

His eyes narrowed.

"Waiting for the test to begin, I mean, and I couldn't shake the feeling. I tried to calm down in the restroom, but it just got worse and worse." I tried to set my lips into something other than a grimace. "I never have experienced anything like this before." He didn't say a word, so I continued nervously, "Is there any chance of making up the test? Or some of the points, at least, with an extra essay?"

He let me wait it out. "Afraid not. That's my policy. No make-ups, not without proper prior notice or a note from a physician. As for an additional essay, I see no reason why your inability to perform in class should result in more work for me."

Desperation. Such unreasonableness. The midterm was worth a quarter of the final grade. "Well, maybe I could get a note. I'm not feeling well. I think that's clear from what happened."

He shrugged. "I'll only accept one that documents a legitimate physical ailment, and then we'll see what can be done. I forewarn you I shall contact your physician personally to verify your excuse."

I had to make him comprehend the viciousness of his inflexibility. "It's been rough since my mother's death." As I said this I regretted it, feeling ashamed, but the memory of Professor's Plavic's kindness convinced me it was all right.

He zipped shut his case. "Yes, I've heard talk in the department about your mother. Unfortunate situation, that. Of course, my condolences. Happens to far too many entertainers."

Implying what? That her death was perfectly acceptable, expected even?

He shook his head musingly. "Americans and their pop stars. Good morning, Miss Wilde."

Standing there alone in the room, I replayed the way Rennet's accent made pop stars sound like poop stars. Americans and their poop stars.

Pop stars, poop stars. Interesting association.

The bastard.

His impassivity was an abyss I had to circle carefully, lest I, drawn irrevocably to it, fall in.

I concentrated on the tree outside the window, the shadow of its leaves softening the dark stripes cast on the wall by the slats of the window blinds, the maroon-and-cream swirls of the linoleum floor worn comfortably by generations of chairscrapers, blackboard powdered with a yellow dust so remarkably like pollen, fertilizing minds with life-giving thought.

No matter what happens to me, I thought, I will never lose my compassion for any person who deserves it.

At home, I went to bed and fell asleep immediately, waking in darkness to the sound of a familiar voice coming over the answering machine, pissed off but loving. "Nita, you have less than twenty-four hours to call your long-suffering, understanding Aunt Kathy back to explain why you stood me up for lunch. Appropriate apologetic gestures include volunteering to sponge-bathe the Fairlane or taking the Joanne Deere out for a spin on the back forty!"

Shit. Forgetting the lunch date made me feel like even more of a frosted flake. I couldn't take any more evidence of how much of a fuck-up I was. I rummaged through the medicine cabinet for the bottle of sleeping pills prescribed for me when my mother had died. I'd never taken any. I swallowed two, and went back to bed.

Sometime later, I was again awakened by the phone. This time it was Jane. "Hi, Nita, it's me, just calling to say— "

I dropped off, not waking until midnight. After zapping some Bagel Bites in the microwave, I opened my Italian book to prepare for tomorrow's midterm. I studied for a couple of hours, then shut off the light. Three o'clock, four o'clock, five o'clock passed as I stewed about the test.

The Italian teacher was this hottie originally from Rome who came to class dressed head-to-toe in leather with a motorcycle helmet under her arm. The class was twenty drooling dykes, myself included, and a couple of frat boys who hadn't a clue. How was I going to get through this exam? What if I screwed up in front of this cute woman?

Nine a.m., test-time, heart pounding, mouth dry. But this time, safe in bed. I stayed there, heart hammering, until ten, when it was over. Then I got up, trekked to the medicine cabinet for more pills, and went back to bed.

All that day, and all night, whenever I woke I kept worrying about the tests, thinking about my mother, and I kept taking more pills. They took the bad thoughts away. My insides were gnawing with hunger; I didn't care. I had the worst breath of my life, my armpits were sharp with perspiration, and I was as cunty as a washed-up fish on the beach, but fuck it. It occurred to me that instead of taking two pills at a time I could just finish off the bottle, but I didn't do it. I slept right through my last midterm, Survey of Eighteenth Century American Literature. And another call from Kathy. And several from Jane.

I am in Hollywood looking for a bathroom; I have to pee royally. I see an exclusive club called The Wild Animal, and push my way inside saying my mother is the original wild animal and people laugh. The air is filled with pot smoke. There's a long line for the bathroom. I see the stalls are wild animal pens with wild animals in each one and straw on the floor; I ask the attendant what's all this shit about wild animals, and when she turns around—I don't believe it! It's my mother! She's very thin and pale with terrible breath, and she says in order to raise my consciousness about wild animals she's going to lock me in the stall with one so I can pee in the straw like an animal. This is fuckin' nuts! But I have to go so bad I get ready to do it, and the wild animal like a zebra with antlers looks at me, pleading to get out and kicking the side of the stall bang, bang-bang, bang, bang-bang!

I woke in my bed, someone pounding on the door. I had to pee just as bad as in my dream.

Then I heard Sam's voice. "Nita! Are you in there?"

Jane's voice. "Something's wrong, use the key!"

They burst in. Jane's look of anguish collapsed into relief. "I've left a million messages, didn't you get them? Why haven't you answered, baby?"

I didn't know what to say. "I've been…sleeping." It didn't make sense but it was the truth. I turned over. Just leave me alone. "I'm okay, sorry to have worried you. Could you go now? I'll call you later. I'm not finished sleeping yet."

"Yes, you are!" Jane crossed the room in a whoosh of rustling fabric.

She ripped the covers back, and I turned over, grabbing them from her. "What do you think you're doing!"

She saw the bottle of pills and startled like it was a snake about to strike. "How many of these have you taken? Oh, my God, I feel like I'm dealing with Gina all over again!"

What happened to, "Are you okay, Nita, is something bothering you?" No, she was pissed because I reminded her of my mother. The thought that I was displaying the same type of behavior disgusted me. I closed my eyes.

Sam said, "You have to understand, we've called for three days with no word from you. Then we find you...in this state. We're very worried—"

"To put it mildly," Jane interrupted. "Even if Kathy hadn't called with the news that as far as she can tell, you missed every one of your midterms!"

I turned away with a groan. Fuck busybody Kathy. "It's none of her business."

"Whatever happens to you, good or bad, is our business."

I heard Sam come closer. "Why don't you get up, take a shower, and we'll go have something to eat and talk about this."

"There's nothing to talk about."

"Be a good girl, Nita, and get up and get dressed," my aunt bribed, "and we'll take you to Masa Sushi, and you can order anything you like."

The thought of eating raw fish on an empty stomach right then was nauseating. "No, thank you, I'm not hungry," I lied. "I just want to sleep some more."

"How long have you slept?" Sam asked.

I said the wrong thing. "What day is this?" I opened my eyes and saw a glance pass between them.

"You know from your mom," Sam sounded so reasonable, "sleeping more is not a good idea. Please get up now."

"I'll run your shower for you," my aunt babbled, and went off to the bathroom.

"Let's go, Nita." Sam's voice was gentle, but I heard the firmness underneath. She tugged at the covers. I didn't let go.

Jane returned. "It's nice and hot, just the way you like it. Ready, sweetie?"

I lay there, knowing this was a losing battle.

Sam peeled the blanket down. "We want you to get into the shower now."

A rage erupted in me. I sat up and faced her. "I don't give a damn what you want! When did you ever give a damn what I wanted? You were fine having me raised by a crazy person! Oh, yeah, that was great! I'll call the police if you don't leave me the fuck alone this minute!"

"I'm afraid you have little idea what we've gone through over you and your mother!" Sam lunged at me. With a grunt, she managed to scoop me off the bed and carry me into the bathroom. I was so startled, I didn't struggle. Jane was right behind her, and as she opened the shower curtain, I found my strength and tried to make a good, solid connection to Sam's left eye. It was a miss. She dodged my fist, dropped me in the tub.

As soon as I felt myself falling—incredibly—hot pee gushed down my leg. My face flushed hot. Stop. I can't!

I hit the hard porcelain surface of the tub, not caring how much it hurt, just slid my body toward the spray trying to soak my pajamas with shower water. I turned to see if they had a clue what was happening, but no, Jane had her arm around Sam.

"Are you all right, Sammy? Are you hurt?"

Mortified, I burst into tears. "You bastards! I hate you both! Why can't you just leave me the fuck alone!" I yanked the shower curtain closed, and just sat there. When I was finally done peeing, I didn't know what else to do except take off my pajamas and rinse them out and wash myself off. I couldn't stop crying. I felt like I'd never stop.

Who do I hate more, Jane or Sam?

Who do I hate more, myself, or you, Mom?

I stayed in the shower for a long, long time. If only I could have turned back the clock one week. I had everything so good, good grades, good standing with my teachers, and two people who thought the world of me that I had just called bastards.

The thought of myself preparing confidently for the tests last week, innocent of the breakdown I was about to endure, brought on more tears. I had never felt such shame. No matter how much soap I used, how much water poured over my body, I didn't feel clean.

I heard my aunt's voice. "Come out now, Nita."

No resistance. I was too tired, too hungry, too worn out from sleeping, too scared, having peed.

I shut off the shower. She poked an arm in; I took the soft, thick towel from her, dried off, and wrapped myself in it before coming out of the bathroom.

Sam was sitting in a chair, head back, eyes closed. I felt remorseful and started crying again. "I'm sorry I tried to hit you. I can't believe

64

I did that. Something must really be wrong with me."

"I hope you didn't injure yourself falling." Her voice was flat. She didn't open her eyes or look at me, didn't give any indication that she had forgiven me.

All her tolerance for maniacs had been used up by my mother.

Jane came up behind me. "Get your clothes on. While you were in the shower I was able to reach Joseph—Dr. Gallagher—and he'll be waiting for us in his office." She didn't sound overly friendly either; I couldn't blame her.

I was still fucked up from the week, but I was learning fast how different I was from my mom. I wasn't as defiant. I couldn't take as many drugs. I couldn't hate people who wanted to help me. I couldn't pee on myself more than once.

I nodded through my tears. Okay, it won't change anything, but I'll do what they want. I can't risk losing the only two people who are really there for me. I can't fail my classes, I won't graduate on time. I'll go talk to the doctor. "I'm sorry, I didn't mean it," I kept saying. "I'm so sorry."

Please comfort me, tell me it's all right.

Finally Jane got it, put her arms around me. "Ssh, ssh."

"I'm hungry," I cried.

"We'll stop for something quick on the way."

"Please help me," I whispered, pressing my face into the hollow of her shoulder.

"We're going to get you some help," she said.

The phone rang as I put my key in the lock; I glanced at the message-waiting light blinking on the answering machine. Allie, no doubt. Well, I would pick up the phone this time, give her a break—

"Darling, where in hell have you been?" Julia's voice had a familiar edge of hysteria. "I've been trying you for hours. Didn't you get my messages?"

My sense of disappointment was swept away by embarrassment. It took me a moment to find my voice. "It's a little ordeal called an evening commute. Nothing you'd be aware of—"

"Cut it out, will you please? So can you come?"

"Well, you should know the answer to that one."

"Spare me! Look, how fast can you be ready?"

"I just walked in. I haven't heard what to be ready for."

"Oh." Her exasperation lost its accusatory undertone. "Julia managed to score two of the hottest tickets in town, to the Gay and Lesbian Achievement Awards dinner tonight at the Century Plaza, the place to see and be seen by every California fruit under the sun. And she needs the hottest young dyke on two wheels to escort her, so what do you say?"

I had been to so many of these affairs with her over the years that ordinarily the prospect wouldn't have appealed to me, but right now, I welcomed the diversion. "Sure." She hadn't called me since the morning I'd hurt her feelings by leaving her apartment, and I wanted to make it up to her. I remembered my manners, slipped right into the role of the gallant escort she desired. "Thanks for asking me. Sorry I was so hard to get hold of."

She was pleased by my answer, I could tell by the purr in her voice. "I tried you at work, a young woman said you'd left her only moments earlier."

The fact that Julia, no doubt frantic and demanding, had spoken to Allie about the urgency of locating me was extremely gratifying.

"Wear the black Versace, with the tuxedo pants. And the diamond and ebony stickpin, the one I gave you for graduation."

"I'll sift through my collection of diamond stickpins to find the right one."

"Well, you could have a collection, you're a rich young thing—or will be after you turn twenty-five."

"You forget the bumpersticker made famous by Gina Wilde: 'My daughter's inheritance is up my nose.'"

"Darling, I don't know whether to laugh or cry."

She appeared at my door an hour later, in a shimmery white dress that showed off her cleavage. I let out a low whistle. She beamed. "Not so bad yourself, handsome." When she stepped close, reaching up to adjust the knot in my tie, I gave her a quick kiss. Anything more would result in a hissy about having to redo her makeup.

She turned over the keys to her Mercedes, and as I drove to the hotel, I expected her to ask me about work, but after inquiring in the most general way, she let the matter drop. Fine by me. I was happy to let the memory of the day fade, enjoying the prospect of an evening with this good-looking woman.

Across the street from the hotel a group of protesters bearing signs lettered with quotes from Leviticus chanted, "Adam and Eve, not Adam and Steve." What event celebrating gay pride would be complete without them?

Flashbulbs went off as we walked into the lobby. Julia, a minor celebrity in the local community—and right now, an especially sexy one—was a natural draw for media attention. One reporter asked my name, then looked surprised, but not particularly amused, when I answered, "Mister Julia Reynolds." Julia laughed delightedly.

Once inside, I bought drinks, and we talked, or rather Julia talked, and I listened attentively as an escort is supposed to do. She ran into several people she knew, mostly women her age or older. They regarded me with the same sort of interest they had for the hors d'oeuvre passed by the waitstaff.

The emcee, a lesbian comic, managed to keep the mood light, despite the posthumous awards to honorees who had died of AIDS. I enjoyed seeing so many celebrated lesbians and gays, hearing their acceptance speeches. Yet I was very much aware of those whose achievements were fixed in the past, either by death or because, for whatever reason, they had stopped reaching for success. It saddened me to think Julia belonged in this group. Her claim-to-fame song, 'Sex in a Phone Booth,' pigeonholed her and ultimately killed her career, but its provocative lyrics—so Julia—never failed to make me smile:

> Combine an old-fashioned grab
> With a little sleight-of-hand
> Tell your partner the same rules stand
> If you fumble, she might stumble
> So get a grip, let it rip
> Find someone who likes to watch
> Then kick the action up a notch!

Driving back, she was unusually quiet. I assumed she was debating whether to ask me to spend the night, no doubt reluctant after my leaving last time. I didn't like that awkwardness now between us; there was more making up to do. "I had a wonderful time. Thank you for inviting me."

"You're welcome."

"Did you have a good time?"

"Yes, I did." She stared straight ahead.

"I had such a great time," I said, taking one hand off the steering wheel and brushing my fingers across the silky hose covering her thigh, "because I was with the most beautiful woman in the room."

She turned to me. "Tell me more."

I gently pushed my fingers up under her hemline. "She was wearing the prettiest dress, like crushed pearls. She made you want to run your fingers through her hair, except then she'd have to spend ten whole minutes away from you fixing it in the ladies' room. And she does wonders for her Wonder Bra."

Julia giggled, pleased. I stroked her inner thigh, extending my fingers. She twisted away. "Not in the car, darling."

I drove back to my place to grab my overnight bag, which I had packed earlier, leaving her parked in the Mercedes.

The message-waiting light was blinking again. I'd cleared the machine before leaving.

"Hi, Nita, it's Allie. I'm truly sorry about today. I let you down, you're absolutely right. Won't you forgive me—maybe over brunch tomorrow or Sunday? I'll try you again to see if you'd like to. And if you think I have an ulterior motive for calling, like saving my job, that's not the case."

Hearing the sincerity of Allie's apology, I realized I'd gone overboard earlier. She wasn't a bad person, and I wasn't a fool for liking her. I felt as though a nagging headache had suddenly let up, and a sense of peace came to me.

Julia brushed past. "Got a Coke? I'm terribly thirsty."

I wondered how long she'd been there, how much of the message she'd heard. When she came back from the refrigerator, can in hand, we left. She didn't mention it, and I didn't ask. We drove back to her apartment, her fingers drumming lightly on my thigh, forcing the thought of Allie from my mind.

As soon as she unlocked her apartment door and shut it behind us,

I leaned her gently against the wall and kissed her, knowing she wanted me then as much as I wanted her. She retreated to the bathroom to remove her makeup, while I undressed in the bedroom. On my way to the shower, I passed her at the mirror, and she smiled. "I'll join you in a moment."

I stood under the steaming spray, soaped myself all over and rinsed, and still no Julia. "Hey, your escort's about to drown in your bath!"

"Hush, darling, Rome wasn't unbuilt in a day," she said as she opened the glass door of the shower and shut it behind her. Her face stripped of makeup was beautifully bare. She eased me down to the floor. The last thing I saw as I closed my eyes was a cascade of water glancing off her back.

Later, in bed, she turned to me. "There's something I have to know to satisfy my curiosity, and since you've satisfied everything else, I hope you'll do me the courtesy. Why was that poor chick so worried about you getting her fired?"

Allie was a subject I wished to avoid. "She's someone I work with. We had a disagreement, no big deal."

"Is she cute?"

There was no point in lying. My relationship with Julia was completely open. "Yeah, but her personality leaves a little to be desired."

She seemed to like my answer. "Look in the nightstand drawer."

Nestled there for me, a paper bag from the Sisterhood Bookstore held a generous assortment of trashy romance novels and magazines with a lesbian theme.

"In case you have trouble sleeping, darling."

SIX

The next morning we swung by Julia's favorite coffee house, Latte for Work, for scones and some lethally-charged brew that sent my heart pounding. She drove me home shortly before her tennis lesson at eleven. "Forgive me for not inviting you along, Nita, but this gal has been booked solid by every eligible she-rat in town, and so far no one's been able to score any off-the-court play. I'm seizing the day."

"Don't trip over the net rushing into her arms."

We stopped at a light. "I'll be careful, can't afford to break anything." She removed her sunglasses, flipped down the sunvisor, checked herself in the vanity mirror. "Surely it hasn't escaped you, Julia's not getting any younger. Finding another she-rat to settle down with before her fangs fall out isn't too much for her to ask, is it?"

I laughed, but felt a pang of concern. "Thirty-nine's hardly ancient, Jules, and you know you look great."

"Thanks for the vote of confidence, babe, but after four-oh it gets harder to convince the ladies you're the marrying kind." The light changed. She gave the car more gas than it needed.

"Sam was over forty when she met Jane," I volunteered.

She smiled and patted my knee. "What a nice girl. And people say the young are selfish. I find them generous and kind. Unfortunately, though, so very young. What makes you so goddamned young, Nita? Why the heck can't you be ten years older?" She continued blithely, before I had a chance to feel too uncomfortable, "Your aunties are both very fortunate. But I don't want a lawyer. Too talkative, too brainy. No, I want an ath-a-lete. What do you think about that?"

I glanced over at her; her white tennis outfit contrasted temptingly with the salon-engineered bronze of her thighs. "I think if your skirt were any shorter it'd be around your neck."

She stopped the car to let me out. I went around to the driver's side to kiss her through the open window. "Anybody who wants to marry you has to ask me for your hand, don't forget it."

First thing after I got in, I played my messages: Jane wanting "to make sure everything is all right," somebunny-or-other I dated briefly at U.C.L.A. soliciting donations for the alumni association. I considered calling Jane back, but because everything really wasn't all right, I thought I'd take a little time to think about exactly what to say.

I hung my suit in the closet, unpacked my bag, brought my laundry to the hamper. Not enough there to justify a trek down to the laundry room. Of course the bed was made. No dishes in the sink, no lint on the carpet. My ficus tree was well-watered, not even a dying leaf to pull off. If I wasn't this kind of person, neat to a fault, I certainly would hate people like me.

I was considering the idea of taking the Wrangler to the U-Do-It Auto Spa down the street—to satisfy my need to make something clean—when the phone rang. I assumed it was Jane again, and picked up the receiver feeling resigned to a confrontation.

"Nita, it's Allie. How are you? Did you get my message?"

My surprise changed swiftly to a sense of happiness that seemed a little out of proportion, but I could handle it. The anxious edge in her voice held an intriguing intimacy. "Yes, I did. How am I? Hungry."

First thing Monday morning Allie and I drove to L.A.P.D. headquarters at Parker Center to interview Detective Glynda Gilmore, spokesperson for the Lesbian and Gay Peace Officers' Association. My aunt preferred commentators from the gay community, and had chosen the detective to appear on the show to explain how evidence gathered by police might add up to suicide. I discovered Allie had a galling fondness for Detective Gilmore. "She's kinda tough, but with a smile even the most die-hard criminal might find disarming."

Enough of that. "When you introduce me, why not leave off my last name? She'll be more candid."

"Right." She smiled slyly. "Watch out, you're beginning to think like a reporter."

Parker Center is an old gray box of a building, with green glass

71

bands that only slightly relieve the monotony of the masonry. A memorial fountain in front consecrates the danger of being a peace officer in the streets of L.A.

The lobby looked like a hospital, with lines of tape directing visitors to different divisions. The place was jumping with cops, some in uniforms, countless others, no doubt, in plainclothes. Allie and I seemed to be the only ones who had no idea where to go. She gave our names to the blunt-faced, hawk-eyed officers manning the massive front desk, and one of them paged the detective to come get us.

Gilmore was a tall broad-shouldered butch unit who greeted Allie with an interest seemingly more personal than professional, her eyes sweeping the length of Allie's tailored gray suit. She was in her early thirties, with California-cool looks: Nautilus-trained muscles that gave her navy blazer and slacks the right definition, a gingery tan, butched blonde hair, and big blue eyes. After pumping my hand indifferently, she led us to the elevator, and then down the third-floor corridor, where she opened the door to her office.

One wall was a row of scratched and dented mustard-colored filing cabinets, some with clipboards hanging from their fronts, to keep track of the file contents as they were checked out. Stacked on top was all the filing overflow. The shelves of the bookcase opposite sagged under the weight of looseleaf binders and penal code books and procedure manuals. Detective Gilmore seated herself at the nearest of two gray steel desks, and motioned us to take seats. My vinyl-upholstered chair was pumpkin, Allie's olive green.

The detective opened a drawer and took out a spiral notebook, flipping through the pages. "So Jane's on the warpath again, going after the media? What they're saying about her sister's a disgrace. Well, here's where you come to get—the facts, ma'am, just the facts." She winked at Allie.

My gag reflex was in working order.

She consulted her notes. "I've reviewed the police report, as well as the autopsy report on Gina Marie Wilde, female Caucasian, age forty-two, deceased. Toxicology came back positive for barbiturates and alcohol. Cause of death, cardiac arrest."

"What about the claim that accidental overdose wasn't adequately investigated, Detective?" Allie asked.

"Call me Glyn." The tone was flat, but her eyes narrowed. "Our records document over two hundred hours covering that possibility. That's what we do when a celebrity checks herself out of the Hilton. And it wasn't like Gina Wilde's problems with alcohol and controlled substances were unknown to us. She went DUI every time the moon was full."

Shame made my face a hot mask. I looked down at my hands.

Allie glossed over it, firing off another question. "What about police contaminating evidence to ensure the ruling of suicide, Detective?" She sounded annoyed.

"Now tell me, who in post-O.J. L.A. wouldn't voice that opinion?" Glyn leaned back in her chair and chuckled. "Hey, nobody in the department gives a flyin' fidoodle whether the lady meant to pull her own plug or miscalculated her high. Is suicide any more prestigious than an O.D.? Either is a respectable death for today's rich-and-vacuous, no offense to your boss."

You're talking about my mother, asshole! The words reverberated through my mind as if I'd leapt up and shouted them. Allie bristled on my account. "I wish I could say no offense was taken. Look, these speculations are pointless. All we need from you is verification that police might have—or could have—made this case look more like a suicide than an overdose." Geez, I had never seen her like this: ninety percent hardnose, ten percent bitch. Intoxicating.

Glyn didn't seem to appreciate it. "Okay, anything's possible. Is that what you want to hear?"

Allie rested an elbow on the detective's desk. "Are you going in front of our cameras to tell millions this kind of distortion of facts is rampant on the force?"

"I'm telling you what you think you already know, what those millions of people believe, regardless of what I know to be true. By and large we're squeaky clean, with officers and detectives who are topnotch."

"You've had no problems with dirty cops—as a patrol officer, a detective, a woman, a lesbian?"

Glyn met Allie's challenge with a keen intensity. "No problems." She leaned forward, and I saw the metallic gleam of her service revolver under her blazer. "Of course, I don't mind kicking some butt if I have to."

I smiled, but Allie didn't. Glyn persisted, "A joke, Allie. At least your assistant got it."

The remark had amused me, but I honestly hadn't assumed it was made in jest.

Apparently realizing she may have crossed the line, the detective became conciliatory. "You can play with the particulars of any police report. Some manipulation of evidence is theoretically possible, but unlikely."

Allie resumed her questioning. "How much time elapsed before the coroner was called in this case?"

"All high-profiles take priority—"

"Since the Simpson case?"

"Do you want this information from me or do you not?"

Ms. Glass had finally succeeded in shaking Glyn's beads; she gave a slight smile. "Think of this as preparation for the response you're likely to get from our studio audience." She returned to her subject. "Distinguishing an overdose from a suicide can be a tough call, can't it?"

"I'm no toxicologist."

"You have investigated suicides?"

The detective rifled through some papers. "Of course."

"And you can tell us who is at risk?"

"Yes, I can."

"Will you please?" Allie sounded justifiably exasperated.

Glyn folded her hands on the desk. "Since you ask so nicely, anyone suffering from a psychiatric disorder or substance abuse is at risk. And drug poisoning, the means used here, is the second most common after firearms. Often it's drugs prescribed by their own doctor."

"Not in this case."

Glyn continued, "They get them from a friend. Or at a party, they go to the john, pop open the medicine cabinet, and voila."

This jerk wasn't telling me anything I didn't already know. I couldn't help interjecting, "People make a plan. They get the weapon or drugs, put their affairs in order, give away prized possessions, draft a suicide note. Here the will was outdated, the belongings remained with the owner, there was no note. Women usually leave one. Someone in the arts—it's rare they don't."

I thought I saw a flash of recognition in Glyn's cold blue eyes. Undoubtedly I was mentioned in the sheriff's report she'd just reviewed. Had she guessed who I was? Glyn said to Allie, "Your assistant seems to have done her research."

"That's what she's paid for."

"What people fail to realize about suicide…" Glyn took up where she'd left off, her tone subdued, her focus on the wall behind us, "It's a crime of passion. If it's a serious attempt, it's usually overkill. A fifteen-story leap. A heavy-load shotgun blast angled straight up through the roof of the mouth. The whole bottle of pills. This one is a tough call, in my unofficial opinion. I'll have to defer to the coroner."

"But the possibility could exist…"

A grin. "Anything's possible."

Allie stood. "I think this is where we came in. We'll schedule your appearance at a time convenient for you." She extended her hand, and the detective rose to shake it before offering Allie her card.

"Call me in the meantime if I can be of service." Another wink.

She walked us to the door, took my hand, and shook it firmly. "Be sure to tell your aunt hello from Glyn," she said.

We left Parker Center and headed toward the Hollywood Freeway back to the studio without talking or even looking at each other—as though she was trying not to draw attention to how humiliating that encounter might have been for me. Of course her overlooking it so pointedly had the opposite effect. I kept seeing that smug look on Glyn's face, replaying her little barbs. Rich and vacuous. DUI every time the moon was full. That's what we do when a celebrity checks herself out of the Hilton.

Who was it who said that it might actually be possible to die of embarrassment because you want to so badly…

Then I glanced down at the console between our seats where Allie had tossed her purse and Glyn's card. The back of the card was visible to me, the word LUNCH? scrawled across it.

Fuck you! Asshole!

One fuckin' day when someone talks shit about somebody you care about, see how you like it, then maybe you'll understand—

Then I turned on myself: Who's the asshole, thinking she'll understand? All she understands is her own Hollywood topcop take on Gina

75

Wilde's pathetic life. All she understands is making a move on Allie!

Well, back off, Jack, I seethed, this one is mine!

Cancel that. I mean... Oh who the fuck cares. I'm used to my mother being ridiculed—why should it bother the shit out of me this morning?

Because Allie had been there to hear it, of course.

I'm the daughter of someone who chose boyfriends based on how much coke they gave her. Someone immortalized in the *National Reporter* buying beer at the Seven-Eleven in a bra and slip. Someone who regularly went to court for a slap on the wrist with me in tow as Dutiful Daughter, Symbol of Parental Obligation. Shit, she once threw up all over me and didn't even remember it. So what if she went out and bought me a remote control Ferrari to make it up to me. I never once the fuck could bring myself to play with it. Maybe I was just being a brat, but I never considered those consolation prizes real gifts.

How can Allie not see that there must be something wrong with me, because there was so much wrong with my mother?

And how can I ever explain, after the things my mother put me through, why I miss her? How once in a while I still cry at unexpected, humiliating times—in public, not just alone in the shower, when I can really let go?

"Like some music?" Allie's voice startled me. I shrugged; her eyes lingered an instant on my face. She left the radio off. After a moment, she said, "Being obnoxious is part of a cop's job description. Don't let it bother you."

"It's not that. It's..."

She waited, and when I couldn't continue, she finished my sentence for me. "It's the way she talked about your mother."

An insect obliterated itself on the windshield. What to say? Just the truth. "Yeah. I've heard it all before, but somehow it sounded worse with you sitting right there."

"I can understand that..." She glanced at me, holding my gaze for a moment, then she looked again at the road. "But just for the record, I'm on your side. If you tell me your mother acted awful toward you, I hate her. If anyone else says rude things, it makes me mad. I know you loved her, and you're incapable of loving anyone who doesn't deserve your love."

I just stared at her, unable to speak.

She smiled ruefully. "Don't forget, I have lots of experience with mothers."

I jumped at the chance to refocus the conversation. "I can't really know you until you tell me what happened."

Her eyes briefly met mine. "There isn't much to tell. We had a great relationship. Then my parents found out about Cheryl—they flipped."

What was the matter with people? Not wanting to dwell on the outrage, sensing Allie was already beyond it, I asked, "How did they find out?"

She paused a moment, as though trying to organize her thoughts, or maybe get a handle on the emotions underlying them. "Cheryl was my first lover. We lived together, were a couple for six years, since I was nineteen." She slowed the car as a traffic signal went to yellow, and stopped at the crosswalk, scanning the faces of the passing pedestrians as though searching for someone in particular. "My parents eventually got wise, demanded I end it, arranged counseling with the rabbi—to become normal. I went a few times, to show my heart was in the right place. As you may have noticed, Nita, I'm fairly normal on my good days."

"I noticed."

"They threatened to cut me off. I told them to go ahead. They sat shiva for me, and that was that. About two months later, Cheryl left me."

God. "Any special reason for the betrayal?"

"Some little idea about sleeping with another person."

"She sounds completely off her rocker."

Allie smiled. "You're good for my ego." She continued, "She married him, they have a kid."

That just floored me.

The light changed, and she accelerated smoothly. "I wasn't invited to the wedding. Too bad, I had a beautiful set of broken dishes I wanted to give them."

Her poise was amazing. How long for her to find it after the stark, screaming rage she'd hinted at? "Allie, how did you ever make it through?"

"Oh, for a few months I got drunk and made myself available to any woman who showed interest. But for the past two years I've been pretty sober, and celibate. The end."

We drove along in silence for a minute or two, down Temple Street toward the Hollywood Freeway, which would take us back to the studio south of Vine at De Longpre.

But Allie sailed right past the freeway onramp. Before I had a chance to ask, she said, "If I don't return directly to work, you won't report me, will you?"

I caught her spirit of adventure. "Depends where we go."

"Chinatown. I love wandering around, browsing the souvenir shops." She paused, giving me just enough time to take to the idea. "And maybe I'll even make you do lunch. Who can tell how long Glyn might have bored us?" She reached over and gave my hand a quick squeeze; a happiness surged within me that took away the gloom of our conversation. "Shrimp with lobster sauce, roast pork over pan-fried noodles. Bottom-feeders and cloven hooves."

"Everything denied a good Jewish girl?"

Her smile was lascivious. "You got it."

SEVEN

Later that afternoon, while Allie and I were trying to locate the private eye who claimed to be the architect of my mother's new life in Mexico, my aunt came to our door. "Nita, if you can spare a moment, I'd like to see you in my office. Nothing to do with business, just family. I'll bring her right back, Allie." Jane's tone suggested she was borrowing me from my rightful owner.

As we walked down the hall, she added in a low voice, "Actually, I want to talk to you about business and family."

The portent of her tone raised my antenna, but I could wait until we got to her office to hear what was up. She told the receptionist she wasn't to be disturbed, but almost immediately Tonia buzzed. A look of annoyance crossed Jane's face as she took the call.

I wandered over to the mahogany and glass cabinet that showcased a lifetime's collection of awards. I'd looked them over so many times that even the three Emmys placed top row, center, inspired little awe. I let my eyes trail to the shelf below: The Association of Television Critics Award for Outstanding Talk Show Host next to a pink marble triangle from the National Lesbian and Gay Arts Foundation, inscribed For Outstanding Cultural Contribution: Jane Wilde. Beneath that, a gold trophy in the shape of a drum major commemorating Jane's stint as Grand Marshall of the Christopher Street West Gay Pride Parade towered over several Golden Mike statuettes. The lowest shelf held a small pyramid of marble dedicated to The National Association of Broadcasting's Woman of the Year: Jane Wilde; a glass obelisk that read Network Executives for Television Excellence: *The Jane Wilde Show*; and a plaque from Los Angeles Gay and Lesbian Community Services Center recognizing the show.

The cabinet was immaculate, each trophy precisely placed. I saw my own reflection in the streak-free glass, and tried to imagine how it would feel if the awards were mine. It would mean doing my job—and being gay—in front of an audience. I had never wanted either.

For the first time it occurred to me how Jane intermingled the souvenirs of her achievements in the Business and the Life. My aunt had carved out her own corner of the world: mainstream success as a lesbian. Those awards—the group of them together—meant she'd satisfied her demand to be accepted on her own terms.

My mother's Grammys and platinum albums had been displayed at Capitol Records until after her death. Hugh, her agent, had thought it unwise to keep them at the house with all the druggies drifting through, so he never fought that provision of her contract. The awards were in a Beverly Hills bank vault now.

I heard Jane bang down the receiver, and turned to see her shut the door. She motioned me to the couch. "What a woman has to do to get five minutes with her favorite niece."

I gave her the obligatory "I'm your only niece," and sat down, last Friday's confrontation suddenly heavy on my mind.

"Thank God—one's all I have time for." She yawned and pinched the bridge of her nose. "You know, when you started working here, I imagined I'd see more of you than our weekly lunches and an occasional Sunday at the house, but lately we've even skipped lunch. I miss you."

It wasn't as though her tone was accusatory—I knew she meant only to be affectionate, but somehow I felt as though I had to explain myself. "We spend time in the same building, we're together every day, but you're right, we haven't talked much."

"Exactly. So let's play a quick game of catch up now, and then maybe you can stop by on the weekend." She nestled against the couch cushions. "Needless to say, I know you weren't happy about the interview. I broke my promise to myself that I wouldn't cause you a moment's distress with this project."

I stared at her, thinking: Can you really fuckin' believe I'm not going to be affected by it? That there's some magic wand you can wave and all the crap will just disappear? "I appreciate your saying so. Maybe that's an unrealistic expectation."

She sighed. "Maybe. But we're this far into it..."

You want to know if I'm sufficiently pissed off to pull the plug on your stupid motherfucking project? This friendly little chat is just damage control!

I tried to stay calm, but my anger spilled out. "I don't need reminding how much you want this to go forward."

Her eyes narrowed. She looked puzzled, hurt. "What's this wall that's gone up between us, Nita? I don't like it one bit."

I said nothing.

She leaned closer, placed a hand on my knee, tried to get me to look at her. "Just tell your old aunt what's going on, sweetie. There's nothing the two of us can't talk about. The interview really was a bad idea. I was wrong, and I'm sorry."

I knew I had to find my voice right away, before she had the chance to melodramatically blow the whole situation up like a Thanksgiving Day parade float. "It wouldn't have been such a big deal, except everyone but me knew I was supposed to be narrating the bio. What's the point of that? Look, maybe you feel guilty about my being uncomfortable, and you're trying to protect me, but you only end up hiding things."

Her expression turned thoughtful. She folded her arms across her chest. "That could be true."

"It's damn true."

"And it also could be true—" She looked away from me, across the room, to the awards cabinet, "that for the past twenty-one years I've done a pretty lousy job of protecting you."

Was it really necessary to bring up this old stuff now? Weren't we okay about it? I appreciated her stepping in when Mom was so shit-faced she didn't know her ass from the moon. In therapy we talked about all the times I was left alone. We cried, you said sorry, I said fine—God!

Relax! Forgive! It's all over!

"I just want to do something right. I think the show can give us the perspective we've both been lacking. I'm tired of being angry at my sister—and myself."

No reassurance from me this time. Nuh-uh. So sorry. I said nothing.

She tossed her head. "You say maybe I feel guilty. Oh, baby, you have no idea!"

Well join the freakin' club. You weren't at the house when it happened, I was! You weren't the one who didn't get there on time, it was me! Try that on for guilt—

Jane gave a bitter laugh. "I was always threatening to take you from her. So what, big deal. I went to the top custody lawyers, they said, 'Prove Gina Wilde unfit?' In my dreams. Could I do that to you? Would that be fair?"

Excuses, excuses, we all fall down!

She went on. "Not to mention me being a lesbian on top of everything. Even Sammy lost faith in the system. Screw it, we should have just kidnapped you!" She glanced sideways at me. "What do you think, Nita? How about going on the lam with your two old lesbian aunts? Hacking our way through the Peruvian jungle, making midnight passages on the Orient Express—skulking around Paris in matching trench coats and fake moustaches!" With her finger she brushed the skin above her upper lip. "Well, in my case, maybe not so fake."

Despite myself I giggled, her so-close-to-the-bone combination of silliness and sincerity softening me against my will. My family 'tis of me. I composed myself. "I think I didn't need my only sane relatives taken to the Bastille."

She smiled, not just amused but really and truly relieved I had said something nice. That made me feel bad—her expecting me not to be nice. Why am I such a mean biddy? Always taking things the wrong way.

"Whether or not I did the right thing, I have to live with it. I did what I could, even if it wasn't enough." She made her voice falsetto. "'I'll never have kids, can't Nita stay over a couple weekends a month? Need time alone? I'll take Nita. New boyfriend? Nita doesn't need to be there. European tour? Have a good time, don't forget to write, Nita stays with me!'"

I grinned, remembering just how much she had schemed to take me away from all the craziness. So she hadn't been my knight in shining armor, maybe that wasn't possible. What am I, some wuss that can never get over it? Will I be creaking over to Joseph's when I'm ninety, and he's—

"But after Gina died, the outgoing, fun-loving girl I watched grow up disappeared." My aunt turned gloomy again. "I didn't know what to do."

"There wasn't anything to do except keep an eye on me by giving me a job."

"You got the job because you have a lot to contribute to my team, and because I enjoy spending time with the people I love. Anyhow, it seems to me the girl I missed is finally coming back."

"I do feel better," I admitted.

"That's wonderful." I let her take my chin in her hand, lightly touch the tip of my nose. "All right, back to more important matters... Can we expect you on Sunday? I'll get Sammy to fire up the barbecue, and you could bring your swimsuit, use the pool."

"Sure. It'll be fun." She released me, seemed about to add something, so when she didn't, I asked, "What?"

"If you'd like, ask Allie to come along." My jaw dropped, and she laughed. "Am I wrong to think you might want to?"

"Yeah, like, all wrong."

"Well, I can wait, heaven knows I've had practice, for you to find a proper girlfriend." A teasing note stole into her voice. "Oh, by the way, did you notice that I refrained from mentioning how lovely it was seeing you on the news?"

EIGHT

On Monday Allie and I appropriated Tonia's Compaq and ran up her online bill, using a worldwide database called DIALOG to track down Jack Sklar, the private eye supposedly hired by my mother to take her to Mexico. An article we read said he was L.A.-based, but Information hadn't yielded a phone number. Allie typed a few keystrokes.

"The trick," she said, "is to customize your search while allowing as many hits on the name as possible. Depending on whether he owns a business, is married, has gotten a traffic ticket, or spends his time selling stories to the tabloids, we should come up with something we can trace." Once she had accessed the database, she typed "?e = sklar, jack" plus a long code of letters and numbers.

Not only was I fascinated by the process, but by her expertise. "How'd you learn this stuff?"

"The first *Jane Wilde Show* I worked on, when I was an intern, dealt with finding missing persons. Tonia shelled out fifty bucks for a book about conducting on-line searches, but no one could be bothered to figure it out. So I did. A plus at hiring time." She concentrated on the monitor, waiting for the data to come up.

I rolled my chair a little closer to hers. "Your intelligence, perseverance, or not letting Tonia waste the fifty?"

"The money, honey." She giggled, adding several keystrokes.

Within moments we had the number. Allie called him, and put him on speaker phone. He jumped at the chance to appear on the show.

"Two years ago," he related, in a New York accent softened by years in the California sun, "I was contacted by a woman who wouldn't identify herself, but said she was a celebrity tired of living in the limelight, and begged for my help. Eventually she revealed she was a singer, and being the die-hard fan that I am, I guessed I had Gina Wilde on my hands. Faking her own death was her idea. I counseled her against it. It's bad for the family, you know, but she convinced me if I didn't help her disappear she'd commit suicide. I asked for my standard fee, a thousand dollars a day plus ten grand up front. The money was delivered in twenty-four hours." Sklar interrupted himself. "Speaking of money, what kinda compensation do you offer?"

He did not pursue the idea once Allie explained it was the show's policy never to pay guests. "But," he added, "I won't discuss the particulars of how I helped Gina over the phone."

"Fine. We need to pre-interview you before we sign."

"I'm free today."

Sklar worked out of his mobile home in Santa Monica. After Allie got the directions, we let Tonia know what we were up to, then jumped in the Wrangler. His unit was modern and well-kept, with a white metal awning that ran the length on one side; birds-of-paradise and banana trees thrived in pots underneath.

The private eye responded promptly to our knock. He was at least six feet tall, with thinning salt-and-pepper hair and aviator glasses. Casually dressed in a brown cardigan, checked shirt, and camel-colored slacks, he appeared cordial and, despite the surroundings, professional. Still something seemed slightly amiss. He looked like a college professor—or, more precisely, the way someone who hadn't set foot on campus in twenty years might imagine a professor to look. We sat in the living area, furnished with a rattan sofa and chairs. The big-screen TV was tuned to ESPN, with the sound off. "Salt air is terrible for the ol' tube," Sklar said, adding, "hafta keep it on night and day." He sat back in his chair, putting one leg up on a footstool. "Since we talked, I've been thinking about what you might want from me."

Allie leaned forward. "We want you to come on the show, explain what you did and why you did it."

He passed a hand over the top of his head, as though to reassure himself that there was a substantial amount of hair remaining. "Hell, I won't pussyfoot around, I'd done that kinda thing before, but not for anyone in a legit-type business. I was surprised when Gina called, 'cause I didn't know my reputation had spread to the industry. Well, everyone knows there's ties that bind the industry to all kindsa businesses, legit or not."

He flashed a toothy grin which faded as soon as it had appeared. "But I felt for the lady, and, like I said, I'm a fan. Saw Gina in concert a buncha times. In concert, on a record, the lady has it all. No need whatsoever to use the past tense about it."

I felt uneasy. Could this cheeseball really have knowledge that my mother was alive?

He continued, "I know she left her kid and all, but I'm not sorry I helped her. Gina wanted in the worst way to be gone, and I helped give her the dream. I won't take it back now. No effin' way am I gonna lead your people down her trail. Not for all the dough in the world—not that you're offering." He sat up straight in the chair.

Allie was calm and reassuring. "No one will ask you to do anything you're not comfortable doing. Right now, just please tell us what exactly you did for Gina—to give her that dream."

"I got her the medication—"

"What did you give her?"

"The whole world knows it was Seconal. Didja think I'd say Valium?" Sklar slid the footstool away and crossed his legs. "She had some experience with drugs, and I know a little about pharmacology. I dosed her the right amount for her height and weight. When the time came, I called a friend at the morgue. They took her there, put her in the celebrity lounge—"

"The what?" Allie interrupted.

"The celebrity lounge. The high-profile slab room. I picked up the body bag, put her in the car. I got her a wig, make-up, clothes, fake i.d. By the time we hit the border, she's Miss Jane Doe."

Then who was it in the hospital—who was it in that coffin, eyes sealed, chin sunken? It had to be you, though it really didn't look like you. You were very definitely someplace else.

The idea of my mother out cold in Sklar's custody really creeped me out. I could just see him unzipping the bag and slipping his hand inside her bra—

Thankfully, this scenario was cut short by Allie. "A fascinating story, Mr. Sklar, but so farfetched, I have a hard time believing it. Your tabloid readers might hang on every word, but I don't think our audience will buy it."

His hand stole again to the top of his head. "There's nothing stranger than fact, but you may be a little too young to realize it." He leaned forward suddenly. "So how about I give your audience some cold, hard proof."

Dread spread from the pit of my stomach. He's going to pull a gun on us! But Allie was absolutely unruffled. "That's exactly what's needed."

He stood, again offering us that grin. "Like her signed contract with me? Step on into my office, I got what you need." Allie and I exchanged a look. He laughed, a short bark. "Hey, I just played that one back, seemed like a pretty bad come-on. I assure you, ladies, I mean no harm. I'm a one-woman man who's already got his girl."

He walked down the hallway. Allie followed—stupidly, I couldn't help thinking. My mind raced trying to come up with something to divert our course, but I couldn't, so I had no choice but to tag along.

We stopped at a closed door; behind it I heard music faintly playing. "My office," he announced, then flung open the door.

Allie gasped. As I peered over her shoulder, a jolt of adrenaline took my breath away. Then my vision got slow and kind of grainy like I was watching an old home movie...

What the fuck was this?

Posters of my mother covered the walls, the windows, even the ceiling. CDs were tossed onto a table. From the CD player her voice emanated with a ghostly wail—a song called "Paralyzed."

> You criticized
> I apologized...
> Don't you realize
> I'm paralyzed?

Concert tee shirts were draped over the couch. And most un-fucking-believable, in one corner, a mannequin in an blonde wig cut in my mother's favorite layered style wore one of her trademark stage outfits: black leather 'boyfriend' jacket and miniskirt, black lace bustier, and stiletto ankle boots. Here Sklar had modified the bustier to suit his fantasy: the mannequin's nipples jutted through slits in the lace. On the floor were wads of what looked to be used Kleenex.

The psycho spends his days in here jacking off!

Sklar laughed—a laugh terrible in its naked delight and triumph. "There, ladies, what further proof do you need?"

All of a sudden I stood at my car with no memory of walking to it. I tossed Allie the keys. She drove as I unrolled the window. The breeze cooled my face.

Oh God, somebody, stop me before I reach over and grab the steering wheel and plow right into that bus. When my dad hit the wall in Daytona did he think of me? The second we get on the freeway I'm going to pull up the emergency brake. My hand...

Put it down!

Allie caught my hand, thinking I was seeking hers. "Let's go somewhere," she suggested. "The beach, or back to your place?"

I left my hand in hers for a few seconds, then let it drop. The only place to go was work, to resume our normal routine. That's the only way back from a brush with insanity.

The music gives each and every nutcase access to the most vulnerable place in my mother's being, like the tabloids gave them access to the private scenes of her life. She couldn't have kept anyone out, even if she had wanted to. The sickest human beings in the world rape my mother over and over in their minds, and there's nothing I can do about it.

I'd sensed from the start that the situation with Sklar wasn't right, yet I'd gone with it, hoping he'd be normal, doubting my own perception instead of his sanity. The story of my life. It freaked me out, how we'd just been sitting there for a half hour talking, while the music had been playing, my mother's face and body plastered on the wall. Right now, as a matter of fact, Sklar was probably sitting there, with the tunes blasting, dick in hand.

Allie was unusually quiet and stayed close by me all afternoon. At the end of the day, she asked me to dinner. I told her I didn't feel up to it. Disappointment registered on her face as she said she understood. I promised to call, but she still didn't look too happy.

I went home, took a shower, flopped down on my bed, stared at the ceiling...

The rosedraped coffin. Knock-knock, who's there, nobody, no

body who?

Jane, her face runny with tears.

Flesh darkens under the cover of flowers; the hushed blood spoils.

The two of us love the meat dead in its box—

Shut up—that's gross, disgusting! God how sick!

How can I love anything human ever again...

How can I eat a hamburger?

Stop it! This minute!

The human body! Shitmachine bonebag bloodpool lungclog brain-clump painprison deathcamp—

Stop! Don't think about this now. Just think about Allie. It would be okay to love her, she's pretty, doesn't smell, doesn't shit, will never die!

Shut up! Now!

I sat up, heart pounding, and picked up the phone and dialed—not Allie, but Julia.

"Darling, what's the matter?" she said after I'd spoken only her name.

"Well, Allie and I went to interview—"

"And who, may I ask, is this Allie?" Julia's voice was throaty, her tone intimidating.

"Don't you remember, somebody I work with? And—"

"Somebody you play with?" she needled, then gave a short laugh. "Go on, Nita, I'm sorry."

I told her the whole disgusting story, and when I was done she was silent for a moment before offering her take on the day. "Of course what you describe is an extreme situation, but understand—the whole world really is crazy. The only thing standing between people and a mental breakdown is their dandruff. You're too young to realize this, but if you stop operating as though everyone is rational, you'll be a much saner person."

"This is supposed to comfort me?" I said, recalling my impulse to crash my car while Allie drove it.

"No, it's meant to educate you. If you want to be comforted, call up your girlfriend."

"She is not my girlfriend."

"Whatever you say. Now if you recall what I told you about Gina—"

I don't want to talk about my mother now!

"—don't expect her to be sober, and you'll save yourself a lot of pain every time she turns up drunk. Expect her to be high, and if she's not, great. Assume the world is crazy, darling, and if you actually meet somebody halfway sane, you're ahead of the game!"

After we hung up, I turned on the TV, not so much traumatized by the guy's sickness anymore, but pissed off at my mother. Joseph says this anger is normal, and even desirable, but I hate it.

I knew she couldn't help herself, but why was a nice life out of the question? People liked her. She was talented, affectionate, a lot of fun. Okay, she suffered from depression. But the addiction seemed so unnecessary; medicating yourself never works. On an emotional level I couldn't forgive her behavior. Joseph says it's a matter of time, but I doubt it.

Her last stay at Betty Ford, she wouldn't talk to me—or Julia—for a week, though for once she'd gotten into the car to go there without calling us names, without pleading or tears. When she allowed me to visit, I arrived with the usual care package: a carton of Winstons, some chocolate eclairs from her favorite bakery, and her old acoustic guitar that for some reason we called Alfred. She looked like shit, her hair pulled back into a greasy ponytail, her gray sweat outfit not disguising how bony she was underneath. She hugged and kissed me, went on about how sorry she was. At least she knew better to promise that this would be the last time. But it was.

We ate the pastry in her suite, then she went to smoke in the TV room where nine or ten other wealthy fuck-ups were killing time. When she came back, she picked up Alfred. "Tell me what you think about this, Nita. I've been working on it all week. It's called 'Time.'" She began to sing:

> In this private, empty room
> I can't tell night from day
> Doctor, can you wish me more
> Than just a pleasant stay?
>
> You say all I need is time
> Time to get my life on track

Time to work things out
Time to get it back

So Doctor, can you tell me
Why joy can't spare a minute
But sorrow works a double shift?
In terms of anguish
Time—what is it?

I was so hacked off, I said maybe she should stay in rehab forever, if she could write like that here. We'd both be better off. That made her cry. I waited a few moments before putting my arms around her...

Oh Mom, the song is wonderful, everyone will love it, there's no reason for such a great artist with so much talent to be drinking and doing drugs like this when being able to write and sing so kickass is a natural high.

—Do me a favor and lay off the horseshit!

Do me a favor and get yourself straightened out before you make us both insane. Don't you love me, Mom? Don't you see what this is doing to me? Don't you care?

—Of course I love you, of course I see it, oh Christ, if you're going to cry—

Then why do you keep doing it? You're not only hurting yourself, you're hurting me.

—I know I am. I'd give anything to stop. Sometimes I hate myself so much, Nita, I feel like killing myself.

Now I'm supposed to feel sorry for you, right?

—You just don't understand. You never have and you never will.

So it's all my fault because I don't understand you, Mom?

—No, it isn't your fault. Just please stop crying! It's my fault, my problem, and I don't understand it. How can I explain it to you?

For a moment I let myself believe that she was still alive and living in Brentwood. I closed my eyes and envisioned our house, the heavy front door with the stained-glass panes bearing a coat-of-arms and her initials, hearing the thunk it made when it shut. Seeing the living room with the grand piano at the far end, the keyboard and mike set-up. The cream-colored rug with the faint pinkish stain in the center that never would come out after someone smashed a pitcher of sangria at a party and it soaked in the entire weekend. The white lacquer end table with the black Coach address book... My last time there—

"Ready, Nita?"

"Janie, don't you hurry her, she needs to take her time."

"Nita, have a moment alone, we'll wait for you outside."

'Bye bedroom, kid playing, 'bye window, tree growing, 'bye hall-way, open door, empty room where It happened—Don't go in there! Oh God No! Get out, leave right now! Stairs—down—better...Out! Slam! Breathe!

Jane! Sam! Somebody! I'm Ready!

What an asshole I was today in front of this woman for whom I'd like to appear strong and romantic and sexy. Instead I was totally out of control, totally embarrassed. She just felt sorry for me, at the mercy of a crazy person. So much for swearing never to let it happen again.

I watched MTV for a few hours before reaching for the phone to call Allie. I dialed, then put down the receiver, grabbing my keys and jacket.

I called from the convenience market down the street from her apartment. She picked up on the first ring. "I want to come over," I said.

Her building was a two-story stucco job with arched windows, the apartments set around a courtyard; the night air was lush with the scent of magnolia blossoms from the tree in its center, the cuplike flowers gleaming like white wax in the darkness.

When she answered the door I saw how worried she'd been. She invited me to sit on the couch, asked me if I'd like a drink. I shook my head, taking in my surroundings. The living room was casually fur-nished with the sofa and two matching comfortable-looking chairs in blue-and-white campstripe, a blue rug over the blond hardwood floors. On the wall opposite was a large painting of a clear azure swimming pool, a woman in a white bikini on the concrete beside it, one arm trail-ing lazily in the water. In the background rose the Hollywood Hills, the famous sign barely visible. I liked it, and I told her so.

"I bought it to remind me what's important in life."

"In Southern California anyway."

At the far end of the room, drapes were pulled back across a sliding glass door leading to a balcony, where I could see a settee, a few chairs, and some plants. The wall space was taken up by bookcases that contained mostly paperbacks, shelved a little haphazardly. I also noticed quite a pile of newspapers on an end table. The room had an air of being extremely hastily straightened. But it was cozy.

Lana put in an appearance. She seemed to be all fur, no meat, white, with a tiny, worried face. She seemed prissy, even for a cat, but maybe I'd feel different if I ever got to know her better.

"About today..." Her voice startled me, even though it was low and gentle. I turned and looked into her eyes, less anxious now. There was no pity in them, only compassion.

She took me in her arms, whispered comforting phrases, tried to tranquilize me with words. "What a bad day. I know how upset you must be. Talk to me. It's fine if you just want to let go and cry."

If only I could have.

NINE

We were a month away from Labor Day, when the show's fall season would open with the series "Death of a Sister, Death of a Star." Our operation went into high gear. Seated at the conference table to screen Karen's bio, we learned that we would meet daily to report our progress. "And be ready for emergency confabs, some at extremely inconvenient hours," Tonia reminded us.

Jane cut to the chase. "In other words, General, our personal lives are on hold until we air."

Everyone groaned.

Tonia smiled. "In a nutshell. Now, if you people are through griping, Karen, we're ready."

I slumped in my chair as she crossed the room, video cassette in hand, and slid it into the VCR on the TV cart. After much soul-searching, I'd explained to Jane that I didn't feel comfortable helping narrate the bio. I knew she was disappointed even though she smiled and said it didn't matter, and not to give it another thought. She was so nice about it I got a terrible case of the guilts.

The screen was dark except for my mother's name and the dates of her birth and death glowing against the black of the opening frames. Then came snapshots from her infancy and childhood, accompanied by the sound of a camera shutter clicking and Jane's voice-over narration. "I was three when Gina was born. When my parents brought her home from the hospital, I ran outside announcing to all the neighbors, 'I have a sister!'" In rapid succession came photos of Jane holding my mom as a baby on her lap, my mom squirming, slipping down through Jane's grasp, then the two of them sliding from the sofa to the floor.

Jane's narrative continued, "This is the way I will always remember my sister." Onscreen a home movie captured my mother and Jane as adolescents, dressed in outlandish hats and old evening gowns someone had given them, lip-synching the Supremes' "Where Did Our Love Go?" How many times had I seen this before?

My aunt's voice resumed, interrupting everyone's laughter. "You may now realize why I made the spoken word my career. But Gina always loved to sing—and write songs." Pages of handwritten musical notation dropped, one upon the other, until sheets of her most popular published songs landed on top.

"Gina formed a band in high school called Angel City." A photo of the members flashed on the screen, grunge cases before their time. "With my sister as lead singer, the group worked the L.A. scene, and she met and eventually worked on her own with several greats, including Carlos Santana, Jefferson Starship, Fleetwood Mac." Concert footage rolled, scratched and overexposed, of my mom in her late teens singing backup behind Grace Slick, of her onstage taking a swig off a bottle of Jack Daniels before passing it to Stevie Nicks.

A picture of my parents and me, as a baby, followed. "Gina fell in love with race car driver Brian Crane. They had a daughter, Nita."

When you hit the wall did you think of me—

The baby picture remained onscreen a little long for my liking. "Brian died before his daughter's first birthday."

"At the age of twenty-five, my sister signed with Capitol Records, and she went on to record eight albums, the ninth released on the first anniversary of her death. She received myriad awards for artistic achievement, including five Grammys. Gina made several appearances on *The Jane Wilde Show*. This was her first." Jane and Gina, perched on stools on the talk show set, showed an unmistakable familial resemblance. Their genetic sameness—blonde hair, expressive eyes, prominent cheekbones, and slender physiques—played against superficial differences suggestive of an elemental dissimilarity in their personalities: my mother's hairstyle was a tad spiky, her makeup heavier, her clothes tighter.

"Well, Janie, your show has become the hottest ticket in town, sure took you long enough to invite me on! My agent kept asking me if you and I really were family." She leaned closer to Jane and put an arm around her.

Once there was no place safer than your arms.

She turned to the audience. "You with sisters or brothers know sibling rivalry does exist, and we've had our share of squabbles, pulled out a fistful or two of hair—"

Jane reached a hand to her head, pretending to check her hair. We laughed.

Jane's voice narrated, "She surprised me during a landmark taping for our staff and crew." There was a clip of my mother walking out onto the set with a hand-lettered banner reading "Congratulations, Jane, on Show One Hundred!" My mom and I had made the sign the night before.

Let me write it, Mom, your handwriting is the pits.

—You have glitter in your hair, Neet, it's pretty.

You have it on your face. Quit inhaling the fumes off that magic marker or I'll tell your sponsor.

—Yep, I guess it's a teenager's job to be obnoxious.

Jane continued, "And a few times she appeared in front of our audience to do what she did best."

The next cut was a close-up of my mother's face. The room filled with her voice singing, "Take a Bow:"

> Take a bow, they loved you
> When the show is over
> What will you do?
> You haven't a clue
> So for now
> Just take your bow...

Tears—fuck no!

She took a deep bow and the screen faded to black.

Our applause began before a production assistant flicked on the lights. Tonia was beaming. "Jesus, what a great job!" She high-fived Karen.

For the first time, I saw a smile on the crank-muffin's face. "You can just call me Karen."

Allie caught my glance and rolled her eyes.

"Terrific," my aunt added.

96

I completely agreed with them—not only was the piece creative and technically flawless, it completely lacked sentimentality. I realized why, for emotional reasons, Karen might have been selected for this project. Her absence of sensitivity had served her well. Anyone less cold might've turned the whole bit into a real tearjerker.

Now that I'd seen the bio, I felt like a royal ass, sweating it the way I had. There was nothing so scary about it. I could have participated. Instead, I'd only succeeded in showing Jane what a wuss she had for a niece.

Tonia's voice interrupted my thoughts. "After we roll the bio, Jane will give a factual account of Gina's last days, and discuss some of the gossip surrounding her death."

"We're sure to hear from her fans as soon as the real publicity begins," Jane added. "Maybe we can salt the audience with some of these folks, have them talk about the rumors."

Sam swiveled side-to-side in her chair. "Red flag, hon."

Jane scowled. "You and I will personally pre-interview these people. We will script whatever they have to say in their own words. Okay, Sammy? See me waving a white flag?"

The attorney cracked a smile. "Just doing my job."

"So," Jane continued, "after this segment you think you can bully me over—"

Everyone snickered, including Sam, then they put their hands together—three quick claps.

"After that segment, let's show the audience how the tabloids craft their stories. And Linda," she turned to the senior associate producer, "before counsel drapes you in red flags, though by the way, red is a good color for you..."

The woman, who happened to be wearing a red-striped blouse, flashed a nervous smile. "I have a former editor of Celebrity Outlook and two fact-checkers on tap. Every question I've written is ready for Sam's once-over."

"Perfect. That leaves only the Pandora's box of pulp fiction. Allie?"

Allie began to fill her in on whom we'd lined up, and then—I have no idea what possessed her—she began to relate the incident with Jack Sklar. There was no reason to do it; needless to say, he wasn't appearing on the show. Everybody—my aunt, Sam, Tonia, Linda, Bob,

Karen, plus five production assistants—sat spellbound as she described the sight we'd been treated to in the mobile home. At least she skipped the Kleenex.

Now why the fuck did you go and do that?

People glanced in my direction, then looked quickly away. Jane sat there with her eyes closed. My heart began to pound.

Well, if I thought I was embarrassed just being there with Allie, it's a bazillion times worse now!

I knew she hadn't thought about what she was saying, because as soon as she saw my expression, she faltered, ending lamely, "I can't believe his story actually went to press."

Oh God, somebody, what can I say! "Would've made a great scene in a horror flick."

Thanks, Allie, really 'preciate it!

After the meeting broke up, my aunt trailed us out into the hallway. "Nita, come to my office." She took my arm.

Shit, if she says one word about how sorry she is, I swear I'll lose it completely—

She banged the door shut and led me to the couch. "I'm very thankful he didn't try to hurt you or Allie." She shuddered. "In the future, anyone involved with the tabloids will be interviewed here. There's no reason to take such a risk. Sweetie, you must let me know about things like this, painful or not. Didn't we learn that the hard way last fall?" She caught my hand between hers and held it. "Remember our deal? No secrets. When you grow up with so many of them, you get used to not telling, but the only way to stay strong is if you do."

The minute I got back to our office Allie apologized. I interrupted her, "I know you didn't mean to, but right now I'm too upset to discuss it." Why I didn't stick to that, why I let her persuade me to drive down the block to talk, I don't know.

As soon as I killed the engine, she moved closer and put a hand on my shoulder. I shrugged it off. She sat back in her seat, played with the seat belt catch. "I wasn't thinking. You seemed okay about it, and..." her voice trailed off. "I wasn't thinking, I'm sorry."

I was silent.

"It was such a strange scene, it got to me. I know it was awful for you, but you wouldn't talk to me. Why did you lead me to believe you were all right when obviously you weren't?"

"Please shut up!"

Allie looked stricken. I had to control myself. I was already ticked off at the way I'd acted over the bio, and knew she didn't deserve me taking that out on her, but I couldn't hold back. "I'm sorry. Yes, it was awful for me. Now everyone we work with knows exactly how awful! It was bad enough it happened in front of you!"

She turned from me to stare out the window.

I still couldn't stop myself. "What in hell went through your mind to make you tell them about it?"

Allie sighed. "I enjoy being around you, Nita, but it isn't always easy."

I resented what seemed an implied threat. "And that's supposed to mean..."

She turned back, eyes flashing. "As difficult as it may have been for you to have me there, did you ever stop to consider it was hard for me to be there?"

I hadn't, and her calling me on this only made me defensive. "You haven't answered my question."

She countered with hostility. "What question was it again? Did you ask whether the experience was horrible for me, too? Or whether I'm embarrassed to have made the mistake of telling everyone about it?" Her voice broke. She opened the door and got out.

I sat there for a moment, then unrolled the passenger-side window, started the engine, and followed her down the street. "Come on, Allie, don't be silly, get back in the car."

She sped up, hands jammed into her pockets. I saw tears streaming down her face.

Oh God, I made her cry. "Maybe we both made some mistakes." She just kept going.

Enough. I parked the car, jumped out, and ran after her. "Stop, please."

She stopped. I caught her arm. "Get back in, please?"

She tried to twist away, but I held her firmly.

"Let's get in the car and continue our discussion."

"Take your hand off me." Her voice was toneless.

Ice water filled my veins. I did as she asked.

TEN

At a little before seven that evening, I walked down a brightly lit corridor, the gray-and-maroon checked carpeting muffling my footsteps. The place had a pleasantly clean smell almost like a freshly-chlorinated swimming pool, but there was no pool here. I stopped in the middle of the hallway at a door with a brass plaque engraved with Joseph Gallagher, Ph.D., pushed it open, and took a seat on the sofa in the waiting room. Magazines were scattered on the glass-topped coffee table; I picked one up, then tossed it back. Even when I had nothing particular on my mind, I couldn't really concentrate on reading before a session. Tonight I had an excuse for being distracted.

After Allie left me standing there in the street, I had driven back to the office. She showed up shortly. My back was to her, and I heard her shuffle through some mail and collect her notes from the day. I thought she might've been stalling, seeing if I would speak to her, but when I looked over, she snatched her purse from her desk drawer and left without a word.

The clock on the wall opposite chimed seven. Bits and pieces of my first session came to mind:

...So—where am I supposed to sit? I mean, it's not like I've ever done this before. I never thought I'd have to. No offense, but I don't know you at all, and I'm supposed to tell you personal stuff?

Suicide—me? Uh-uh, no way, never! You have to be totally selfish and irresponsible to do that to the people who love you. My mother might've made that decision, but I wouldn't!

Sure, she hugged me a lot. Of course I couldn't always be affectionate with her when I wanted to. It was always like, careful of my lipstick, watch my hair.

100

A couple of times, but I probably deserved it. It's not like it really hurt or anything...

When you're in love, it's important that people you care about know. I figured she'd be cool. I mean, she was the poster child for alternative lifestyles. And she really wasn't shocked at all. Whatever made me happy was okay with her. Only don't automatically rule out all guys. Don't miss out on having a kid.

Did I cry when my mother died? Of course! I still cry every day—I mean, sometimes I cry every day. What kind of a stupid question is that? I loved my mother, sure I cried.

Having a famous mom there's always a comparison being made. If you go into the business you spend your life competing with this legend. If you want a normal job, everyone assumes you're a loser...

At the age of four or five I was hanging out at parties taking hits off people's joints.

Well, on a whim she bought me this puppy and I got really attached to him and then he like peed all over the house and chewed shoes, and one day when I got home from school she'd returned him to the breeder. And another time when she grounded me, and I missed the junior ski trip. Oh, you mean did I hate her for that? Well, addiction is a sickness, can you hate someone for having a cold...

The door to Joseph's office opened, and he welcomed me with a smile. Joseph is handsome, in his early fifties, with a forehead that wrinkles when he's engrossed in what you're saying or whenever he smiles, which is a good deal of the time. He's always impeccably dressed. Today he wore sharply-creased tan slacks, a white shirt still crisp-looking for his last appointment, a blue silk tie with beige and cream stripes, and tasselled loafers.

I could've spent the session just bitching and moaning about the argument with Allie; Joseph focused on the crazy scene in the mobile home instead. "You will admit it was hard for you?"

"Of course I admit it."

"Did you admit it to Allie?"

"Yes. Well, not exactly." I knew he deserved a better answer. "It was obvious I was upset, but I handled it. I was fine until she opened her mouth and told everyone about it."

"And that was what you couldn't handle?"

"Exactly." A pause. I waited it out.

A characteristic wrinkle of the forehead. "Would you consider the possibility that the guy upset you, and instead of allowing yourself to be upset, it came out at Allie?"

I started to feel uncomfortable, the way I did whenever I thought he wasn't understanding what was really going on. "Wouldn't that hack you off? Shouldn't some matters be private?"

"She didn't use the best judgment, but no harm was meant. As soon as she realized it, she stopped. She apologized to you." He straightened his tie even though it didn't need straightening. "What did Jane have to say when you told her?"

"She made me go back to her office after the meeting—"

"You didn't tell her earlier?" He looked exasperated.

What am I supposed to do, get a megaphone and immediately blast everyone with my embarrassing problems? I said nothing.

He gave a little grunt of disapproval. "How were you right after it happened?"

"Well, when I went home I called Julia, as a matter of fact. I talked to her about it." There, maybe he'd be satisfied that I had opened up my yap to someone. "But she wasn't all that helpful. She just said that the whole world is crazy, and if I stop expecting everyone to act sane, I'll be a lot better off." And I remembered she told me to call my 'girl-friend.' Maybe it really was wrong of me not to have talked to Allie...

"Oh, that's not so terribly unhelpful... And then did you call Allie?"

I started to feel really guilty. "I drove to her apartment later that night."

"And you talked it over? She comforted you?"

"She tried to, I guess."

"And you wouldn't allow it?" I shook my head. He sat back in his chair. "Forgive me if I'm wrong here, Nita, but I think we're back to that old behavior of yours of clamming up, stuffing your feelings, say-ing you're fine—maybe because you feel you have to impress Allie by staying cool."

I guess that made sense. Anyway, I liked the picture of myself stay-ing cool for Allie. "You think?" I said, all dweeby.

"Yeah, I think. And I have a suggestion—"

I couldn't help myself. "You always do." Then I quickly added,

"Thank God."

He smiled. "So what are you trying to prove, that therapists aren't immune to flattery?" He straightened in his chair, a look washing over his face that meant I was about to learn something, probably accompanied by that excruciating sensation like bone and muscle separating that I know is a sign of true personal growth. "I'm giving you an assignment. Ready? The next time you find yourself in an intolerable situation, listen to the voice inside. Is it saying, 'This is awful, I can't stand this, I hate myself, I'm going crazy, I'm going to die?' Write everything down and bring it to the next session. I want to see how you talk to yourself."

It sounded totally off-the-wall. "Only crazy people talk to themselves."

He scowled. "Everyone talks to herself, Nita, but it's the way that you do that makes a difference. Trust me. And another thing—if someone is concerned about you, please don't just say, 'I'm fine.' By saying you're fine, you deny your friends their role. They cannot comfort you, they cannot protect you."

I understood what he meant, but I didn't like it. "And if I don't let my friends protect me, I have no right to be angry if they expose me?"

"Take into consideration that an association with you comes with a whole lot of complications Allie has never dealt with." He sounded impatient again, as though he couldn't believe he should have to explain this to me. "You're the child of one celebrity, the niece of another, who just happens to be her boss. You're still grieving for your mother. You're very involved in this project. And you're heading for trouble if you don't keep the communication lines open with your aunts, as well as your friends. Don't take for granted that anyone knows what goes on inside your head, especially if you don't let them in."

I left his office confused and upset, feelings that, after nearly a year of sessions, I'd gotten accustomed to, even come to expect. His ideas challenged me, often in ways that weren't exactly comfortable. When I'd confessed my frustration to Jane and Sam, my aunt had nodded knowingly. "Many times we came out of there and had a screaming fight, or cried in each other's arms. Oh, the joy of therapy!"

If I'm resistant to anything Joseph's said, experience tells me not to jump to the conclusion he's wrong. On a rare occasion, he's not on the mark, but most of the time, he is. Dead on.

Tonight I knew he was right, but I had trouble accepting that my denial over the incident with Sklar had made Allie disclose it. That she'd brought it up because she needed to talk about it, and I wouldn't.

By not allowing Allie to comfort me, I'd been acting weak, not strong. It depressed me that I couldn't see this without Joseph pointing it out. Not taking the time to find out her feelings was selfish. When she'd brought up the incident at the meeting, again I thought only about myself. She'd gone out of her way to apologize and to talk it over with me in the car, and I'd yelled at her and made her cry. It scared me that I hadn't a clue how awful I'd acted. Was it any different from being drunk or on drugs and not realizing what I was doing?

Well, Mom, I lived with you long enough to act just like you. It's an illness I've caught. I'm just as sick as you—

Hey, I'm talking to myself! How freaky! Joseph's right. Now what the fuck did I just say?

Shut up, asshole. Who the hell cares?

What could I say in my own defense to Allie? Would she even listen to me?

I drove to Burbank, where I stopped and bought her a bouquet of tiny pink roses, then went to her apartment. It was only nine, and I was surprised to see all the lights were off. It occurred to me she might not be home, a discouraging thought, but I rang the bell anyhow.

She undid the lock without asking who it was; of course she knew. She was in her pajamas, her hair a little tousled. Could she have been asleep at such an early hour?

I extended the roses. "I'm sorry...I don't even know how to begin apologizing." I was afraid to look at her, to see the expression on her face that meant I was no longer welcome at her door, in her life.

She let me in.

ELEVEN

Advertising for "Death of a Sister, Death of a Star" began two weeks before the taping, and Jane's time was tied up in meetings and calls from reporters, many from the pulp media. Sensing a pre-emptive strike was about to be launched, they figured the best defense was to infiltrate the enemy camp before the campaign actually began. Pushed to the limit by the turmoil, Tonia wanted to fire Matthew, the publicist. "He's the only mouth in town who doesn't know the meaning of the words 'press conference'!" But my aunt intervened on Matt's behalf.

The closer we drew to the airdate, problems seemed only to increase. The scenic shop, having rebuilt the set during the summer, was late installing it in the studio. Empty, the room seemed cavernous with its twenty-foot high ceiling, but once the set was loaded in, it seemed to shrink. Carlos, the director, had difficulty getting used to the new dimensions. A camera operator would have to stand right up against the back wall in order to get what was called the 'beauty shot,' showing the entire set, that was used in the program opening. The lighting crew worked overtime hanging instruments from the grid before the techs could come in to complete the electronic setup. All this caused the budget to skyrocket; Tonia went around looking like death warmed over, but there wasn't much she could do about it.

Jane started intensive rehearsals with Carlos, while he finalized the shooting schedule. Tonia and Sam tweaked scripts with the writers. As the countdown began during the last week before we aired, panic set in. There was just too much to do. The production staff was supposed to keep all the show elements going as Carlos had ordered them, make sure that the guests understood their segments and what they were to do on the air, update scripts and keep cue cards in the correct order, label videotapes properly, order flowers for Jane's dressing room. It was so overwhelming, we began to specialize. I had the pleasure, along with Yasmin, a fellow production assistant, of arranging hotel accommodations and transportation for nearly sixty people. Yasmin's sense of humor made the job bearable. "If TV production doesn't work out for us, we could always make it as tour directors."

The day before we aired, Carlos put us through rundowns of all five shows. There was still so much that needed to be finalized, I began to wonder how it would all come together. With the camera placed so far back for the opening shot, Jane couldn't read the Teleprompter. Some of the lights were hung too low, blinding her. There was a boom shadow on Camera 3's medium shot. Connections on the wireless mike transmitters kept breaking. Two sequences ran long and had to be rewritten. My aunt was exhausted long before we finished, becoming irritable as the temperature rose under the lights. During the dinner break, she, Carlos, Tonia, and Sam became embroiled in a screamer about the last show's content. Jane wanted to scrap one or two segments and leave them 'flexible'—or unscripted—in case an unexpected matter developed that should be addressed in front of the camera.

The idea made sense to me, but evidently it was unheard of to the people who mattered. Carlos tried to impress upon her the importance of staying within the time schedules of the shows as they had been fixed. Tonia asked her to consider how much money would be wasted over last minute changes. And of course Sam worried my aunt would get herself into some unforeseen legal trouble. "I'll just tell the court I couldn't run a red flag through my client's TelePrompter, and pray that all actions against us will be dismissed."

They retreated long after they should've to Jane's office to have it out, or finish having it out, returning quite some time after the break was supposed to end. I could tell my aunt had won—she was beaming, overly solicitous of the other three, who barely glanced in her direction. I was pleased she'd prevailed. Concerned, however, that the row might have taken on a personal dimension, I managed to catch Sam a moment later to ask her if everything was all right. She just rolled her eyes.

We wrapped just before eight. Tonia's last words to us were ominous, "Tomorrow morning's call is at seven, which means get your butt in here by six forty-five. Be on time, or consider yourself fired. Surgically attach your phone lists to your hand, in case there are any last-minute changes and you need to contact someone. Get whatever sleep you can. You'll need it. That's it, people."

Allie and I walked out to the parking lot together. I was dead tired and assumed she was, too, so I was surprised when she suggested we grab dinner. Without thinking, I declared myself too tired.

"You have to eat," she said, looking down at her shoes. My eyes followed, and I watched as she traced circles on the pavement with the toe of one pump. Under her hose a thin gold chain accentuated the thinness of her ankle. "Otherwise, you'll be trashed tomorrow. I just feel so wired... Look, why don't I follow you back to your place, get a pizza delivered, we'll eat, I'll leave, and you can fall into bed."

If she didn't mind the commute, I wouldn't mind the company. As we drove off the lot, she kept pace with me, flicking her lights so I'd wave to her when we stopped at traffic signals. When we got on the freeway, she pulled in front briefly, only to drop behind again to follow me down the off-ramp. By the time I met up with her in the parking garage of my apartment building, I realized I had this stupid grin on my face, even before she asked me what I was smiling at. "You." I didn't think twice about the wisdom of my honesty.

I called for the pizza and salad, remembering just in time that I was completely out of soda, and added it to the order. When I hung up, she seemed amused. "Ever the bachelor. Nothing to drink?" She pointed with her chin to the refrigerator. "What's in there, science experiments?"

Her gazed roamed the room, taking in my desk that held only a computer and a pencil holder filled with up-ended needle-sharp pencils, bookshelves organized within an inch of their lives, ficus tree, a dead leaf in the pot. She shook her head wonderingly. "How long has this been home for you, anyway?"

"Since I started school. Four years."

"It's like a barracks, so bare. Anyone could be living here. Don't you believe in posters, knickknacks, even a piece of paper crumpled in the wastebasket?" She plopped down on the futon that doubled as my bed, put her arms behind her head, and gave a languid stretch.

I tried not to linger over the lovely way her breasts filled her creamy ivory sweater, didn't want to be caught staring. "I'm holding off on the clutter until I get married."

She cocked her head to one side. "And if you find a woman who's as tidy as you?"

"Fat chance," I said.

We ate in front of the TV, and when the eleven o'clock news came on, she yawned and said she should be going. "You're welcome to crash here," I said reflexively, never thinking she'd say yes. My surprise registered on my face, I was sure; she pretended not to notice, and asked to borrow something to sleep in.

I took my time in the shower, getting far too turned on by the thought of climbing into bed with her. If I was a rung in her ladder, I didn't want to believe it right then.

The sight of her reading under my covers set me right off again. Her head against the pillow, the swirl of hair rich and dark against the stark white case. Her fingers spread like the delicate branches of a tree holding the book angled to her face, her lips slightly parted. Her eyes darted across the lines in a quick sexy rhythm, scrolling images through her mind. When she noticed me, she put the book down and smiled.

I got in beside her, put out the light, and we said a stilted good night. I lay wide-awake, and after a few minutes, stole a glance at her. The light that filtered in from the street lamp turned her chocolate hair to silver. The glitter confined usually to her eyes now spilled all over her skin, inviting me to discover the abstract beauty formed by the angles and planes of her face. I had to close my eyes for a moment, simply for the pleasure of opening them again to see her. And when I did, she moved into my arms, brought her lips to mine, claimed my mouth with her own. Her tongue began a slow stroking, creating paralyzing surges of desire, flooding me with waves of arousal. When she sat up to pull off her clothes, I lay there helplessly, just watching, until she was nude. I waited, enjoying her vulnerability, the sense of my own power returning, coursing my bloodstream.

But then a deeper realization hit me: she was the one in control, by showing herself to me first. She knew I'd be unable to resist her lead. And this challenge was more exciting than the feeling of power that'd come back to me only an instant earlier.

As I undressed she made no move to help, watching me with an electrifying frankness. Then she leaned over me, her breasts tantalizingly close to my face. Naturally I reached to touch her, but she caught my wrist. That sly smile started. I saw how much she wanted to satisfy me, and how she knew it wouldn't take much effort. She lowered her naked body onto mine, her hand coming instantly to me, lightly breaking the surface of moisture, then glided slowly up. No woman had ever touched me first. But I angled my hips to guide her where she was needed: when she got there I moaned. I filled my mouth with her tongue and pitched against her, drawing her fingers down deep. She found my natural rhythm, then began teaching me a new one.

Then, that moment of inevitability. From the way she intensified my pleasure, she realized I was there, too, and she sent me spiralling toward an incredible release.

I opened my eyes to see hers were closed; a spasm raised her eyebrows that I felt the echo inside me. Then I had to see more, make the full range of pleasure her body was capable of register on her face. As I maneuvered her onto her back, her hands moved through my hair, gripped my shoulders, raked my skin, crushed me against her. I asked her whether I was too heavy even though I knew she would say no, because I had to hear the sound of her voice which I had grown to love for itself, apart from her words, accented by sexual need.

"Oh... Nita..." she whispered, groaning in a way that almost made me cry out with her. Her breasts overflowed my palms, her nipples fat and firm between my fingers. I trailed my hands down her body, grazing her inner thighs. She opened wider, and I brought a hand to her lightly and came away wet; I returned again and again until she was straining for my touch.

I spread her with my fingers and moved up to give her the intensity of sensation she needed. She moaned and pressed against me, so that my palm covered the entire surface of her pleasure. I let her push and rock and show me what she wanted, until a shudder stopped her undulations and she tensed. Then I caught her and cradled her and shook the last tremors from her. She smiled as her eyes fluttered open. "There aren't words to convey how good that was."

"Maybe you shouldn't wait so long between drinks."

She stroked my hand, still covering her. "Don't confuse how much

I want you with the fact that I haven't wanted anybody else, not for so long."

"Never again, I promise," I said, flicking my fingers.

She giggled and twisted away from my hand, then pushed me against the pillows. "All right then."

She held me in her arms, told me she wanted me again, as soon as I was rested.

"I'm fine," I said, but I didn't have quite enough breath in my voice and it came out a croak.

She snickered. "You can't even talk."

I sat up, put her under me, straddled her. "Talk isn't what's important here, now is it?"

TWELVE

I woke in the darkness as the radio blared on, and lay there, my heart hammering. Allie's "Oh, no!" made me jump out of my skin; incredibly, I'd forgotten her presence. I reached over and turned the switch, last night a sudden flood of memories, of doubts.

The experience had been unexpected but so powerful, there was no way to characterize it as a casual encounter. I cared about her too much to be a trophy notch in her lipstick case. Fun to be so for the girls I dated in college, but the thought distressed me terribly when it came to Allie. Would she use my trust in her against me? Could last night have been the winning play in the game she was running?

She sat up, stretched, and I caught just a glimpse of her breasts in silhouette before she covered up. She studied me for a moment, concerned at first, then her expression brightened inexplicably. "Ordinarily, I'd ask you to hold me, but since I have six spare minutes to run home to change clothes and make it back to the studio, you're off the hook."

I relaxed just a little, and she could tell. She kissed her fingertip and placed it on my lips, then got up. "Don't worry so much, Nita." She disappeared into the bathroom.

I arrived at the studio before night seemed truly over, and met up with Allie and the others assembling for Tonia's crack-of-dawn 'prayer meeting.' She sat down beside me, and I felt so conspicuous I whispered, "Maybe we shouldn't sit together."

She scowled and shot back, "Will you relax? We always sit together." Her poise unnerved me even more. Wasn't I supposed to be the one in control, and here I was losing it all over the place? I leaned back in my chair, stretching out my legs and crossing my ankles—a pose meant to convey a sense of ease.

The air conditioning was on full blast, the temperature freezing, yet Tonia seemed a little flushed as she filled us in with what lay ahead. "This week will be a bitch, but the results will be worth it. Thanks for your hard work—I'm proud of you. You make our team the best in the business. Before I turn this over to Janie, lest you think I've reformed, my curmudgeonly ways will make a comeback as soon as we wrap."

A change had come over my aunt since I'd last seen her. She no longer seemed frazzled. I sensed her utter concentration and control, the way my mother had been before a performance.

Jane's demeanor led me to believe she was about to deliver a cross between a pep talk and a call to arms, so it surprised me when she began by revealing her vulnerability. "This project scares the hell out of me, but I operate on instinct." Her eyes swept the studio, ensuring our personal commitment by quickly locking gazes with each and every one of us, taking the courage she needed from our loyalty. "My instinct tells me to take what I'm afraid of and turn it around. It tells me this project will keep our show going strong. It's more rocket fuel to boost your already high-powered careers. We know from the pre-show hoopla the reaction will be huge. Thumbs-up, the glory is yours. Thumbs down, the responsibility is mine alone. Your effort has been superb. It means more to me than you can imagine."

We gave her the requisite three claps, then Allie and I headed off to control the green room.

A green room is not green. It's drab. When I was a kid, I pestered the hell out of my mom for an explanation, but she didn't know. Our studio's interpretation of green-room drab was taupe, soothing for the nervous or temperamental. The carpeting had a shiny look to it, polished, no doubt, by quite a few floor-pacers. On the coffee table we'd set a tray of doughnuts, bagels, and fruit. The food would go fast—people like to get whatever they can if they're not being paid for their time.

My awareness of my new relationship with Allie was diverted by the group that waited to go on, the memories they brought back. Guests for the first panel included a psychology professor from U.S.C., a gossip columnist known for her oversized harlequin glasses, and Kristina Randy, my mother's former publicist, resurfacing from whatever swamp she'd submerged herself in after Mom died. They would discuss the public's fascination with the lives—and deaths—of celebrities.

There was a ton of medical personnel: paramedics who'd begun the resuscitation attempt in my mother's bedroom, nurses on duty when she was brought in to the emergency room, the doctors who worked on her, including the one who pronounced her dead. A tiny, troll-like lady in uniform came up to me and tearfully introduced herself as the dispatcher who'd talked me through CPR. I didn't know what to say, so I just thanked her. This opened up a whole floodgate about how brave I was, how I never should think my mother's death was in any way my fault, that I was included in her prayers each night, that she had a granddaughter my age she hardly ever saw. Maybe she was only caught up in the moment, but it was weird to be in someone's thoughts when to me she was only a disembodied voice over a telephone line, one that I'd rather forget.

All these people had been key players in the worst night of my life, yet I didn't recognize a single one. We could have passed on the street, stood in line together at the supermarket, gotten into a car accident, without my ever realizing who they were.

I didn't want to know who they are. I didn't want them to know me.

Along with them, there was one other guest in the room, coolly eating a doughnut and drinking our lousy coffee—Detective Glyn Gilmore, here to talk about the possibility of police contamination of evidence, and make eyes at my new girlfriend.

Just before the taping started Sam called me to my aunt's dressing room. I paused in the doorway. Eric, Jane's hairstylist, and Lauren, the makeup artist, were performing their ministrations, having a difficult time choreographing their movements to stay out of each other's way.

Jane saw me in the mirror, smiled, and turned in her chair. Lauren muttered, "Move again, and I quit." Eric sighed.

"Sorry. Nita, wait just a moment so I can talk to you."

I sat with Sam, who explained, "She only wants you to tell her how pretty she looks, and say break a leg."

Had Sam forgotten how many times I had sat backstage with my mother, pumping her up before she went on? I knew how to handle a pre-performance celeb—

—Three minutes, Nita. I'm ready for you to say it now.

Okay. More than all the times the sun will rise and set...

—And?

More than all the stars that light the sky at night...

—And?

More than all the ages that will ever come to pass...

—Yes?

You will go out there and be great and they will love you.

—Do you really think so?

I know so.

—Thanks, Nita. Be good while I'm gone—

"Ten minutes," the floor manager barked into the room.

Last-ditch blotting and spraying completed, Eric removed the smock protecting Jane's clothes, and she stood.

"Thanks, guys." She turned to us, and, when Sam gave her a wolf-whistle, broke into a wide smile.

"You look great, Aunt Jane."

"I hate stage makeup, but when I haven't slept, I'm grateful for the camouflage."

Looking frantic, Tonia burst in with one of the assistant directors, who handed Jane some index cards. "Cueing changes!"

Sam took my elbow. "Let's give her a gentle hug—don't crush anything—and get the hell out of here."

Allie and I went to watch the taping on the green room monitor. The endless weeks of preparation had finally boiled down to this moment. My pulse began to race; I turned to Allie, and she furtively squeezed my hand.

At first, all cameras were focused on the back wall of the set, where a lighting technician projected the show's logo, created by placing a stencil in front of a floodlight and rotating shades in various hues over the lens. The colors went from pink to mauve before turning lavender. We were on.

The audience applauded as Jane stepped onto the set. She sat on one of the chairs placed center stage, smiling as camera one came in for a close-up. "Welcome. Today's show is about the effects publicity can have on your life. The late Andy Warhol claimed that everyone would be famous for fifteen minutes, and we'll be talking today about getting burned during your quarter hour in the limelight. This issue has touched my life dramatically. As you all know, nearly two years ago I lost my sister, singer Gina Wilde. Her death, a barbiturate overdose, was ruled an apparent suicide. Her voice and songwriting talent were, and still continue to be, beloved throughout the world."

She paused briefly for applause. "Over the five incredible years we've been on the air, I've been fortunate to have had my sister on many times. One of my producers, Karen Kincaid, has compiled some highlights of these appearances for you." Jane scanned the studio. "Where are you, Karen? There she is! Can you get her on camera, Carlos?" Karen managed a quick smile and waved. Jane gives credit where credit is due.

The bio played, and then the audience, after a hushed few seconds of silence, went absolutely wild. Jane continued her monologue with difficulty. "It's still hard for me to believe my sister is no longer with us. Your support since her death has been tremendous. I very much appreciate all your letters and telephone calls. They offered me comfort when I needed it—as well as the idea for this show. Once I began to recover from the shock of losing my sister, I became angry about the ensuing media frenzy." She continued, looking directly into the camera as it dollied in for a close-up, "As a child, Gina was extraordinarily sensitive and had great difficulty defending herself. If someone called her a name, she ran home crying. I sometimes had to step in to protect her. It's up to me to do this one last thing for her."

Her comment was met with another round of applause, and she prepared to launch into the next segment. "I'm certain people will misunderstand my motives. They'll insist I'm disgracing my sister's memory in hopes of a ratings sweep. When we come back, I'll let you decide for yourselves."

Well, here we were at ground zero. Allie and I brought out the professor, the gossip columnist, and my mother's publicist, and when they were done, the medical personnel. As the paramedics sensitively yet matter-of-factly described the events of that night, my mind fired image after image like a disjointed music video.

Scissors slicing through the tee shirt, laying bare her breasts. Defibrillator paddles slapped down. Her body jolting obscenely from the charge. I can't look, turn away.

A male voice shouts, "Okay, here we go again! Again! Again! Again! Nothing!"

What are you saying…she's gonna die?

Allie put a hand on my shoulder. "You okay?"

I stifled my instinctual 'I'm fine,' and nodded instead.

Jane, finished with the doctors and nurses, set up the next segment. "When we come back, we'll have an LAPD detective explain how police picked up the investigation."

Glyn went on looking confident and relaxed, and I realized why the Lesbian and Gay Peace Officers' Association had chosen her as their media spokesperson. She loved the camera, and, though it pained me to admit it—the camera loved her. I couldn't resist kidding Allie, "Hey, close your mouth."

She grinned sheepishly. "Glyn's a jerk, but…"

"That's okay, I have Uma Thurman."

Jane made little headway with the detective. After going over the basics of police procedure in a high-profile investigation like this one had been, Glyn reiterated what she'd said to Allie and me in her office. "Anything's possible, Jane, but why would police care whether it was suicide or an overdose?"

"The idea of suicide is painful for our family."

"Of course." Glyn sat back and crossed her legs. "More than two hundred hours were put in on this case, so the police finding was no rush to judgment. Plus, we had the autopsy report…"

Jane turned to the audience. "The coroner will be with us later in the week, after we go through some of the more creative theories of the cause of death."

Glyn continued, "Certainly it's occurred to you, as the sibling of someone with a long-standing and dangerous addiction, essentially she was involved in a slow form of suicide."

"I'm aware of that, Detective. It just might be easier to live with the idea she made one final, terrible mistake, rather than a conscious decision to leave us."

"Every time she popped a pill or took a swig, she made that decision," Glyn said firmly.

She was right.

We took a two-hour break before beginning the afternoon's taping, and then wrapped by five o'clock, after the first segment had aired. Then Jane, Sam, Carlos, Tonia and the rest of the production staff gathered in the conference room to watch the local news broadcasts. The atmosphere was tense but optimistic. That changed shortly.

"Do we really care about the sordid private lives of Jane and Gina Wilde?"

"Today's *Jane Wilde* program was innovative, but hardly in good taste."

"As this sister act navigates reality TV's uncharted waters, we wonder, will Jane sink or swim?"

"That's okay, we can handle it," Jane reassured us, but I could tell she was disappointed. The six o'clock news was worse: her integrity was viciously attacked. "Those who tuned in to *The Jane Wilde Show* today watched trash TV in action. Evidently Jane has decided exploitation is the name of the game, and she proves herself a top player in what is certainly a crowded field."

My aunt sat back in her chair and closed her eyes. Still in stage makeup, her face looked like a too-rouged corpse. "Someone turn off the goddamn set." Her voice sounded gravelly. All the production assistants rose, but I got to the TV first.

Tonia, by contrast, was like an uncoiled spring, immediately calling a meeting with Jane, Sam, and Carlos. She bellowed at the cowering Linda returning from yet another cigarette break, "Get the writers back here immediately!" before striding toward my aunt. She stopped in front of her, hands on hips, eyes flashing. "You and I have been through worse. We have the talent—and goddess willing we'll find the money—to fix this." Still Jane had no reaction. The expression on Tonia's face softened slightly, but when she spoke again, her tone was threatening. "I will not have you sitting there like a whipped French poodle. Where's that poker-up-the-butt backbone? We won't get anywhere if you cave."

Jane drew a deep breath, got up and started for the door. "Give me a few minutes to recoup first," she said in her best celebrity voice.

Tonia sighed. "Please, Janie, recoup for no more than five. It'll be an all-nighter as it is."

Sam and Tonia exchanged a glance, then Sam was instantly by Jane's side. Time to shore up the old ego. I was surprised when Jane

117

called over her shoulder. "Nita, are you coming?"

Apparently the ego required two people for shoring purposes.

I caught up to them and we went into Jane's office; all three of us sandwiched together on the couch, my aunt in the middle. She wasted no time. "Screw those network anchor wannabes, trying to humiliate me! I'm not exploiting my sister for ratings, I'm saying the time has come for that to stop! Of course my point is lost on them. It makes them nervous. If they can't exploit someone, they'll find themselves out of a job!"

"Hon," Sam said, modulating her tone to reel in Jane's hysteria before it gained full momentum, "this isn't about them. You're disappointed in yourself, and I'm not sure why. We all recognized the potential risk, and whatever tweaking we have to do for tomorrow's show, no biggie."

I took advantage of Jane's slightly relaxed expression to interject, "Yeah, chill, you were good."

The look I got said she wasn't in the mood for anything that would undermine the seriousness—or melodramatic potential—of the moment. "Well, maybe I've been a fool to imagine I could push the genre to a new place. I certainly haven't done Gina's image any good today."

"Janie—and forgive me for saying this, Nita—rehabilitating Gina's image is hopeless. She was what she was, yet you loved her. Your outrage at the media picking her bones is your point here. How often must I tell you, you aren't responsible for your sister's actions."

The remark reminded me of Julia's advice. "Like Julia says—"

Jane wailed, "It must be my darkest hour because she's quoting that woman to me!"

Sam looked amused. "Jane, how many times do I have to remind you that Julia Reynolds is just an empty vessel our niece helps to fill?" She turned to me. "What does Julia say?" she asked politely.

"No one is so important to anyone else that they can make them live or die."

Both of them stared at me, surprised, I assumed, to learn that Julia and I occasionally took a breather from our marathon sex sessions for a serious discussion.

But still Jane exploded, her general outrage finding an avenue of expression at the mention of Julia. "How someone with half a brain can decide to sleep with a teenager—"

Sam cut her off sternly. "Leave it alone. We have enough to think about now."

Silent only a moment, Jane came back with a "Neither of you has said 'I told you so' about the show." She was obviously miffed at being made to shut up.

Sam rolled her eyes. "We don't have the energy to reassure you that your two best friends aren't monsters."

Exactly the right thing to say. I shot Sam a smile; she winked.

"My only two friends."

"You won't have any friends at all if you keep up this attitude." Sam reached to put an arm around her, and she grabbed me as well. We all hugged. "She's so much trouble, Neet," Sam said, "maybe now would be a good time for us stop loving her. What do you think?"

"I will if you will, but I don't think I can do it on my own," I said, and Jane laughed, the sound muffled against Sam's shoulder.

We returned to the conference room. Allie and I offered to stay, but Tonia told us to go home and get some rest. We left reluctantly, stopping at my place to pick up a change of clothes before heading to Allie's to spend the night. When we reached her apartment, the message-waiting light on her answering machine was blinking.

"Allie, Glyn here. It was great seeing you today. The show was terrific. How about going out Saturday night to celebrate? I know a place in Malibu, right on the beach. Name the time and I'll be at your door!"

Jealousy stabbed through me. "Did you give her your phone number?" My tone wasn't too nice.

Allie shrugged. "I'm listed." She came to me and took my hand. "Don't worry, I'll let her know she's barking up the wrong tree." She grinned. "Yours."

After a dinner of Chinese takeout, feeding each other on her balcony in the evening light, we went in to sit on the floor drinking wine and watching TV, my back against the couch, Allie between my legs. I held her loosely against me, my arm just under her breasts. She followed the show closely; I could've happily watched a test pattern. The commercial breaks were what interested me, when she would lean her head back on my shoulder, bringing her mouth to mine.

Much earlier during the day, I had resolved that tonight I would restore what I considered the natural order of things, i.e., please her first in bed. After we got under the covers, I took her in my arms; she responded to my kiss by trying to steal my air. I decided there wouldn't be much warmup; this had all the earmarks of a shameless quickie. Wrong. When I slipped my hand under the waistband of her pajamas, she twisted away.

"Uh-uh, I never go first." Her tone, a little domineering, turned me on even more than the answer surprised me.

"Why not?"

"Do you want me to tell you, or would you like to find out? Now, listen to what I say." She boldly switched the bedside light back on.

I winced, reached again for her pajamas, and again she moved away. Apparently this was going to happen her way or not at all. "I want to touch you, too."

"If I handle this right you'll have to. Just listen to me."

"I'm listening." Believe me, I was. When she told me to take off my tee shirt and shorts, I complied immediately.

"First, I'll tell you what I'm going to do to you, and then, depending on your answer, I may or may not go through with it."

"You're already doin' stuff to me."

A smile played on her lips. "That was a very good answer." She lay beside me.

"I'm glad it pleased you. Isn't the rule if I please you, you please me?"

"The rule is, I'm making the rules, you're following them. Now, I'm going to find out if you're wet, and exactly where. When you're very excited, do you get wet on top, all over your clitoris?"

"I don't know," I whispered. "I never bothered to notice, and no one ever told me."

"Another good answer." She ran her hand through her hair, obviously enjoying her own game. "And if I find you wet, and bigger there than I think you must be normally, it would mean you're ready for what I have planned for you next."

"I seem always to be in that state when you're around, so you may never have a way of knowing what I'm normally like."

She smiled. "Shall I check you out anyway?"

"Yes. Please!" I moaned when her hand came to me, but she took it away again just as quickly.

"Well, you seem ready. So, I'm going to start lower down, draw my fingers up through the middle, and circle you once."

"Just once? Go slow." I raised my hips to her hand as it left me, chasing the sensation.

She kissed me softly and lightly. "I'll start in the same place, but I'm not going to slide up the middle. Would you like to know which side I'm going to touch?"

"Yes," I managed to breathe.

"That was the right answer, but I'm not going to tell you. Instead just experience it. Here we go." I watched, fascinated, as she took two fingers, one on either side of me, and brought them slowly up. When she began her vibrations I closed my eyes. Then she stopped.

I wailed, "You're killing me!"

She laughed. "Don't be silly, I'm just talking to you." Her expression became serious. "But if you'd like, I could stop talking. I could stop right now."

"You could stop now, but I can't."

"That's very true." She came closer. "And because you admit it, you're going to get a reward. This time I'm going to move up, circle you, and then I'm going to stroke you ten times on your favorite side. Do you know which is your favorite side?"

"N-no."

"Your left. Do you know why?" I shook my head. "It's your favorite because you're left-handed, and when you touch yourself you concentrate on the left side, so it's more sensitive. It's the opposite for me, because I'm right-handed."

"That's very informative," I said weakly.

A sly pleasure stole across her face. "And I know you think about girls all the time. I imagine you touch yourself when you think about them."

"There's no need to do either now."

She brought her hand to me, and actually counted out the strokes she was giving me. By the time she hit three, I was praying, Let me come before ten.

121

No such luck. "Would you like another ten?" I nodded. She did it slower this time. Then she paused, removed her hand. God, almost! "Another?" This time she went faster. Just when she stopped, I started to come, and she expertly finished me. It was so good, having her touch me as much as I needed, I forgot the exquisite sense of deprivation leading up to it.

I held her and kissed her, told her what a fabulous lover she was. She rolled over on top of me, gently balancing her bones on mine. "There you have it," she said. "The power of talk."

THIRTEEN

Taped to our office door the next morning was a piece of paper torn jaggedly from a legal pad. "N—I must see you at once—Aunt Jane," was carefully penned in her best autograph-endorsing script. What had developed overnight? She never signed herself 'Aunt' Jane. It made me suspicious.

Allie looked concerned. "I hope nothing's gone haywire."

Keeping my misgivings to myself, I told her I'd meet her in the green room, gave her a kiss, and headed for Jane's office. I paused at the open door; at first all I saw was the desk, phone buttons lit up red like tiny emergency flashers cutting through the darkness, then I heard her call my name. I could barely see her lying on the couch. "Be a good girl and open the blinds for your old aunt." Her voice came out with a croak.

The early morning sun filtered thin and bleak through the slats. She sat up. Her hair was out of place, and a crease from the seam of the couch cushion divided her face into asymmetrical halves. She clutched Sam's houndstooth blazer as a makeshift blanket. I sat beside her. "You guys never made it home, I take it."

She yawned, covering her mouth with her index and middle fingers, both stained with red ink. "Nope. I slept maybe an hour. Sammy couldn't rest at all." She reached up to touch her hair. "Geez, I must look like the top of a pineapple." She pulled her hair straight up. "Attention!"

I giggled, glad that her mood had improved from last night. "Shall I call Eric and let him know he's got an emergency?"

She threw off the jacket, stretched, and groaned. "I had a terrible dream that the studio was as big as a stadium and there were a hundred thousand people in the audience." She paused a moment and shook her head. "How your mother managed that, I'll never understand. Any-hoo, I was trying to interview guests, and they were all mumbling, except this one surfer kid who kept calling me 'Dee-ude.' Everything on the Teleprompter was coming out in code, and when I looked at my cue cards, the letters ran like blood and dripped off the page." She shuddered.

"How about some coffee?"

"That's very sweet of you, not right now." She patted my knee. "We only have a sec, and there are a few things I want to go over with you. I was so upset last night, I didn't get a chance to ask you your feelings about the show yesterday."

The inquiry put me on red-alert. I played it cautious. "I thought they went fine, especially considering all the things that had to be dealt with at the last minute."

She shook her head. "No, no, how did you feel? Was it okay—listening to the doctors who tried to help your mom?"

Her impatience was hardly conducive to me opening up, telling her how I'd wakened during the night, replaying in my mind the paramedics' frantic orchestrations in my mother's bedroom, the cold finality of the emergency room, my vivid recollection of inside-out rubber gloves on the floor beside the garbage pail near the E.R. double-doors. Only sheer exhaustion had brought me back to a light sleep that left me unrefreshed.

But stronger even than any impulse not to trust Jane with my feelings was a resolve not to keep hiding them from everyone. The incident with Allie over Sklar had shaken me. "It was hard," I finally said.

She studied me for a moment, then looked away. "I'm sorry."

I wondered why she'd even asked. Did she imagine I'd shrugged it off? "Should I have said something else?"

She looked surprised. "No, of course not." She stroked the collar of Sam's jacket.

"The doctors made it seem so traumatic to them, how devastated they were because they couldn't save her. I kept thinking, what's the big damn deal? I felt that way for the last ten years. You, probably even longer, right?"

Those clear, light gray eyes that caught mine were so similar to my mother's it freaked me out. Lack of sleep wove a spidery network of bright red capillaries, like Mom's eyes after a coke-wired night.

She drew a deep breath, then slowly released it. "Right."

"So yes, it bothered me. And I knew you couldn't show much emotion on the air, but you had to be feeling pretty strange."

She kept running her hand over Sam's blazer like she was petting a dog. "I was having a hard time controlling myself. I'm used to feeling composed in front of an audience."

"You did fine."

"Thank you."

Again her eyes caught mine. The conversation dwindled into silence, and I thought she was being too polite to tell me to shove off. "Well, you have another big day ahead of you." I stood. "Or—wasn't there something else you wanted to say?"

A look came over her face that I couldn't quite read, sheepish maybe. "It can wait."

"Ready for your coffee now?"

She bit her lip, the offer seeming to touch her. "You're a nice girl, Nita."

I grinned. "That's my job."

"You're good at it." She returned the smile.

During the morning we learned of a programming change. A new guest had been added to the morning lineup: Jackie Landis, Channel Ten News entertainment reporter, who had pronounced yesterday's show "trash TV in action." I knew the drastic measure—with the attendant technical backflips required—indicated the necessity of addressing the bad reviews immediately. Only by confronting her detractors head-on might Jane recover some ground.

The middle-aged reporter broke through fashion barriers with her round, red-rimmed glasses and shoulder-length hair shellacked by spray into a helmet shape; her expression suggested her face was carved of oak. She sat impassively in the green room, responded to my offer of coffee with the single word, "Black," and didn't bother to thank me when I brought it over. She had all the charm and warmth of a Nazi prison guard.

Jane began the interview in a conciliatory manner. "Your statements on last evening's news were thought-provoking, to say the least.

Would you summarize what you said?"

"Certainly." The Chihuahua was straining at the leash. "Your show yesterday was one of the worst examples of trash TV I've ever seen. You talkers will stop at nothing to hook an audience—even exploiting the death of your own sister."

My aunt responded graciously. "I could waste a lot of time begging to differ, but I believe the shows' content will serve as my defense. You'll see my true motivation has little to do with self-promotion."

Landis yapped, "Nevertheless, your ratings'll go sky-high."

"Exactly why do you think so?"

"Isn't it obvious? Celebrity dirt sells."

Jane was waging a small battle with her temper. If she ever shot me a look like the reporter got, I swear I'd pee in my pants. "'Dirt,' as you call it, implies secrets. There are no secrets here. I'm a successful woman who happens to be a lesbian. My sister was a successful woman who was a drug addict. Despite our differences, we loved each other, and that's what should come out about us." The camera feed showed Landis sitting back in her chair, her wooden face looking a little splintered. My aunt continued, "And I'll tell our secrets over and over, so they won't become an issue ever again."

That evening's *Entertainment Tonight* praised the show and local news stations declared Jane was "fighting back," urging viewers to "tune in to judge for yourselves." We even made the national news: Peter Jennings proclaimed that controversy was once again brewing on the West Coast, where avowed lesbian talk show host Jane Wilde was going where no talk show host had gone before by airing her own dirty laundry. Jane wasn't exactly thrilled with the image, but Tonia grinned. "That's the kind of publicity I like—free publicity."

The afternoon's taping began with a person whose appearance I'd dreaded: Darren Cruz, the pathologist who'd performed the autopsy and released the results. My first sight of him that morning came as a shock. He was...a very cute guy. I never considered that the coroner's office would send their own version of a media god to appear on camera. Attractive in a frat-boy way, he was like a real-life paper doll who owned a socially correct outfit for every occasion. His Armani for today's show would have been appropriate for the funeral of any dignitary.

From the very first question, it was evident he had experience addressing a television audience, explaining in words any layperson could understand how blood-level concentrations of the toxins found in my mother's system were consistent with an intentional overdose. "Speaking in very general terms, she ingested several times the usual dosage of Secobarbital taken for sleep, swallowing the pills with vodka."

"Given my sister's bent, that could've been part of a day-long party. Except, dammit, she'd been sober a year."

Cruz pyramided his fingers; it was only then I noticed his gold-and-onyx pinky ring. A gay pathologist? Why the heck not. "I understand your frustration, and, yes, some addicts do indulge to that extent. As you undoubtedly know, alcohol tends to increase the toxicity of other drugs. In your sister's case, there was also liver damage, which boosts the sedative effect. Barbiturates may be taken in small doses, accumulate in the system, and cause a reaction similar to a larger dose, but that's extremely rare. I believe the pills were not spaced out over a period of time, but ingested all at once."

"Dr. Cruz, can you state definitively that you agree with the police finding of suicide?"

"There is, conceivably, room for a difference of opinion in this case, but, given the circumstances, and her history, there's likelihood." He'd replied without hesitation, but his answer was equivocating.

"She left no note. She seemed happy; her life was going well. And when she was depressed, everyone around her knew it!"

You could say that again.

"Suicide, especially for those who have a history of mental imbalance like substance abuse, is often an impulsive act."

Jane pressed him, "But it might have been an overdose."

"It's possible."

"Could you estimate, say in terms of percentages, how certain you are it was a suicide?"

He looked a little uncomfortable, pulled at the cuffs of his suit jacket. "No, I will not. Many courts of law have qualified me as an expert in forensic medicine, and my opinion is that she probably committed suicide. Shall I tell you what I have told other families in similar situations?" He leaned forward, ran a careful hand through his hairstyle.

"It's only human to seek the truth, Ms. Wilde. But if the factual information you're offered is too hard to take, you may decide to welcome a little doubt into your life. You can choose not to accept the ruling. There is a possibility that the death was accidental. In time, you may find it easier to say, 'I will never really know.'"

Good God, is that what they pay him nine bazillion dollars a year for?

There was a brief pause before my aunt answered. "Thank you for your words, Dr. Cruz. Right now I can't do that."

Shortly before we were about to pack it up, Yasmin caught up to me and told me to check in with my aunt. I found her seated at the conference table with Tonia. When I came in, the executive producer said hello, rose, and walked out.

"Hey, General," I called after her, "what do you know that I don't?"

Jane smiled, but something big was brewing. "Sit."

I took the chair closest to her. "What's up? Is this what you wanted to talk to me about earlier?"

"No." There was a manila folder on the table in front of her. She traced a zigzag pattern across it with a finger. "Listen very carefully to what I'm about to tell you."

She had my attention. "I always do."

"We've assumed this project would generate a lot of publicity, good and bad. The tabloids especially would...retaliate. Did you understand that?"

"Of course." I wondered where this was going.

"I received a tear sheet from this week's *Observer*. It's designed to do some damage."

"What further damage could be done? God knows there's nothing left to say about Mom, and there's a whole scrapbook full of really nasty stuff published about you, too."

"This one may upset you, Nita. Because you—and Allie—are the focus of it."

My heart began to speed as she opened the folder. The full-page article was captioned in inch-high type: "ALL IN THE FAMILY." On one side of the page was a photo of Jane and Sam holding hands as they walked somewhere along the beach. Next to it was a picture of me kissing Allie on the balcony outside her apartment only the previous evening.

Oh fucking shit.

A Wilde Interpretation of Family Values!

Recent studies have indicated sexual deviance to run in families, and that certainly seems to be the case with avowed lesbian talk show host, Jane Wilde, seen here with female companion Samantha Diaz, one of Hollywood's top entertainment lawyers, who goes by the nickname Sam.

Fearful her niece, Anita, might succumb to the fast-lane lifestyle that killed her mother, Gina Wilde, Aunt Jane gave the troubled teen a summer job on her show, and it seems aunt and niece have some shared passions. Young Anita makes no secret of the fact that she and associate producer Alice Glass find the fringe benefits of working together very exciting!

It concluded with more bullshit about my mother and the show's main mission "to expose to the public the private trials and tribulations of singer Gina Wilde, in order to counteract last season's ratings' slump."

I slowly raised my eyes from the page, afraid to confront my aunt. But there was no anger on her face, only concern. I got up and put my arms around her. "I'm sorry. I don't know what else to say."

She sighed, hugged me tightly. "Don't be. It's not your fault. They're going to come at me any way they can, and I'm sorry you and Allie got caught in the middle. For the record, about Allie—you couldn't have made a better choice." The article had been photocopied; she pressed one into my hand. "Talk to her immediately. Remember, because you and I are used to the media documenting our private moments doesn't mean she is."

"I'll handle it."

She studied me. "I know you will. But before you go, an idea occurred to me. You might call it a favor."

"Anything," I answered, anxious to hear her suggestion.

Her tone changed, sounding parental. "You're a sweet girl, Nita, so you need to pay attention to what people are asking of you—myself included—before you say 'anything.'"

I don't mind someone who loves me lecturing me a little. She continued, "I was thinking you might like to come on the air to talk about the project and Mom. That's what I was going to bring up this morning, only the time wasn't right. Now, though, you have an added incentive, to give your reaction to this article. How about it?"

Go on the air with you? You have gotta be out of your fuckin' mind. I said nothing.

She took my chin in her hand. "Such a serious face."

Take your damn hand off me. Annoyed, I stood, suspicious of her motives, and moved away from her. "Do you think it needs to be dignified by a response?"

"Surely you must have an opinion."

Her tone seemed patronizing, and I really started to get angry. "If you want my reaction, why not ask me right now? Why make me tell you in front of—"

"I didn't mean to upset you. I must be under too much pressure to propose this in the right way. Don't talk about the article, then. Comment on whatever you wish. Tell what this project has meant to you, good...or bad."

Her insistence made me even more unwilling. "Why? Aren't you, Sam, and Allie the only ones who need to know what it's meant to me? Why does the whole gossipy world need to hear?"

"It doesn't." She wouldn't look me in the eye.

"But you still want me to do it."

She gave a short, fake-sounding laugh. "I guess I should've known better, after the way you reacted to the voice-over on the bio. Look, it's merely a suggestion. Don't get yourself so worked up about it."

"I'm not worked up!" But I felt guilty not being able to do what Jane wanted, and resented her asking in the first place.

She forced the issue. "In fact, one reason I kept time open during the last show was to give you an opportunity to tell your initial feelings about the project, and how they've changed. And since you've had a moment in the hot seat..."

What an asshole I was to have cheered when you won that battle. Now I see what you're up to. There goes all my respect for you. "Don't ask me to be your insurance against failure."

Her eyes were like steel, her voice just as cold. "Never imagine yourself to be other than what you are."

Tears came to my eyes, and I willed them back. Her expression softened immediately. "Our first fight." She smiled, held out her arms.

Fuck you for playing with my emotions this way.

I didn't go to her.

"Sweetie," she said softly, "Say what you wish, as long as it's the truth. Talk about your mom, talk about the tabloids, talk about the show. If you want, you can go on the air and slam-dunk your old aunt."

"No, I can't," I said, pushing past her.

FOURTEEN

I went directly to our office to get Allie.

"Nita, what's wrong?"

"I'll explain in the car." As I drove off the lot—my head still reeling—I went for it. "A picture of you and me kissing made the papers. Jane wants me to go on the show with her tomorrow to talk about it, but I've had enough personal involvement with this project, thank you very much."

Allie was agonizingly silent. When she finally spoke her tone was clipped, almost aggressive. "I need to see it."

I tried to tweeze from my pocket the copy I'd taken from Jane, weaving toward opposing traffic.

"Park," she said.

I pulled over, gave the article to her. Her face was emotionless as she read. "I can't believe this, I just can't believe it," she kept repeating. "Everyone will see this."

"Well, it isn't unexpected," I said, my blood still sizzling at Jane having put me on the spot. "What I never expected was my aunt pulling this last-minute bullshit on me."

"Maybe you assume your life is fair game for the media, but I never thought too much about it—"

"What gets me, Allie, is that I should've seen this coming from the moment she wanted me to narrate the stupid bio. Did it occur to you she might ask?"

She looked distracted. "I...don't know." She kept staring at the picture.

Her lack of reaction to what I was saying made me anxious.

"Don't you think it's outrageous?"

132

She drew a deep breath and glanced at me. "Yes, it's outrageous. I feel violated. Disgusted. Like trash."

Back to the article, of course. I tried to reassure her. "Oh, don't get yourself in an uproar. It's something you get used to."

Her hands begin to tremble, and the color rose in her face."Don't get myself in an uproar? Do you see the way you react when the papers talk shit about your mother?" She raised her voice. "Damn it, you and I are drawing paychecks because Jane is in an uproar!"

Bringing up my mother—and parroting me to make a point—brought us dangerously close to a huge fight. Maybe if I tried to see things from her perspective... "I'm sorry this upsets you so much." Somehow the words came out snide.

She didn't give me a chance to explain. "Yeah, you sound really sorry. What did I expect, anyway? You wouldn't know how I feel. You haven't lived a normal day in your life."

Her words were a slap in the face, but I reminded myself not to take it personally, she was only angry about the article. "Look, it upsets me, too, but what can we do? It's already in print. Anyway, no one will remember it beyond next week."

"I'll remember it—every time I'm with you!"

This sounded distinctly like a threat: because of this one dumb photo nothing would be the same, or as good, again. She'd constantly be on her guard, never free with me, always mindful that paparazzi might be lurking. "Allie, don't you think you're overreacting?"

"Of course you think I'm overreacting—to you it's nothing appearing on the nightly news as Mister Julia Reynolds dressed in butch drag!"

Enough. I decided not to dignify that bullshit with a response. I started the car. She stared out the window, silent all the way to Burbank. I tried to put our little tête-à-tête out of my mind. Instead, I dwelled on my aunt's underhandedness. When I stopped in front of Allie's building, she remained in the car long enough for my frustration with Jane to explode. "Appearing on the show would be good for me—yeah, right. Am I too stupid to notice it's for her benefit? Let her find a loudspeaker and discuss matters better left private, I'll be damned if I will."

Allie turned to me. "Oh, your reluctance goes beyond the issue of privacy." Her tone was cutting. "Don't you agree?"

I'd antagonized her by bringing up Jane. It wasn't what she was upset about. "What would be the point in my going on the show? I can't convince people that Jane is doing the right—"

She started to interrupt, then stopped. Calmed a little by my own venting, I tried to persuade her to finish her thought. "You won't like it, so I'd better not," she said.

"Let me be the judge."

"Okay... Sometimes, Nita, you're a terrible judge."

I felt myself becoming hostile. "What do you mean by that?"

"You have so little insight into yourself, you can't see your motivations. The thought of going on the air scares you, but it has nothing to do with privacy. You're afraid you'll have to discuss your mother, and if you do, you won't be able to protect yourself. You spend your energy preserving how hurt you are, nurturing it. You keep it alive, but you don't ever deal with it. The truth is, and as I said, you're not going to like it—your mother fucked you up, and goddamn it, you just keep standing there like a pussy letting yourself be fucked up." I just sat there looking straight ahead. I couldn't believe she would say that to me. Even if we were arguing, I expected her to act like my friend.

From the corner of my eye, I saw her glance quickly at me, then away. She reached for her purse. "You said to tell you." Her tone was brisk, as though being unapologetic might somehow negate the viciousness of her words. She opened the car door. "I'm exhausted, and I'm not saying this in the nicest way. You're preoccupied with yourself, and it's not your fault, but unless you begin to see why, the situation's not going to improve. God, that article was the last thing I needed right now." She got out, slammed the door, and walked away.

Geez, just peel out, peel out, peel out! Why won't the fuckin' key go into the ignition. My hand is shaking. Fine, just sit here a minute— like a pussy—maybe she'll hear her words sink in as she goes off.

Right asshole, yup, like she gives a damn—

I'm talking to myself again!

I finally got the car started, driving awhile in the wrong direction before I cared enough to turn around, wandering into a residential neighborhood. It was about four o'clock, not a lot of people around. A couple of joggers huffed by, guys were hunched over an old muscle car they would never finish restoring, a mom yelled at her kids to come in now.

Their daily routines underscored how empty my world had just become.

Tears stung my eyes. I just let them come.

Okay, Mom, this isn't as bad as the night you died, when everything seemed so unreal. When I felt like I'd gone into the otherworld with you. When your death was a drug hallucination and I could never come down.

Fuck you for doing that to me! Fuck Jane! Fuck Allie—Allie...even if there's truth in what she said, why was she so mean about it? Does she enjoy hurting me? And Jane—she just out-and-out lied to me all along. Can she be that afraid of not succeeding? Her ambition—I'll never understand it. Not hers or mom's or Allie's. I'll never understand anything that makes you put people second, not in a bazillion years—

Calm the fuck down!

Where am I going, who can I talk to.

Never tell anybody what Allie said!

There's no one I could tell. Not Jane not Sam not Julia—

Joseph?

No, it's too pathetic to pay someone to hear how my girlfriend—I mean the woman I thought was going to be my girlfriend—called me a pussy!

Fine then, suit yourself. There's nobody.

No body who.

What must your body look like now—your favorite dress in tatters—your face a mask of bone—your heart a heart of stone—

Stop!

I have got to write some of this stuff down, so Joseph will stop bugging me, and let him check it out. I told him no meds, never, no way, but maybe I should try them. I keep having such freaky thoughts.

Suddenly, a plan. I got on Glen Oaks Boulevard, driving past the stucco and glass facades of stores no one had much use for anymore— a coin laundry, shoe repair, tailor, slowly being edged out by convenience markets and video production labs. When I hit Olive I turned, heading for the Golden State Freeway. The early evening commute was starting, but traffic wasn't bad enough to convince me to just go home. I took the freeway around the back hills of Griffith Park with its sooty-leaved, tinder-dry trees, and connected to the 134 going toward Hollywood.

Friday afternoon, the Forest Lawn Drive exit was desolate. Not a popular time for visiting. At the gate an attendant with the agitated self-importance of a Shrine Auditorium parking valet on Oscar night asked the name of my "loved one," did a double-take when I told him, and then offered me a map of the grounds. I said no thanks. I'd been there only twice since the day of the funeral—for her birthday and the anniversary of her death—and wasn't sure where I was going, but fuck needing a map to find my own mother's grave.

I drove around a little while before recognizing the right area, feeling guilty as I noticed the bouquets of flowers, balloons, and teddy bears left by people more conscientious than me. Then I parked, and walked uphill along a smooth asphalt path past what were referred to in Forest Lawn terms as "serene groupings" of willow trees. I broke out in a sweat in the broiling hot Indian summer sun as I approached the gravesite. Into the top left corner of the pink marble headstone my mother's portrait was etched, a trifle too angelic-looking, I thought, with demurely downcast eyes and swirling tresses of hair. Under her name was the title of the song—my song—that I chose as her epitaph: "You Can't Tell a Gift When to Come."

Collapsed in the heat was the floral arrangement Jane had ordered delivered weekly. Fans had left roses, photos of my mother in concert, a handmade card that said 'Rock On In Heaven.' Tears dripped from two half-notes drawn to look like eyes.

I scooped everything up and dumped it in a nearby trash can. Maybe it was disrespectful, but I just wanted to be alone with her with no distractions, no reminder of anyone else's attention. I sat on the marble bench, elbows on knees, and stared down at the ground.

Hi, Mom, it's me.

I imagined that she could see up at me, like when you dive to the bottom of a swimming pool, open your eyes, and make out a fore-shortened, wavy image of people at the surface...

You're the only one I can talk to about what happened today. And after today, I don't want to think about this ever again.

Okay, maybe I am afraid to go on the show, but that doesn't mean I'm a bad person. Wasn't Jane wrong to make it seem I was neglecting you—and her—by refusing? I'm allowed to say no, and I don't have to justify my reasons to anyone.

And does Allie have to be so mean about it?—She really doesn't get it how scared I am.

A tear rolled down the bridge of my nose and plopped into the dust between my feet. With the toe of my shoe I rubbed it into the ground.

What if I went to our house, and you were there?

I can hear you now, saying if this chick what's-her-name thinks you're a pussy after all you've been through in your sweet young life, she has another think coming.

Don't worry, Nita, you just had a bad day. Everything's gonna be all right, just give it some time, chill yourself out. Jane's Jane, there's nothing you nor I nor God can do about it. It takes her a while, but she always admits when she's wrong. Allie was out of line, she'll apologize. If she went too far, just send her on her la-de-dah way. No matter what happens I'm always on your side. Remember you're not just Neet, you're Really-Really-Neet!

I'm so mad at you, Mom, sometimes I forget you could be nice. Maybe that's why I'm so angry—then I don't have to be sad. What will happen to me once I start feeling sad?

Here, I'll say something without any anger. Okay, I miss you, Mom, and I love you.

I sat there for a while, listening to the hum of the freeway below, the rhythmic whir of lawn sprinklers, the shrieking bluejays searching for food in the grass. The vapor trail from a passing plane streaked the sky.

The day after you died, a skywriter drew a huge heart enclosing your initials above downtown L.A. I was stuck in traffic with Jane and Sam on our way to the funeral home. All around us, people were laying on the horn and flipping one another the bird, talking on the phone and retouching their makeup, totally preoccupied with the reality of the moment, totally unaware that for people in the next car, reality had become a nightmare from which they thought they might never awaken.

Maybe you thought I never understood you were in pain. I went off in my own world and just got angry whenever you tried to make me deal with your sickness. Still, I knew you weren't having a good time here, and it really bothered me. I wish it could have been different, but now I know that it wasn't possible. I can't feel guilty anymore. I accept that I may never be as artistic as you or as famous. Yet I will have a good time.

Well, I guess I'll go now. Thanks for listening to me today.

As I headed down the hill, Spielberg's enormous Dreamworks studio with its magician's cap tower looming across the freeway came into view. How L.A.—right next to a cemetery, the entertainment business was going full tilt.

Even Forest Lawn was a tourist destination, my mother one of its attractions—I'd have to live with it. The place where she's buried was still special to me.

The sun was just setting, the sky butterscotch and pumpkin and magenta, electric against the descending black. The evening breeze carried a hint of the sea, a mineral undertone reminiscent of blood. I drove home after stopping at a convenience store for a six-pack. Jane had called, and, playing by the rules we'd established last fall—no ignoring phonecalls—I left a voice message on her pager saying I'd talk with her tomorrow. As I expected, or steeled myself against hoping, there was no word from Allie.

I popped a Bud Lite and flipped on MTV.

When the alarm woke me at four-thirty the next morning my first thought was, How much had I drunk and my next was, Did Allie and I really have that terrible argument? I contemplated just not showing up to work but decided against it. If something even worse lay in store for us, better not to avoid it. And Tonia would turn my ass into hamburger if I stayed home.

At six forty-five I sat shivering in the freezing studio waiting for the morning meeting to begin. Before I realized what was happening, someone slipped into a seat behind me.

"Morning, sweetie." Jane sounded a little anxious.

I turned. "Hi."

Her eyes, crawling again with those red spider-lines, searched mine. Her pre-makeup face seemed extra pale. "How are we?" she asked carefully.

I hesitated. Her willingness to approach me when she had such a tough day ahead of her was enough to show she cared; hashing out our stuff could wait a while. "We've been better, but it's all right. Why don't we talk later, when you don't have so much to think about, maybe on the weekend?"

She nodded, reassured, I thought, that I'd had the consideration to put things in perspective. "It's a date." She squeezed my shoulder. "Things go okay with Allie?"

"We'll talk on the weekend," I repeated, my voice catching. She looked concerned, obviously wanting to know more, but respected my privacy, and moved off after squeezing my shoulder again.

Sitting there I dreaded seeing Allie, wondering how we'd manage to work together. The moment she arrived, I averted my eyes, concentrating on Tonia as though she were delivering the Sermon on the Mount.

Day Two of damage control would start with people who had sued the tabloids for defamation and lost. Jane would use them to prove that because lawsuits usually fail, other ways of taking the pulp media to task were appropriate—such as airing my mother's story. Also booked was the widow of the vocalist of the alternative band Golden Mean who had recently died of a heroin overdose; she was furious at the media for the character assassination of her late husband.

I had put off facing Allie as long as possible, but when I returned to the green room, there she was. Her nervousness made mine worse. "Nita, what can I say—"

"Later, okay?"

As people arrived, I tried to make them comfortable. The unsuccessful litigants were mostly Hollywood celebrity poachers who namedropped shamelessly with one another. I felt sorry for the widow. With her big hair and Barbie-doll figure she looked like the typical rock star wife, yet her swollen eyes seemed to indicate she wasn't just grieving the death of a meal ticket. She sat away from the others, trying, no doubt, to shield herself from their gawking, and said "Thank you, honey," when I brought her coffee.

I focused on the show, remembering how many times Jane had threatened to sue the tabloids, how many times Sam had counseled her against throwing away money. Celebrities had to endure any gossip that is 'newsworthy.' Journalists duck behind the shield of the First Amendment, claiming their outrageous lies serve the public interest. Damage to your reputation was hard to quantify to the satisfaction of the law, especially for someone like my mom, who did so much of the damage herself. By the end of the segment, I was utterly convinced a lawsuit would've gone nowhere.

Next up, the widow. Scenes from Golden Mean's music videos showed her lead-singer husband in a variety of fashions and poses, destined to make him the heir apparent to the grunge-throne. Skintight, dirty jeans. Sweatshirts with the sleeves ripped off to display heavily tattooed arms. Pierced nose, ears, eyebrows—when I meet someone like that, I can barely resist leaning over and yanking on something. With each end-beat, he tossed his shaggy dyed hair into his eyes. Body tremors were his singular solution to the problem of keeping time. I was relieved when the final shot of him faded, showing him back-lit and Jesus-like with his acoustic guitar high above his head.

Yet his wife's seemingly genuine grief reminded me that snap judgments were really unfair. After the studio lights were back up, she blinked a couple of times, as though bringing herself back to a reality she would rather not have to see, and it was a struggle for her to speak. "When Jason died, the world fell apart, and the tabloids helped smash it into little pieces." She fought back tears; Camera 2 zoomed in like a lion chasing prey. "The decision to put your own story on and go after the tabloid monsters—that's a decision of the heart as well."

No, no, no! As much as I wanted to believe her, I knew she was dead-as-a-doornail wrong. Everybody in this business was driven by one burning question: 'How do people feel about me?' 'They love me' was the answer they had to have. Jane was doing these shows because she disliked the way 'they' were judging my mother. On the surface, that seemed unselfish, but deep down it was just ego, this all-consuming need for external validation. The same ego that would trail forever in my mother's wake like a sickening perfume.

I was tired of every person I cared about wanting to be worshipped by the whole fuckin' world. I needed to get away from them all.

The studio was quiet when my aunt came out for the closing monologue, a white rose in her hand. Two chairs were placed center stage; during rehearsal, there had been only one. She sat, then tossed the rose onto the empty chair. The audience exploded in applause.

It was corny, but it got to me. Jane and I would miss my mother until the day we died. I couldn't be angry with Jane; she'd always been nice to me—what more did I expect? Just because we were family didn't mean we were anything alike.

She began, "So much time has passed since Gina and I lip-synched to the Supremes in our parents' garage. I'm happy with the shows this week, although the verdict is not yet in, and already the tabloids have started retaliating. I've opened myself up for it, but I regret that my family and staff have also been targeted."

I got nervous all over again, thinking about the conversation that lay ahead with Allie.

"One goal this week was to find out how exactly my sister died. Many may feel the medical examiner's word was definitive. I'm not sure. I still can't accept the idea of suicide."

O.D. or suicide—maybe the coroner had given us the key to understanding, even if we couldn't buy the police finding. Since yesterday, two people I really cared for had turned on me. Maybe certainty—about my mother's death, about anything at all—didn't exist. Maybe in time I would accept that I'd never really know...

"Some call the tabloids harmless entertainment, but I can't, and neither can my family. My sister led a troubled life, but she didn't deserve the treatment she got. So the next time you're at the checkout reading a paper while you wait in line, think about the person behind the headline. Thank you for making this a very memorable week."

After we wrapped I went to Jane's dressing room to exchange air kisses and drink a plastic tumbler of warm champagne. Before I left, she came over and asked if I'd care to spend the night at their place. I hesitated, not sure what would happen with Allie, and she said the invitation would be open all weekend.

Later, Allie and I drove down the block for our talk. I sat there, heart pounding, while she played with the catch of her seat belt, until the uncompanionable silence prompted her to apologize. "About yesterday—I'm sorry. I was feeling frustrated, and the article pushed me over the edge. There are some problems with us being together, as I not-so-nicely mentioned, and I'm sure you have issues about me you haven't brought up."

She paused, I guess, to give me my chance to lay it on her, but I couldn't think of anything other than her blasting me yesterday. Then she had seemed like a totally different person, not the Allie I knew and was beginning to love, not like any woman who could ever love me. I shrugged. "Other than what you said—the way you said it—as of yet, I have no complaints."

"I realize now how upset Jane made you, and that the article about us meant nothing to you. Yesterday I wanted you to show you could understand my feelings and advise me how to handle the situation, but you could think only of yourself. That's why I got angry. I'm sorry I lashed out at you. You didn't deserve it. As much as I might like to, I can't take back what I said."

"I can't change the fact that I acted thoughtlessly, either."

"So now we have to decide whether we can go forward together— unless you've already made your decision." She glanced at me, then looked away.

Twenty-four hours ago, those words might've sent a chill through me, but now the possibility of breaking up wasn't so intimidating. "There was truth to what you said. I probably can learn from it. Regardless, when you turned on me, I felt so alone." I paused, my throat suddenly tight. I swallowed hard, fighting back tears. "What's so hard is that I was just allowing myself to feel less alone... Maybe you can't understand me, but what pushed you to the point where you no longer cared how you expressed it?"

Her lips curved down into a thin, tight frown. "The world you belong to owns you, Nita, and I don't think I can get comfortable just being along for the ride. You need a lot of time for yourself. It isn't your fault, you never asked for the life you've been handed. But maybe you're not ready yet to think about someone else."

"Maybe not." I glanced up, looked in her eyes.

They filled. She blinked. "I think you could have given me a lot. I mean, you did. Even before..."

The weight of her words seemed to settle on my chest. "No less than I received."

"More orgasms in fewer days than any other woman."

I knew she wanted me to laugh at her joke, but I couldn't. I struggled to say something positive, to do my part to lighten the mood. "As for you being along for the ride, well, one day you may find I'm okay in the passenger seat. Don't forget the back seat has its charm, too, when I'm in the car."

She smiled as two tears broke loose, and she moved nearer. Her arms went around my neck, mine around her waist.

Strange, to realize with a touch meant to be healing that too much damage had been done. To acknowledge an ending with an embrace.

FIFTEEN

In the next few hours existence slowed to a crawl, like right after my mother died. I had to talk myself through everything: Here's the offramp. Put on the turn signal. The light is yellow. Slow down and stop. Pull into the Seven-Eleven driveway. Take a six-pack of Bud out of the cooler. Is a six-pack enough? Pay the lady. Wait—don't forget the change.

At home I lay on the couch watching MTV like a beached whale, obsessing over an urge to call Allie that was interrupted only long enough to make excuses not to.

What would I say? I made a mistake, please come back, let's try again? Or—you'll always be special to me, I hope we can stay friends? She's not ringing my phone to tell me that. Why should I?

I fell asleep—a beer-induced stupor—about midnight and woke the next morning with a pounding head, dry mouth, and aching bladder. I showered, poked around in the refrigerator. Even if it held anything appealing, I couldn't eat.

Where can I go, who can I talk to? Nobody. No body who. Oh, hell. Not now, not today—

I reached for the phone, speed-dialed Jane and Sam. It was Sam who answered. Jane apparently had a rough night over the show; she'd left early for a women broadcasters' convention in Long Beach and wasn't expected until early evening. "In case you're wanting to say hi."

"That's okay, I can wait. I'm a little cheesed at her right now."

"Yeah, the interview. She just couldn't stop herself from steam-rollering you..." She sighed, sounding exasperated. "Sometimes your aunt is so determined to have her way, she literally will stop at nothing to get it. Call her on it. I've had to more than a few times. She doesn't mean any harm, but she has to be truthful with you. In this case, if she's not being honest with you, she's lying to herself."

Sam's reaction was reassuringly logical. "That makes me feel better."

"Well, good. Hey, aren't you supposed to come over here this weekend? Or maybe the two of you have better things to do?"

Having to explain that the relationship was over almost before it had begun only added to my hopelessness. I fought my natural impulse to go hide under a rock. "How about I come over now?"

Jane and Sam live in Benedict Canyon, which winds through the Hollywood Hills between Bel Air and the San Fernando Valley, fifteen miles from my West L.A. studio apartment. A few minutes onto the 405, surfing the radio, I picked up on "Home," one of my mom's few slow songs; the lyrics were about loss and defeat, but the raw, nervy edge of her voice suggested something else. I cranked it:

> I come out on stage strung out from the road
> Wasted by strangers just scared of feeling old
> Surrendered my fortune to get a little gold
> And I can't find my way home
> No I can't find my way home...

I knew her voice would bring me to tears. I wanted it to.

As I turned into the driveway, I was conscious of arriving alone when I should have had Allie with me, and wondered what this familiar place might look like, through her eyes. The two-story gabled house, painted gray with red trim, was nestled in a grove of California oaks. It was well-cared for, the home of two people devoted to its upkeep—and to each other. Inside, the requisite wall of fame you find in the home of anyone in the business, the carefully chosen artwork and knickknacks that evoked a sense of old Hollywood. Jane and Sam's bedroom, intimate with its four-poster bed and fireplace opposite. The motto painted in Latin above it was 'Si non petes, non futueris' —without perseverance, one has no future. I used to think it was a testament to their ambition, but I know it's the theory behind their relationship. They work on staying together—and staying in

145

love—day and night.

A few days and nights—all it took to end the possibility of Allie and me. Nope, I sure couldn't wait to destroy that one.

By the time I shut off the engine I was more or less okay again. I parked, fished through the glove box for a Jack-in-the-Box napkin to wipe my face, and checked in the rear view mirror for any snot that might be hanging out of my nose.

I went around to the kitchen door. "Anybody home?"

"In here," Sam called from the den. As I came in she glanced up from her desk, a massive block of rich cherry wood topped by beveled glass. Thick stacks of what looked to be contracts were laid out before her, illuminated by a lilac and leaf-green Tiffany lamp. She removed her reading glasses and gave me a look that seemed to indicate she suspected something was up.

"Am I interrupting you?"

"Not in the least. I was hoping for a distraction when you called." She switched off the lamp, rolled her leather chair away from the desk, and stood. "As a matter of fact, you could provide me with an excuse to make a couple of root beer floats. And we have plenty of time to enjoy them before your aunt gets home and starts bugging me about my cholesterol." She put an arm around me as we headed for the kitchen counter.

Rolling up the sleeves of her shirt in an exaggeratedly meticulous manner, she made me giggle. "Attention to detail is critical. Splash the cuffs, cholesterol police shove a celery stalk in your mouth so fast you don't know what hit you." I laughed out loud, grateful for how hard she was working to amuse me. We sat at the table, and she scooped the ice cream and poured the soda. The sweet, spicy drink was comforting. For years Sam and I had indulged our shared passion for ice cream. I gulped it.

Eying my nearly-empty glass, she suggested, "Another?"

"No—I'm okay. A glutton, but okay."

A pause. "Are you okay, Neet? The article...was Allie all right about it?"

Again the papers had made my life a mess. Jane and Sam would never have known we were lovers without that photo. Without the photo, we wouldn't have broken up, at least not in such an embarrassingly brief time…

Oh, fuck, the truth was I'd made a mess of things, denying Allie—again—the right to talk about something she needed to discuss.

I stared at my hands on the table. "No, she was not okay about the article."

She continued, "Didn't mean to pry. If you want to talk, just let me know."

I tried to laugh. "It was the shortest affair in history." Making light of it didn't seem right. "It's not…" I was going to add, "a big deal," but why make myself a liar.

She was silent for a moment, then reached over and grasped my hand. "I'm sorry."

On her ring finger was the platinum and diamond band identical to the one Jane wore, and I felt sick that I hadn't made it even one week with someone I liked so much. This time, I'd really thought… How long would it be before I found a woman to love, who really wanted to love me? A tear streaked down my face. Fuck it! I promised myself I wouldn't! I quickly wiped it away.

"Everyone gets her heart broken," Sam said gently, with a knowing toss of her head. The angles of the fine lines etched around her mouth told me they'd not all been put there by laughter.

But it was more than a broken heart, like my spirit or something had been stolen from me. She would have no way of knowing this; I didn't want her to. I just went ahead and told her what had happened between Allie and me, sans being called the p-word, which, I imagined, would impact more negatively on the caller than it would on me.

She listened carefully. "Well, she's probably right about you needing more time to deal with your mom. You always try to show everyone you're fine, fine, fine, but it's equally, if not more, important to let yourself feel loss, to grieve."

I shook my head. "It's time to move on."

She smiled as if my impatience was only a sign of how long a way I had to go. "It doesn't work like that. Usually, you're not conscious of feeling better until…" She stopped in mid-thought. "When you lose someone, you wonder how everybody around you is going along with their daily lives, preoccupied with which pair of jeans they should buy, whether to have pepperoni or sausage on their pizza." I nodded. "But then one day, months or years later, it's you agonizing over pizza, and you realize you've come out the other side." She stared off through the window, her eyes searching the yard, resting on one of the old oaks. In it, maybe she saw an image of herself, having endured.

"Before Janie met me," she continued, bringing her gaze back, "she had some rough times..." Her voice faltered; she cleared her throat. "She wasn't ready to love me, or anybody else. It took her a while to allow herself to open up again. Of course, I had ways of inspiring her to accelerate the process." She gave me a wink, and I smiled. "Remember when your aunt moved to New York? Network news offered her a great job. We were very much in love, but I knew she had to have it. I understood why—I'd just made partner at Blaylock, Anderson & Meyers. Ever hear of them?" I shook my head. "Big entertainment firm. I was their triple-token: female, Chicana, and gay. Hell, I know how it feels to want success so bad you'll take whatever else they're serving just to fill your plate."

That surprised me, to say the least. "I never thought of you as ever having compromised yourself."

Her sleek eyebrows lowered over her dark, friendly eyes. So what if I still had a couple of things to learn about the world. "Few people get anywhere in life without compromising along the way. The trick is to be honest about what you want and weigh it against what you're giving up. That's what Janie and I tried to do when she made the move to New York, too."

"It seems like you were sacrificing your relationship for her career," I blurted out without thinking. Then I wondered whether I'd said too much. "I mean—"

"That's what it boiled down to."

"So how did you get back together? Why would you want to, after she showed you her career was more important?" I gave a quick glance around the well-appointed kitchen, testament to a domesticity that seemed a miracle, given what Sam had just described.

She sat back in her chair, pyramided her hands, flexed her fingers. "About six months went by, and I got kinda involved with someone else. One day I get a call: Janie's back in town. As soon as she tells me where she's working, I figure she moved back because she found some great woman. The new job here was the pits." She rolled her eyes.

"What was she doing?"

"Some cable extravaganza on Sundays at three in the morning, interviewing teamsters-turned-ballerinas and the inventor of taste-free potato chips, making downwards of zip a year. Her own show, though—the first."

I giggled. "So who was she dating?"

"Nobody. She'd had a little fling down the line, but it was over. She missed me. Said after I told her goodbye, she wasn't as fine as she thought she'd be. When I let her know I had a new lady in my life, there was silence on the line. To tell you the truth, the silence was music to my ears."

For one second I allowed myself to imagine how sweet a triumph like that over Allie would feel. "Serves Jane right."

"Even though we broke up, I'd never stopped loving your aunt, and I knew she loved me, too. It took a while, but we got back together." She patted my hand. "So you never know. Maybe you and Allie—"

"Won't happen," I answered firmly; just entertaining the idea hurt too much.

"Well, it could be it's not meant to. Or maybe the young woman just needs some time to think about what a dope she'd be to let you get away."

I feigned indignity. "By association, are you calling my aunt a dope?"

"Not me, but I'm a good catch she almost missed out on." She paused for effect, then continued, "And my life wouldn't've been all that much without her in it. I've been lucky, and you'll be, too. If it doesn't work out with Allie—"

She wasn't getting it. "It's over with her."

"Then it'll happen with some other nice girl. There are plenty out there."

"I can't even think of that right now."

"Of course not, you've had a rough couple of days. You need time to recover. Your aunt'll be home soon, and she'll have some insight into the situation. Janie's good at talking about emotions, does it for a living, you know."

But Sam's presence was special in its own way. Her self-assurance and common sense made me stronger.

"It feels just right talking with you," I said. "Thanks. I know every-thing you told me you must've learned the hard way." I got up and gave her a hug. I'd never spoken this directly to Sam before. "Sometimes I just need another butch woman to talk to."

She held me at arm's length, reached up and tousled my hair. "Forgive me, but it's a stretch of the imagination to conceive of that skinny twelve-year-old tomboy who always conned me into playing one-on-one as a 'butch woman,' but I'm working on it, give me time!" She chuckled. "Well, butches are supposed to be tough, and femmes some kind of shrinking violet, but the reality is more complicated. Butches are strong on the outside and soft inside. Femmes are soft on the outside and like steel inside—and sometimes you can't talk to them. Thank God we find better things to do together."

Before dusk I took a walk behind the house, up along the ridge where I could catch the last rays of the sun and get a view of the lights coming on in the canyon. It had been a hot day, and as the shadows stole down the slopes and hollows of the hills, the sharp smell of weeds and wild mustard and sagebrush rose around me. I heard the laughter of people at a barbecue in a yard below and crickets and the last songs of birds before they rested.

From where I stood I could see Jane and Sam's house, and I watched as my aunt pulled her Jag into the driveway. I knew she'd interrogate Sam about what I was doing there—and once she started in, the victim was a goner. I was five minutes away, and started to come down the hillside. Then I stopped. Let Sam tell her. I didn't need to go over it again.

I stayed up there until it was dark, until a couple of coyotes yipped and yowled close by—like they'd just found dinner, and it was me, and all they needed was some warm tortillas, hot salsa, and a cold beer to go with. It was an ungodly noise, and it sent me hurtling down the hill-side, crashing through brush and sending pebbles skidding, back into the safety of the backyard.

Through the living room windows I could see them seated togeth-er on the couch, Sam's arm around Jane. Sam was speaking, my aunt listening raptly.

It was a loving, tender image of the two of them, but I couldn't help seeing it reproduced on cheap paper, on sale at the checkout for a dollar and change.

I came into the room, and Jane held out her arms. "I'm sorry about Allie," she said. "Want to talk?"

"Later, if that's okay."

Over dinner at my favorite restaurant, I made the mistake of asking Jane how the broadcasters' convention had gone. She scowled. "Oh, I was pretty much lesbian non grata. The only reason they didn't cancel my appearance was that my peers needed someone to spit-roast. After my keynote, madame chairwitch asked if I minded taking a few questions about my latest exploits, and like a dummy I chirped, 'Sure!' First they accused me of losing journalistic objectivity, then, when I paraphrased a few choice headlines, they charged me with launching a personal vendetta."

Sam got hot under the collar. "Does any one of them have a show in all the top ten markets? Are they out-and-proud and still pull in enough dough to keep their distributor happy?"

I changed the subject.

When we got back to the house, we watched TV in the den. The tan leather-upholstered furniture, Adirondack-style end tables, and wood paneling gave the room the feel of a mountain lodge. Sam and I lay on the rug with its pattern of pine branches and pinecones as we always did; Jane sat on the couch with her feet tucked up under her, staring at the screen's flickering images without ever fully losing herself in the plot. As a matter of fact, watching TV with my aunt could get kind of irritating. I understood it was a busman's holiday for her, but did she have to spoil it for everyone else by constant interruptions with suggestions for improvement?

After an hour or so, as she usually did, Sam fell asleep, the remote dropping from her hand. Jane shot me a glance and laughed, waking her.

"Bedtime for me," Sam said, getting up and kissing my aunt. "Love you, hon. 'Night, Neet."

When the next commercial break came, Jane wasted no time. "Let's talk a minute."

I turned off the TV, and took a seat on the ottoman in front of her. Her black silk kimono contrasted dramatically with her blonde hair. It was rare to see her without make-up these days, so conscious was she that when her face was bare, there could be no doubt she was forty-six. The slight puffiness of her eyelids, lacework of lines around her eyes, and slackness to her skin that she endeavored to hide from the California sun—all had led to the proclamation that a facelift was imminent when the show was on summer hiatus. Looking at her now, I felt kind of sad, not that she was aging, but because I would no longer see her as she would have appeared naturally.

"I imagine you must be having a hard time over Allie," she said, "and I'm sorry to add to it by making you upset with me."

I'd forgotten telling Sam this second part, but Jane needed to hear from me how I felt. "If you want my help, don't pretend it's for my own good. There may be some benefit for me, but that's not why you're asking. It's insulting."

She looked uncomfortable. "In my business honesty isn't always best. Occasionally, when there's something I badly want, that's the policy I go by. I wanted you on the show. So…"

I could tell she was struggling to maintain her composure. "Why didn't you simply ask me to consider it for you, then?"

"Because you know what happens? It doesn't get done, and you're faced with the fact that the other person doesn't care enough to do what you asked!"

"You don't get it at all," I said in irritation. "That's the only reason I would do it: if you came to me and said it was important to you. And why throw it at me last minute? God, you planned for weeks to have me on! What a terrific way to persuade someone to take action—don't give them enough time to rationally consider the idea. If they don't have the time to contemplate it, they're sure to go your way."

I stopped then, because I knew I was on the verge of being rude, if I hadn't already crossed the line. She sat there in silence, and I was pretty sure I'd offended her, but all she said was, "Well, it works with people less intelligent."

I laughed, and she relaxed and gave me a smile. "Aunt Jane, you're my only family—and my friend. I have to trust you'll be truthful with me, no matter what. Every time you sit me down for a heart-to-heart I think you're going to ask me to do something I'm not comfortable with. It makes me crazy."

"I'm sorry, Nita." She drew a deep breath, then slowly released it. "I think I understand. I'll try very hard not to be...manipulative with you. Please, if you catch me at it again, tell me to knock it the hell off."

I looked directly at her. "I will." Trying for honesty myself, I admitted, "I might not have gone on in any case. I'm too scared. I couldn't acknowledge it before."

She took a moment to respond, striving to choose the absolutely right words. "It's natural to be nervous on TV. Even a talker like me still gets nervous. And it wouldn't be easy for you to discuss Gina."

She patted the couch. I got up and nestled beside her. "Think about this if you will," she continued, drawing me close. "Before tonight you couldn't admit your fear. Now you can. You have more to talk about, as far as your mother is concerned. Not on TV, maybe not privately with me, maybe not even with Joseph. Try to find a quiet place in your own mind, and listen closely. Tell yourself what she meant to you, what she missed by turning her back on you." She kissed my cheek. "Then, Nita, let her go."

SIXTEEN

Over the weekend Jane followed me around the house like I was on suicide watch. Would I like to take a vacation? Maybe I should come live with them for a while. I must make an appointment with Joseph for Monday.

I said no thanks to the first two offers, but I gave Joseph a call, and started making the list he'd been bugging me for: Things I say to myself when I'm stressed. Hey, this sounds like a category on Jeopardy. I'll take contemporary psychosocial dysfunction for $200, Joseph. It surprised me, though, how much I really do talk to myself.

I decided it was best to stop working with Allie, and Jane agreed I would report to Bob starting Monday. Another P.A., Damon, would take my place. For some reason I phoned Allie at home to let her know. Where was that pride-driven impulse for emotional self-preservation I couldn't shake the night before? Our conversation was short and to the point. She seemed relieved to have me out of her office—and out of her face. When we hung up, I took a shower, the streaming water muffling my pussywussy tears.

I got to work super early and cleaned out my desk, burying myself in Bob's projects. When Allie and I passed in the hall, we nodded and said an awkward hello. I slipped into the restroom, feeling a breakdown looming.

Hey, this is nowhere, this is so fuckin' unfair. Good crap, I was just beginning to put all the mothershit behind me, and now I'm losing it all over again—

That evening at Joseph's I felt like a total failure, and then braced myself for the whole 'don't make other people responsible for your self-esteem' spiel, but he just nodded understandingly. "It's only natural to feel you failed in some way. In time, you'll see blame isn't the issue. No one thinks any less of you."

Maybe I relaxed a little, or maybe I just wanted to change the subject. "Thanks, but you'll think differently after you read this." I handed him the list.

He looked surprised, then pleased, as he realized what it was. Then concerned, as he began to read it. His forehead wrinkled and unwrinkled so many times I started to get nervous. Finally he looked up. "Well, we certainly have something to work with."

What did that mean? I glanced up at his diplomas hung on the wall above his desk. It was a Freudian field day because I was a stupid raving lunatic?

He handed the paper back to me. "Just look at the names you call yourself. 'Jerk, dork, idiot, dweeb, flake, wuss, asshole, fuckup.' If that's what you say about Nita Wilde, what's left for the tabloids?"

Time to get defensive. "I don't really think of myself negatively, if that's what you're getting at."

"Then why refer to yourself in these terms?"

I shrugged. "I don't know, I'm just used to it. Like when you're with friends, you call each other names. No biggie."

He persisted, "Who made you used to it, Nita? Your mother?"

I thought back. "Well, she'd say mean things like that when we argued. But she always told me how much she thought of me, too." I had to nip this in the bud. "I'm not into blaming her right now. It makes me feel like a victim."

"Fair enough." His forehead wrinkled again. "Let me ask you this. If I called you these names, it would be completely inappropriate, right?"

This was stupid. "Of course, you're my therapist."

"And as your therapist, my role is..."

I tried a little lame humor. "To harp on me about the names I call myself?" He wasn't amused. "Well, okay, you listen to my problems, and give me advice. I trust your judgment, and then I get a better perspective. You make me feel better—usually."

He sat back in his chair, looking pleased. I was playing his game. "And our goal here?" He shook a finger in my direction. "Say 'so you can make money' and you are out the door."

155

I laughed. "Besides that, I guess so I can learn to do those things for myself."

His expression said he had me. "Right. You're developing trust in your own judgment so you'll make the right choices. And that smart, capable person making healthy choices is no jerk. Stop calling her one."

He gave me back my list, and a handout describing a gadzillion categories of 'negative self-talk.' Now that I'd been put in my diagnostic place, my assignment was to recognize when I slip into my destructive mental track, and blindside the impulse to do it. Head swimming, I went home.

I actually began to adjust to my new routine of Life After Allie. In only a few months we'd connected so strongly; now, cut loose, adrift, I sometimes gave in to the part of my brain that refused to believe we weren't still together. One more thing I learned courtesy of Gina Wilde. I still saved up things to tell Allie, like funny conversations I'd overheard. Two older ladies talking about their version of poetic justice: "Well, Fran, you know what they say. He who laughs first, laughs last!"

Driving down city streets I brought to my own attention things Allie would have pointed out: cats dozing in windows and cleverly-spelled messages on vanity license plates and boutiques filled with overpriced, pretty clothes. I saw red Miatas everywhere. I was going through withdrawal; my mind and my body craved her, a steady ache that dulled only slightly as the days straggled by.

During the next month, I concentrated on the job, spent time with Jane and Sam, went to see Joseph twice a week, and worked on talking to myself more positively. As he said, the world was a harsh enough place, no need to bring it inside.

The photo of Allie and me kissing made its way into several publications—or so I heard. I had no interest in seeing them myself. I'm sure there was gossip about us, but I didn't get wind of it.

One Saturday morning, as usual, I headed to the studio. Bob had given me a research project for an upcoming show: "Why Do More Men Want to be Women? A Gender Comparison of Transsexuals," and I figured I'd get a head start on it.

Several cars were parked in front of the bungalow when I got there. As I walked past a spotlessly clean, sleek black Camaro I wouldn't have minded owning, I noticed its vanity plate, GLYN. Could she be working for Jane as a consultant again? I wasn't aware of any upcoming shows requiring Glyn's police expertise, but the thought of encountering her today—or any day, for that matter—was kind of nauseating.

I forced her from my mind, made coffee, and went to see what work Bob had left me: autobiographical statements of pre-op transsexuals for me to review for common themes. I admired the courage of these people and found the stories fascinating; reading them made me recall how, at the age of thirteen, I realized I was different from the girls I knew—because I wanted to have sex with them—and I thought for a time that meant I wanted to be a boy.

If truth be told, as a child I'd often wished I was a boy. Loved basketball, soccer, and remote-controlled anything. Hated dresses and Barbies and, frankly, other girls. But by eighth grade or so I'd found the key to my identity—on Jane and Sam's bookshelves, naturally enough—discovering with relief there was a name for people like me. That in my case, liking girls did not mean I wanted to be a boy.

I'd been working about an hour when I heard Allie say, "This is the only Saturday in the last month that I've come in, and now we're leaving, okay?" Seconds later when she passed my door, I caught a glimpse of the tall figure and broad shoulders of her companion.

I glanced out the window to the parking lot. Allie came out of the building, Glyn right behind her. She waited, all smiles, while Glyn opened the car door for her; Glyn gave her a tap on the butt as she got in.

Fuck, what is this! I was seized with jealousy, unable to draw sufficient air into my lungs. I sat back in my chair as they drove off, my heart pounding.

Why does it have to be that cop? Sure, Allie's gonna go out with somebody eventually, but not that jerk. Finding someone else hadn't crossed my mind. Probably Allie and Glyn had been seeing each other awhile; as soon as we broke up, Allie had probably called and told her to come right on over. To think I once trusted her...

Goddamn Glyn. So obvious about her attraction to Allie, she flaunted it in front of me.

It took some time before my thoughts boiled down to one question: Why should I care who Allie slept with?

157

I wasn't over her yet. I could admit that. What hurt so much was that Allie was completely over me.

I worked all day, writing a couple of pages of notes for Bob, stewing about Allie and Glyn. At my desk the next morning, I flipped through a couple of scripts I was supposed to photocopy, when my eye fell on the desk calendar. The date, October first, set off an alarm. I couldn't at first remember why it was significant, but then it hit me—Julia's fortieth birthday was coming up in a week. I figured I'd call, see if I could stop by with a present.

The edge of accusation in her voice made me question the wisdom of the idea. "Ever since you got your picture in the paper, you seem to have forgotten your old friends. Especially the ones who are really getting old."

I ignored the dig and cut to what was bothering her. "Oh, Jules, don't be upset about your birthday. I'd like to see you, give you your present."

"I'm registered at the House of Palsy."

I giggled. "Doesn't a woman hit her sexual peak at forty?"

"So I've been informed—by every Girl Scout in this town."

"When can I come over?"

"I'm accepting gifts at all hours, but shouldn't you ask your girlfriend to let you off your leash first?"

She really had aggravated me now. "You're making me wonder why I'm bothering."

She sighed, realizing she'd gone too far. "I'm sorry, don't mind me. I'm just resentful of twenty-one-year-olds and their romantic opportunities."

Her pity-play worked, and I gave it another try. "You gave me my first opportunity, remember?"

I heard a smile slide into her voice. "Due to advancing age, Julia's mind must be slipping. She's forgotten what a nice girl you can be."

The next day, I bought her a gold bracelet I knew she would appreciate, and that night, after stopping to pick up a dozen cream-colored roses, drove to her building. When I got off the elevator, I was startled by the sight of her—hair blonde and cut short. She grinned. "What do you think? Tart city!"

I didn't care for it, but left my comment open to positive interpretation. "You look like a whole different woman."

She shut the door behind us and returned my hug stiffly. "Relax, we broke up."

She kissed me like she'd missed me, and took her roses. "How beautiful."

Seated beside her on the couch, I gave her the gift. Looking pleased, she unwrapped it, and I slipped the bracelet on her wrist. "It's beautiful, darling, thank you."

"It looks nice on you. Happy Birthday."

She settled against me. "Apparently you've been keeping busy. I watched the shows on your mother, the project was well done. Were you pleased?"

I nodded, but her praise reinvigorated my irritation with Jane. "But get this, Jane wanted me to go on with her!"

She took a moment to reply. "It's not inconceivable she might ask you, but I can understand you not wanting to."

Her answer was a little too evenhanded for my liking. "She tried to make me feel guilty, like she needed me for the ratings. I finally told her to knock it off. She admitted she was wrong." This encapsulated version was slanted to win Julia's vote.

"Well, we all make mistakes, don't we? Especially under pressure. I understand she's been catching a lot of heat. Even you got caught in the fallout." Her lips curved into a smirk. "Everyone should have such an attractive...supervisor."

I didn't want to talk about Allie, and said so. Julia was understanding. "I see losing her has caused you some pain."

I nodded. There was no reason to hide my feelings, nor explain them in further detail.

"Well, a loss like that is a character builder. Now you know why Julia's so loaded with character."

"You are a character, for sure." Time for the conversation to go deeper into Julia's favorite subject: Julia. "So what made you decide to go blonde?"

"Isn't it a cliché that when a woman goes through a major life-passage, she changes her hair?"

"I've never known you to strive for the cliché."

"Nonsense, I've spent my whole life getting there! My moment of glory long gone, I console myself with the trappings of a useless existence—and an occasional young woman too polite to mention it." She patted my knee, and rose suddenly. "How about helping me with these flowers, and we'll open some wine?"

For the first time in my life, I had too much to drink. I'd like to think it contributed to my decision to spend the night, but to be honest, I'd have to blame my own bad judgment.

After some initial excitement, I found myself in a weird predicament: nothing was working. Then, sometime during her efforts I must've passed out, waking to her wail, "You fell asleep!"

Not that I felt like going on with it after being yelled at, but now, wide awake, and stone-cold sober, I let her keep trying. Finally she gave up. "What is it, Nita? This has never happened before, I used to call you 'Easy-Off' for a reason!"

My faced burned with embarrassment.

"Am I finally too old for you, or are you so gone over that little bitch you can't come with anyone else!"

I moved away from her. Not that she deserved an answer, but she was suddenly so hysterical, my only instinct was to calm her. "Look, we both had more to drink than we should have—"

"Oh, no, you can't blame this one on alcohol. You can blame your whole fucking messed-up life on your mother being a drunk, but you can't use that excuse tonight!"

I got out of bed.

"Where in hell do you think you're going?"

I grabbed my clothes and high-tailed it into the darkness of the living room, hearing her get out of bed and crash around, then the sound of glass breaking. I wasted no time getting dressed. I was putting on my shoes when she came out, lunging toward me, her arms filled with perfume bottles from the dresser. She tossed one at me and missed.

"You've gone crazy, Julia!"

"You're the one who's crazy if you can't make it with me!" She lobbed another, and the top flew off. A dark stain seeped onto the white carpet, the sharp fragrance permeating the air. She was loud and nasty. "Who needs you, Nita? All you ever do is bring me your problems and use me for sex! Cry to Aunt Femme and Uncle Butch for a change!"

She threw another vial, this time hitting me in the face, and as I reeled back from the blow, I tripped over the glass coffee table. It overturned, shattering the top and the lead crystal vase holding the roses I'd brought.

"You idiot! You'll pay for this mess!"

I raced out of the apartment, slamming the door behind me, and heard a bottle splinter against it as I reached to press the button for the elevator. A neighbor peeked around the corner, his wide-eyed wife cowering behind. "Nigel, call the cops!"

Forget the elevator. I ran down the entire twenty flights of stairs, recalling that crazy morning after our first time together when I'd done the same. I jumped in my Wrangler.

I made it a good part of the way home before it dawned on me that the police might very well show up there, so I turned the around, considering my options. The only place I could go was Jane and Sam's—but what explanation was I going to offer for showing up like this in the middle of the night? Oh, Julia got mad because I couldn't come, so she attacked me and I trashed her apartment and now the police are after me.

I went to a motel.

Lying in bed, the chorus of my mother's punk anthem, "Lullaby and Bad Night," played in my head as I pictured her swinging a guitar and smashing it on the stage floor at each endbeat:

> Singers never sleep at night!
> They wake up with a scream!
> Quaking in the clutches
> Of bloodthirsty dreams!

It occurred to me how one experience like this should've made her swear off alcohol. But I knew better. For her there had been a dozen nights like this, hundreds, and she'd come back for more. I'd do anything to avoid another out-of-control scene, but she sought them out, created them, until one night she finally found the means to bring her sickness to an end.

That's what it took to be an addict. And I didn't have it in me.

SEVENTEEN

A couple of weeks later I received in the mail a copy of *Paparazzi* magazine, a tabloid that managed a pretext of respectability with a glossy four-color layout and the occasional glitzy TV special: "Paparazzi's People of the Year." "Paparazzi Presents the World's Ten Sexiest Men." "Paparazzi's Oscar Picks and Pans." I turned the envelope over. There was no return address; it was postmarked L.A. Curious, I opened to a page that had been turned down at the corner. A photo captured Jane, fist raised and about to smack into her own palm, with the accompanying article:

TV Talker Jane Wilde's Ratings Gambit Backfires

A Hollywood source close to talk show host Jane Wilde says the embattled lesbian is furious at her niece for not appearing on the show's season opener, an exposé of the fast life and mysterious death of singer Gina Wilde. The controversial attempt to bolster sagging ratings failed because Gina's daughter, Nita, 21, also gay, canceled the scheduled interview, leaving staffers scrambling for a last-minute replacement.

Jane's scheme to put her niece on the air is, per our source, 'pure exploitation that reveals Jane's desperate bid for ratings. Nita was ordered to break into hysterical sobs on cue!'

Widespread publicity of Nita's sexplay with a female associate producer is only the latest of many backstage lesbian liaisons. According to our insider, who prefers to remain anonymous, 'Not only is Jane's current lover, attorney Samantha Diaz, on the payroll as a legal consultant, but Jane and executive producer Tonia Talbot have been romantically linked for more than a decade, as well.'

Nita Wilde's foolhardy actions have done more than ruin her aunt's plans. She's living proof that in Hollywood, blood isn't thicker than water!

I couldn't have been more stunned if I woke up one morning and discovered I was straight. The way the lies mushroomed was mindboggling. Reading the article, I wondered what sick puppy was behind it; before I finished, I had a very good idea. After all, hadn't I provided the inspiration?

It was payback time for Julia.

She'd taken what I'd said and run with it to the far reaches of a truly paranoid left field. By coming up with such an absurd version of Jane's plan—using my insinuations—Julia's pulp media attack held an unintended secondary purpose beyond revenge: it made me realize I'd overreacted.

Jane may have wanted me on the show, but not to exploit me for ratings. Reading it in print made the thought silly. Although I was still glad I hadn't agreed to an interview, I began to see that nothing I might have been asked would have been all that personal. Everybody already knew what a royal ass my mother had made of herself in public. What else to say but that with some exceptions, she was a royal ass in private, too.

And if the unthinkable happened to me in front of the audience— if I actually broke down and cried—they would only think it was staged.

I understood why I jumped to the conclusion that Jane was out to use me, and that the inevitable result would be that I'd completely lose control. Just this once, I forgave myself for my screwed thinking.

And it felt like I was taking another step to really be in control.

I got up, magazine in hand, and went to find my aunt. She and Sam were seated on the office couch. When I knocked, they looked up, their innocent pleasure at seeing me making them seem vulnerable because of what I was about to show them.

I passed it over. After a few seconds, Jane began to make little huffing noises; Sam, who seemed to be further along on the page, said "Ssh!"

Of course Jane flipped off, "You ssh!"

I giggled, but when Sam said, "Be quiet, Janie," I hushed up, too.

Silence on Jane's part was extremely temporary. "Just where did they come up with such garbage about Nita and me? No one except us three even knew I wanted to do an interview! Well, Tonia did, of course…." She exchanged a glance with Sam I couldn't place, then looked around wildly. "Who would leak this stuff to the press? Is my office bugged?"

Sam remained reassuringly calm. "Don't be ridiculous."

Jane scanned the article again, handling the magazine so roughly I thought the pages might tear. "Imagine printing that I would use you so calculatingly, Nita." She looked up at me, eyes wide with distress. "Good Lord, I hope you don't believe that!"

Things were getting out of hand. It wasn't fair that my bellyaching to Julia was now coming back to haunt all of us so outrageously. "Of course not." Suddenly I was tired of carrying around the secret of that stupid night. "Look, your office isn't bugged. I'm pretty sure who's behind this, and I hate to admit it, but I had a part in it, too." They both turned to me, astonishment registering on their faces. "But Aunt Jane, if I tell you, please don't get angry. Don't get carried away by your emotions." As soon as she heard the name Julia, she'd be out for blood.

Sam rolled her eyes. "Good luck, sister."

"Okay." I took a deep breath, released it. "I think it was Julia."

Sam did a double-take. "I'm not overly fond of her, but that's hard to believe. She's always been so nice to you."

Jane was predictably livid. "Nice! Oh boy, has Julia been nice! Yep, the one word to describe Julia is—nice!"

I sighed.

Sam took Jane's hand. "You swore you wouldn't get upset."

"I have never approved of that woman, and now look what she's done."

"Janie, knock it off." Sam sounded stern, and I was glad she'd stopped her. "None of this matters now. Nita, what makes you suspect Julia? Did you two have a fight?"

I silently thanked her for redirecting the conversation, though I didn't look forward to revealing the whole imbroglio. "Yeah. Actually she needed someone to throw stuff at, and I happened to be there."

"What? Tell us what went on."

"Okay." I felt my face grow hot. I related the events of that night, concluding with, "She clobbered me in the face, and I tripped over the coffee table and broke it. The neighbors said they were calling the police. I split. Maybe she got into trouble for disturbing the peace."

Sam leaned back in her chair, graciously glossing over the embarrassing aspects of my story. "Well, unless you told anybody else you were upset with your aunt—"

"Just you and Allie."

Jane snapped, "Two people who definitely can be ruled out. It's Julia, all right. Goddamn her..."

Before she could go off again, I broke in. "Julia was just trying to teach me a lesson. The backstage liaison stuff is so absurd, no one will believe it. Only Sam could possibly be bothered by that garbage about you and Tonia, and you both know it's a stupid lie."

Over the next few days, the more I thought about it, I couldn't be pissed off at Julia; I felt sorry for her. Drunk that night, all her insecurities—about growing older, about me no longer needing her—rushed to the surface. I could forgive her. Even when she went out of her way to be a pain in the ass with the article, the message was clear: Don't become your own worst enemy.

Summoned to the conference room the following Monday morning, I joined Jane, Sam, and Tonia at the table. My aunt looked flushed, as though she was barely containing excitement over some new scheme, and her hair was out-of-place, caught, no doubt, in a breeze of her own making. She began rapid-fire. "I want to run an idea past you to close out the fall season. I've been thinking..."

The executive producer leaned back in her chair and stroked her chin. "Isn't there a clause in Janie's contract prohibiting her from doing that, counselor?"

Sam reached over and high-fived her.

Jane rolled her eyes. "If you're finished, what about a couple of shows to follow up on the Gina series?"

With a violent clicking of the beads on her braids, Tonia lunged forward so suddenly that my aunt startled, and then laughed. "Jane, you're out of your fleabitten mind! Look where it got us last time."

"Hon, it did end up just short of a fiasco."

Sam, I suddenly realized, was the triangle point of these two extremists.

"You haven't heard me out." Jane paused. "It's a sound concept, for many reasons. For one, it'll fit in nicely with the theme of the other shows scheduled for the week."

Tonia looked like she suspected someone of trying to slip her a piece of week-old tuna roll. "'Things We Love to Hate'? How?"

"Those shows cover why we hate other races to why women hate it when men leave the toilet seat up, and how to resolve conflict once it's acknowledged. Well, I love to hate the tabloids...and the tabloids love to hate me. This week, of course, *Paparazzi* is at the top of my list—"

Tonia interrupted, "I just can't figure out how in hell their insider picked up on our two-night stand in New York ten years ago. Nobody but you, me, and Sam knew about it." She glanced at me, then frantically toward Jane. "I mean—"

Jane and Tonia really were lovers? She was Jane's fling?

My aunt blasted her with one of those pee-losing looks. "Nita knows Sammy and I once broke up, but she had been spared that gory little detail—up until now!" She turned to me. "Just to clarify, well after Sammy and I called it quits, Tonia and I were together for a very brief time."

It blew my mind, I guess, because I never seriously considered the idea. How could the three of them be so tight now? How could Sam put out of her mind the two of them being lovers? I tried to imagine me and Allie and Glyn one day working together in a business. Impossible, even if Allie and I were to end up back together. If I ever was around Glyn again, I'd crack off her legs and suck out the marrow...

Jane added, "You're forgetting there was at least one other person who knew—Gina. And evidently she spread the word." She scowled at me, Julia's proxy. "Enough. The closing shows. I'm thinking one could be about the recent articles published about us since the Gina series aired." Jane turned to Sam. "Don't red flag me until you've heard me out."

Sam mouthed the words 'Red flag' to me. I giggled.

"And the other?" Tonia said, drumming impatient fingers on the polished wood of the conference table.

"Well, leaving a little time flexible of course…"

Uh-oh.

"Of course," Tonia interjected. "Might as well make things as out-of-control as possible. Might as well spend as much money as we can!"

Sounding annoyed, Jane asked, "Will you let me finish?" Tonia waved a go-ahead. "Talk shows are long on debate, short on resolution. The last show has to focus on resolution. I put Gina's story on the air, now what have I learned?"

Tonia sat back in her chair and squinted up at the ceiling. "Other than how to crawl out from an avalanche of bad publicity?" Jane scowled. "Okay, it's interesting, but it proves you're not taking into consideration the lesson of the original Gina shows. Start a debate about the value of talk shows, and you could literally end up talking yourself—us—right off the air."

Sam reached across the table and covered Jane's hand with her own. "The Gina shows made folks in the business nervous. The rule is…you don't put your own life on TV. Think carefully before you decide to break through that last barrier of self-protection again."

Jane squeezed Sam's hand. "I understand, but my instinct tells me it's the way to go. Trust me on this. I'd like the three of you to be open to my idea. Please." Jane appealed to Tonia. "Remember, even you admitted it's interesting."

"Moment of weakness."

Tonia called a meeting of the associate producers that afternoon to get feedback on Jane's proposal, and asked me to attend. An hour beforehand, Allie, of all people, showed up at my door. "Got a moment?"

I tried to un-register how good she looked in her neon green ribbed sweater and black corduroy jeans. "Bob said the viewer poll won't be ready until two."

"Okay. That's not why I stopped by."

She hadn't 'stopped by' in eight weeks.

"Will you come to my office? I'd like a word with you." She seemed so serious. Should I care what she wanted?

The hallway was hectic. En route we passed Bob, who snapped his fingers at me as though just remembering a task he wanted to assign and asked me please to come back as soon as possible; Karen, who said "Hel-lo, ladies," with a purr that set my teeth on edge; and Linda, who looked back and forth at the two of us in her rabbity manner before mumbling something unintelligible. I felt tense and exposed.

After shutting the office door behind us, Allie invited me to take a seat. I looked everywhere but directly at her, at the piles of paper that now proliferated unchecked, at the tsunami print on the wall that reminded me of the first time we'd met. Was it only six months ago?

She cleared her throat, forcing my gaze to return to her face. Her lips pressed together in a tight line, and when she touched a finger to them I willed myself not to be reminded of her kiss that first morning. As I looked away again, she moved her hand hastily, remembering as well, evidently. "I wanted to talk with you about today's meeting," she began nervously. "Do you know what it's about?"

I nodded. "Yes. I'll be there."

She looked surprised. "Oh. Well, I want to get your opinion on the follow-up shows. That way I can offer mine with confidence." She tried a winning smile.

I resented her attempt to reach out, her sudden attention to what she perceived as my needs. Did she suppose I gave a flying damn what she thought? I couldn't help responding with sarcasm. "That's considerate of you."

"Sometimes I can be that way." The color rose in her face.

"Sorry," I said. By being rude, I'd revealed what a pussy I really was. I had to get out of there immediately. "About the follow-ups—go with your own feelings." I stood.

She rose, too, her face billboarding her distress that her kind impulse was being taken so wrong. "Please tell me how you feel. If you don't support it, I won't. I won't be a part of anything that's wrong for you."

I was so upset, all I could do was wonder how she could remain that focused on the shows. They didn't bother me in the least compared to how I felt about the two of us dropping out of each other's lives.

I stared past her, into the hallway. "Thanks. I know you mean well, and I appreciate it. For the record, I support the project. But I thought we were no longer part of anything having to do with each other."

I left the room.

At the meeting I forced myself to chat with people; Allie sat off by herself, writing something on a legal pad. Nothing required note-taking; maybe she was scribbling Nita Wilde is a ferret-faced fuck-up five hundred times over—not that I cared.

To my aunt's satisfaction, Tonia green-lighted the proposal: "'Why I Love to Hate the Tabloids' will close 'Things We Love to Hate Week.'"

Jane beamed. "And I thought of the perfect musical theme for the shows, Gina's song, 'I Hate Art.'" She went to the stereo on the bottom shelf of the VCR cart and hit the play button:

> I hate dancing, when I do it I feel fat
> I hate poems, they're easy to laugh at
> I hate painting, I leave streaks on the wall
> I hate music, it takes my all
> I hate artists...what a bunch of misfits
> I hate art...wanna make somethin' of it?

This was the one song that really revealed my mother's sense of humor. Why most didn't wasn't a mystery: clever lyrics don't sell. Her audience was more interested in songs about taking drugs and spending money. "Rush" exonerated her hedonism, "Time" gave her the distinction of doctor-validated excess...

Tonia adjourned the meeting with a request that everyone bring her a couple of suggestions to flesh out the shows. "That's it, people."

All that evening I stewed about the encounter with Allie, calling myself every name in the book. After I realized what I was doing, I forgave myself for being a total ass, and then sat down with paper and pencil to get on with Tonia's assignment, thinking I'd have no problem coming up with my share of ideas, but after a half hour the page was still blank.

169

Tonia's assignment: Why I in particular love to hate the tabloids. Or, more accurately, Mom, boiled down into forty-eight more minutes of airtime. How royally lame. I mean, every book says mothershit lasts a lifetime. But I'm supposed to work through it in sponsor-backed segments. Twenty-one years of crap in a nutshell, whatever.

Suddenly, supremely irritated by the task, I began impulsively to write—

> What I Learned from My Mother's Death
> That I'll be fine never seeing her dead again.
> That it'll be easy never going to her funeral again.
> How two hundred roses look on a coffin.
> That it's possible to forgive anything.
> That my lover was turned off by my demons.
> That I created the same demons for my lover my
> > mother created for me.
> That it takes time and costs money to oust demons.
> That my therapist is successful because of how sick I
> > am of my demons.
> He's successful because of how desperate I am for
> > success.
> He's successful because every woman I love will leave
> > me if he isn't.
> How every woman I love will leave me anyway, by
> > choice or by death.
> And I will do the same.
> No matter how unlovable my mother has made me,
> > no lover will leave me because of her.
> That I can crawl out from her shadow.
> No one can make me unlovable.
> That I'm crazy because I think someone else can make
> > me unlovable.
> I can make myself unlovable all by myself.
> How my mother never really knew me.
> How she knew my essence. (She created it.)

Hey, Joseph, get a load of that! All those in a single minute—

The whole concept for the show was something only an asshole would take seriously. Wait, stop! I'm doing it again. I am no asshole! What a dork, calling myself an asshole! All right, here goes nothing:

"Out of the Shadow of Gina Wilde"—The show will address these questions: How can you pursue your own dreams when someone so close to you is famous? How can you reconcile the death of that person and move on?

There, a subject daytime TV can explore in one afternoon.

I put down my pen, sarcasm screeching to a halt.

Jane's original idea—that the show might help us heal—wasn't really bogus. It worked. Not in the way I thought it would. No ratings-driven Beverly Hills mutual-admiration society. Most of the time had been spent standing up to my aunt's bullshit. If there was one thing I'd learned—she was like Mom, tweaked up one huge fuckin' notch. The difference was, when you told Jane things needed to change, they did.

Was I crazy thinking the show might be a way to find the next level of recovery? Why did 'recovery' seem like such a pretentious word for something so important? No, I was not crazy!

Jane and Sam couldn't rescue me, Allie couldn't rescue me. Big whoop! Physician rescue thyself. Allie—

Shut up, shut up, shut up, for one last fuckin' time will you shut up about her! Hey, stupid! Care for some cheese with that whine?

It was way past midnight, time for bed. I had my idea for the show—and something to show Joseph next session, as well.

Either Joseph read very slowly, or he went over the page several times. I counted the number of books in the top two shelves of his Mission oak bookcase—ninety seven—and was halfway across the third before he finally looked up. "So, Nita, you're a poet."

His comment warmed me, but still it felt uncomfortable—too magnanimous. "It's more a list than a poem."

He smiled. "I'd like to see how you prepare for grocery shopping." Then his expression turned serious again. "I was going to ask you to do a similar exercise for the second anniversary of your mother's death, in January."

"I'm ahead of the game. I like that."

"Do you remember how you felt when you wrote this?"

171

"I don't know." I described how I hadn't been able to work, then the list appeared.

He shook his head; I guess I hadn't really answered his question. "Give me a couple of adjectives to describe this list."

What was he getting at? "Well, it's truthful. How I really feel, I guess." I say 'I guess' and 'I don't know' so often with Joseph, he probably thinks I talk this way all the time.

"Sum it up for me. How do you feel?"

"Let me see it."

He kept the page, holding it to his tattersall oxford shirt, navy and white, especially crisp-looking. "Without looking."

It took me a moment. "I guess..." Start again. "I have to forgive the bad, or else it'll make me nuts. I won't be able to trust anyone, I'll believe they're out to get me." I thought of Jane, then Allie. "And I'll drive everybody away. I have to learn from the good, especially when it comes to loving other people."

He nodded. "Nice." Then he looked at me expectantly, his dark eyebrows lifting, and gently repeated his earlier question. "Can you recall how you felt as you were writing this?"

I tried again. "When I wrote it, that's all I paid attention to. I didn't make it sound like someone else might've written it. I thought if another person read it, you maybe, they'd understand what it means."

He handed me back the piece of paper. "Poetry, whether you say so or not."

Early the next morning, I sat in my aunt's office, awaiting the verdict on my proposal. The sun filtered in weakly through the blinds; a space heater took the chill out of the air. Jane, nestled into a corner of the office couch, one leg tucked under her, regarded me over the top of her reading glasses. "Nita, this idea is wonderful, but it scares the hell out of me. 'How can you pursue your own dreams when someone so close to you is famous? How can you reconcile the death of that person and move on?' Whatever makes you think I could pull it off? Most days I cope with Gina's death with absolute denial—I pretend she's just away on tour, or off in rehab, and she'll pop back into our lives at any moment with her full regalia of problems."

"Does Joseph know about this?"

She laughed. "Hey, whatever gets you through." She removed the glasses and twirled one of the sidepieces between her thumb and forefinger. "As for pursuing my own dream...how can I acknowledge on the air envying my sister's success, that it was the motivation behind my career? I can barely admit that to you! And yes, to Joseph, too!"

I tried to choose my words carefully. "You don't have to admit anything of the kind on TV. Wasn't this what you had in mind when you said you wanted the show to reflect what you had learned? Maybe it is a tough subject, but don't people expect that from your show, because it's done with integrity? Because it's the best of..." Oops, not a good insinuation. I continued, "Well, the best. Different from all the rest. Just like you, I mean it. I think this needs to be brought up, and you're the person to do it."

Jane's eyes quickly swept the shelves of the awards cabinet; then she looked at me for a long moment. "Thank you, Nita, it means a lot to hear you say that. It makes me feel I'm a damned good aunt. That's something to be proud of. But if we proceed with this idea of yours, understand you really are leading your old aunt into an emotional minefield."

"Bang!" I said.

She smiled, then her expression changed. "Now, if you were to go on with me..."

Oh, crap!

Yet hadn't I realized as I'd put my idea on paper...

She trapped my chin in her hand. "We'll talk about that later." A sardonic note crept into her voice. "Don't worry, I understand what you mean about my show. I know I'm at the top of my form. And honey, being the best of the bastards suits me just fine."

EIGHTEEN

Rain fell all afternoon, and along Ventura Boulevard, San Fernando Valley's main drag, its effect was transforming—the glitter of glass highrises subdued by the gray thickness of the storm clouds they mirrored, garish neon signs impressionistically swirled into haloes reflected in the glistening roadway. The wet weather ameliorated the strip-mall monotony, lending an enduring quality to the mom-and-pop establishments that had managed to survive despite them. It made the people around us, their rainwear hiding perfect coifs and machine-tanned skin, look a little more human. It made traffic impossible.

Jane patted the Jag's steering wheel with the flat of her hand and let out a low whistle. "Maybe this wasn't such a terrific idea today. I bet you have better things to do on Saturday than take a trip down memory lane with your old aunt."

It'd been my suggestion, after several days of getting nowhere with "Out of the Shadow of Gina Wilde." Why not visit the Tarzana house where mom and Jane grew up? A memory-lane trip just might give us a starting point. "It'll be fun. And afterward, cheesecake at Jerry's Deli. Give me your word."

We hung a right a few blocks past Reseda Boulevard, and continued past a row of stucco apartment buildings to a tree-lined neighborhood of rundown ranch-style houses. She picked out the second to the last. "We have arrived."

Painted a shade of pink reminiscent of underdone calves' liver, the house also sported pistachio-green shutters and a gingerbread trim. You'd think the present owner would hardly be proud of the color scheme. Wrong! The mailbox at the end of the driveway, a replica of the house in miniature, repeated it. Jane sighed. "Your grandfather

174

made that mailbox. Thank God he didn't live to see the paint job."

"Aren't you going to park?" I asked, hoping to learn more about my grandparents, whom I'd never known.

Seeming lost in thought, Jane shut off the engine. I sat back in my seat, trying to imagine the two sisters as kids, leaving this house every morning for school, playing ball in the yard in the afternoon, lying in bed in their room talking before they fell asleep. But the bizarre paint job, weeds, overgrown hedges with the tonsorial flair of boxing promoter Don King, and citrus trees overburdened with fruit made the time-trip nearly impossible. I knew from photos that this was far from what the place looked like when they called it home. My grandfather, a telephone lineman, and my grandmother, who quit teaching school to get married and raise a family, took pride in owning this house, their first and only. I said, "If I had oranges growing on my trees, I certainly wouldn't let them go to waste."

Jane patted my knee. "You're your grandmother's granddaughter. How she loved those trees! We had fresh-squeezed juice every morning. Lemonade with our after-school snack."

"She was a good mom to you."

Jane turned to me, her expression confirming the simple truth of the statement. She nodded. "She was. They were both good parents. Gina and I were very lucky."

I couldn't resist. "So what happened? Her drug addiction, your...dubious sexuality?"

She made a face. "Your mom was always a rebel. Long before she broke into the business, she put a lot of distance between herself and the folks. They were too upstanding, too middle-class, too nice. Her bad-girl image just wouldn't fly."

"Did they ever know you were gay?"

She shook her head emphatically. "Sometimes, selfishly, I almost feel relieved they died without knowing. They wouldn't've understood, and it would have driven a terrible wedge between us." With her forefinger she traced the leather stitching around the steering wheel. "What kind of a world is it when you'd rather your parents die than find that out?"

I knew she hadn't said exactly what she meant. "You aren't relieved they died, only that you didn't have to hurt them. They came from a

175

different era, with different values." I turned back to the house; behind its shutters seemed an intriguing secret that only Jane might be able to reveal. "So now let me ask my question the right way. What about this family, this home, produced two such talented people?"

Her smile acknowledged the compliment. "I've often thought about it. I think we both succeeded because we were made to feel special. We knew we were loved." Her voice wavered with sudden longing. "And we loved each other very much."

The overcast sky, which just before seemed comforting and snug, now imparted an aura of gloom to the street and this house where the ghosts of our family still lived. I was aware as I sat there with Jane, our breath fogging the windows, of how alive we were and how tenuous was our status as survivors.

Living is just temporary resistance. One day we'll be overcome by that relentless force that takes us from the world and from one another—

Knock It Off!

Jane's right here beside me, and she loves me. Her face, Mom's face, variances of each other. Both, permutations of my grandparents' looks. His golden hair and freckles, her slightly hooked nose and dimpled chin. Reach up and flip down the visor, see the face in the mirror reflect those same characteristics, and those of my dad...

So God, somebody, you know what? This might sound weird, but maybe, in a way, everyone is right here in the car with us.

I turned to Jane, hoping she could make me feel less alone. "Tell me the story of the secret friend."

She leaned back against the headrest. "You already know the story of the secret friend."

"So what?" She wanted to tell it, and saying no was part of the ritual. I gently poked her in the ribs, and she swatted my hand. "Let's hear it again."

As always, a look of pleasure shattered that ridiculous air of being put upon. "All right, if you insist... When your mom and I were kids, I used to sneak into our room and leave her little presents of toys or candy, with notes signed, 'from your secret friend.'"

I anticipated her pause, the one that gave me just enough time to ask, "Like what?"

"Oh, a set of jacks, or a piggy bank, or some notecards."

I thought of a brand-new question. "What made you think of doing it?"

"It was Mother's idea, actually. I believe she thought if I got accustomed to delighting my little sister, we would be friends, not rivals. And it was a harmless way for me to enjoy a little power. Funny, but it did set the tone for our later relationship. Even when she got famous, I was still the big sister—and we were friends."

Their adult relationship threatened to intrude into the story, taking away the incipient peace of mind only beginning to calm me down. "So, uh, where did you leave her the stuff?"

"On the window sill near her bed, so it would seem like the secret friend came in through the window, or sometimes, right there in our mailbox."

She pointed to it and, looking away from her, I saw the chubby kid I knew from photographs, with long gold pigtails, knobby knees, and socks that were falling down around the ankles, warily approaching with a gift.

"It drove Gina crazy, not knowing who it was. She rigged up a trap to catch the secret friend in the act, tied a string with a bell to the mailbox. So I very carefully left the gift, then jiggled the hell out of the string. She came racing out to see who she'd caught, and I was long gone, but not out of earshot. Her wails were very gratifying. Almost as satisfying as her, 'My secret friend came!'"

"How did she find out it was you? Did you tell her?"

"When she was six or seven, she started asking if I was her secret friend, but I didn't let on for the longest time. When I finally admitted it, she was extremely disappointed. She said she always thought it was a fairy." Jane chuckled.

I couldn't resist. "So that's the first time anyone suspected you were gay."

The dumb joke made her laugh outright. "If lesbians can be fairies, Nita."

"Only effeminate lesbians."

She laughed again, tousled my hair, started the car, and let the engine warm. "Well, I think I'm reminisced-out. Time for our cheesecake, what do you say?" She gave the car some gas, but didn't pull out. Her expression turned thoughtful. "Childhood is supposed to be such a simple time, simple questions, simple answers. Who was I then? Gina's sister, her secret friend. I never realized childhood would become the source of so many unanswerable questions, like, why did her genius require such self-destruction? How could I become so jealous of someone I loved that deeply? Why did I live, and she die?" She shook her head and sighed.

I wasn't sure what to say, so I just said what came to mind. "I wonder exactly the same things."

She reached over and patted my knee. "I know you do, sweetie."

"And that's one reason I thought doing the show this way might be a good idea."

With a groan, she flipped on the windshield wipers, and eased the car out into the roadway. "The show, don't remind me! How can I approach all this really personal stuff, let the audience in on my real relationship with Gina, without telling too much? Speaking of unanswerable questions, as I've said every day for the past week, where in hell can I possibly begin?"

I thought I knew, now. But I waited to tell her until we were safely inside Jerry's Deli, welcomed by the warm fragrance of fresh rye bread and peppery pastrami, until after we'd slid into opposite sides of the red vinyl booth and were smugly contemplating the arrival of our cheesecake and coffee.

"Why not start at the very beginning, with the story of the secret friend?" I said.

NINETEEN

The response to pre-program advertising was extraordinary. This time, Matt, Jane's publicist, did his job and called a press conference. Most of the reporters dressed like movie stars, and acted the part, greeting each other with air kisses and calling everyone 'baby.' It was interesting how many newspeople my aunt knew by name—and how hostile some of them were. But she proved herself up to doing battle.

"Don't you think people already had their fill of the subject?" a reporter asked, his square chin jutting arrogantly toward her.

Jane slammed him. "If that were true, why would your assignment editor send you to cover my press conference?"

When accused of not learning her lesson the first time, she provoked laughter: "I'm a great believer in remedial education." But she scored the most points with Jackie Landis, entertainment reporter and chief adversary of the first series of shows. Landis, usually so impassive, actually called the original shows groundbreaking. So a former antagonist was making concessions.

Jane met her halfway, graciously. "Tabloid journalism is here to stay. My show is a form of it. But when you take a look at my show, I want you to discover something you didn't know before. I'll tell you a story, my story if need be, not simply to amuse you or make a buck, but because I think there's something worthwhile to be learned." She smiled. "I can't believe I actually said that to an entertainment reporter." Again the room erupted in laughter.

During the post press-conference meeting, Tonia, high from its success, giddily fleshed out the idea for the first of the two shows. "People, it'll be a real audience grabber," she enthused. "We take a few camera-bold folks from the audience and make them the subject of mock tabloid pieces created by our writing team. False rumors in embarrassing detail—sexual escapades, drunk driving, getting caught impersonating their doctor and calling in their own painkiller prescription. They share how crappy it feels being on the receiving end. Janie shares by pitching a royal fit about the recent articles trashing her and Nita. Then, for the audience's delectation, a very erudite, very expensive panel of TV critics. And here I expect some bang for my buck. They'll agree that talk shows, because of their broad-based appeal, have a tremendous potential to influence popular opinion for responsible journalism. Our BBC nabob will report the details of their newest daytime TV survey, that it makes children's behavior less antisocial. Really does a number on the kiddie-shrink business, if television is a force for good."

Tonia's synopsis was given the official sanction of three quick claps, but then her expression turned glum. She waved us quiet. "It's the second show that's the bitch on high heels, people." When she slumped in her chair, I felt a boi-yoi-yoing behind my rib cage. "All we have so far is this: we open with a video montage of highlights from the original Gina series, and Janie trills on about whether she accomplished the goals of those shows. It's hard to accept suicide, it's fun to disprove the dumb rumors, yaddada yaddada yaddada."

"Excuse me," Jane interrupted, sounding haughty, "I do not trill." There was a low-grade giggle. "Neither do I chirp, warble, twitter, gurgle—or babble, contrary to popular opinion."

Tonia bowed with a flourish. "No, but thanks be to the Goddess you can articulate, enunciate, explicate, and pontificate with the best of them, or else we'd all be out of a job."

"Thank you, Ms. Yaddada."

The giggling surged into full-throttle laughter. As I joined in, I recalled my first day on the job: thinking Jane was ridiculing my mom's sad case in crass talk-show terms. Yeah, my mother's life was a fuckin' tragedy, but I can't go around with it reverberating through my bones forever. I gotta make peace with her, find some perspective, step around her memory with a ten-foot pole if I want—or maybe just retrain my automatic red-alert not to go off every time something reminds me of the devastation she couldn't help leaving behind. Take Julia's advice to go ahead and laugh at life's craziness instead.

Tonia's voice tore through my thoughts. "This last show's got to make Janie's commitment to preserving higher standards shine like white on rice."

Jane moved close to Tonia and put a hand on her shoulder, looked into her eyes. The touch revealed the trust they now shared, their reconciliation of the idea that although they were not meant to be lovers, it didn't mean they couldn't be lifelong intimates. I shot a glance at Allie. She was watching them spellbound, her lips slightly parted, her attention held by a history she might or might not have had knowledge of.

Allie...she would always be lost to me.

"What—me, shine?" Jane said, her voice commanding, and adoring, too. "Don't you think my commitment's more the dull and steady kind? Don't worry, Tony. Everything's shaping up fine." Only I knew she was lying, and she sent me a glance that sealed the conspiracy: Open your trap about our show being one outta-shape puppy and your ass is french toast!

I had to smile. We were up a creek, but then again, who else in my life could I trust to get us where we were going—with or without a paddle.

"After all," Jane continued, "I've prostituted my personal life to prove a point. How can the audience not come away convinced of my integrity?"

Tonia rose, took a moment to respond, regarding Jane, shorter by several inches, from a slightly lofty angle. "Take that back, about you prostituting." She placed her hands on her hips. "I'll personally escort the next Prissy Johnson who questions your integrity to a dark sound stage and browbeat him senseless."

After the meeting, Jane caught up to me. "Stay for a few minutes." I joined her at the conference table with a disconcerting feeling I knew what was coming. She began breathlessly, "First, Nita...in order to discuss the media backlash we got from the Gina shows, I need your permission to refer to the articles about you. I won't put the photo of you and Allie on the air, of course, or mention her name."

I shrugged, compelled to counter her excitement with nonchalance. "Go ahead. It's no secret. Is that it?"

"Uh, no." She put her chin in her hand, and clicked her tongue a couple of times, like a clock ticking.

I enjoyed this rare experience—Jane at a loss for words. Well, she wouldn't get any help from me. "Can I go now?" I pushed away from the table, the rolling chair rumbling satisfyingly across the parquet floor. Then with a slow pull I slid back. "Or is there something else you wanted to ask me?"

Exasperation flickered across her face, provoked not so much by me, I thought, but by her inability to be completely in control. "You know damn well what I want to ask you. Are you going to make me come out and say it?" She sighed. "Nita, I can't pull this off without you. Will you please come on my show?"

She wasn't conning me; she couldn't do it without me, and, surprisingly, I didn't want her to. "All right."

Shit o'mighty, what was that! Quick, God, somebody, did you hear? This jerk agreed to go on!

I floundered for conditions. What's gonna make me seem like I'm taking this in stride? "I have to know everything you'll cover beforehand."

"Fair enough. We'll rehearse till we drop."

"And you can't call me pet names, like sweetie or anything."

She saluted me. "Nossir, I won't."

I had to laugh. How quickly she was on to me. Why did she hafta know me so damn well? "And you can't say how you can hardly wait to see me married to some nice girl."

"Honey, after we air you'll be knee-deep in proposals."

"Or honey, you can't call me that."

"Get the hell out of here, honey. I've got work to do." She blew me a kiss.

I started to walk away. When I got to the door, I stopped. "I'm still scared," I said.

I heard her footsteps as she came up behind me. Her perfume embraced me. "Nothing will happen to you. Not while I'm around."

I didn't turn to her. "Someone once said that to me. See where it got us."

Her comeback was reassuringly fast, and accurate. "Just because one person couldn't make it true, don't expect everyone else to fail."

I faced her. "Joseph says that's my new mantra. I hope it's worth the nine bazillion dollars you're paying him."

"Ssh, I don't like that kind of talk from you." She drew me to her. "Be scared. It's normal. You're going to do something new, and I'll be right there beside you. Afterward, you'll feel a little different. You know how that goes already. I've been watching you, and you've changed a lot since you came to work here. You've already become someone not so scared of being scared."

An hour later, boggled by the task of turning "The Secret Friend" into a script outline for the writers, I heard a knock at the door, and looked up to see Allie standing there with two cans of Pepsi and a long, narrow white paper bag redolent of onions and oregano. Startled, I sent my mouse skidding off the mouse pad.

She glossed over it. "I don't know what possessed me to buy such an enormous sub, because I'll never be able to finish it. Care for some?" She sure was trying.

I hesitated a moment thinking of the gossip if people saw us together, then shut the door behind her. We cleared my desk. Allie unwrapped the sandwich, wrenched the halves apart, popped the tops of the Pepsi's.

My heart was starting to pound. I knew she deserved an apology, but was I going to be able to rise to the occasion?

Graciously denying me the opportunity to put my foot in my mouth again, she began to chat, asking me what I was working on, and then she looked surprised when I told her. "That seems awfully personal to put on the air. Are you okay with it?"

"Yeah, I am. But thanks for asking."

She took a bite, chewed, and swallowed. "Would you say it's considerate of me?" She giggled—nervously, I thought.

I floundered for the appropriate reaction. "Uh-huh." Now that was bright!

There was an uncomfortable silence that I knew I ought to break sooner or later, but she, knowing all too well how lame I could be in the communication department, decided to help me out instead. "Want to know what I'm working on today?"

I stopped clenching my jaw long enough to mutter, "Go for it."

"Having a friendship with you." Our eyes met; I put down my sandwich. "But if I'm annoying you, I'll leave, let you eat in peace."

She wanted to make up, despite me acting like an asshole... "Why now?" I asked wonderingly.

"I miss being in your life." She licked a whisper of mayonnaise from her fingers. "What you said the other day really hurt my feelings, in case you're interested."

This concession softened me immediately. "I didn't mean to hurt your feelings. It was the truth. I mean, my feelings were hurt, too."

"No one accused you of lying." Her smile was a little teasing. "Well...maybe you weren't trying to hurt my feelings, only find out whether I have any. I do, you know," she said matter-of-factly. "Maybe you thought I didn't, because of the way I acted before." She glanced away. "I can understand that."

Her approaching me this way was astonishing. After all the shit she had been through with people—with me—how could she just waltz in here, show me she was willing to trust me again? I said, "Maybe you thought I didn't, because of the way I acted. But back to my original question: why are you doing this now?"

She tossed her head, her chestnut hair lustrous even under the insubstantial fluorescence of the ceiling panel. "Back to my original answer: I miss you, and I'd like us to be friends." She paused. "You're looking at me as if you don't believe me."

I laughed, not nicely. "Should I?"

"Trust games, again—still—always." I started to protest, and she held up her hand. "Look, it's all right. How about this: a rung is missing from my ladder, would that be you? Is that more in keeping with my character?"

I was silent.

"And you call yourself butch. Aren't you're supposed to say something gallant now, like 'I never have thought of you that way?'"

I had to smile. "Maybe once."

"No one's perfect." My smile deepened. "And what about, 'We both made mistakes?'"

Hey, I could get into this. "Some real biggies on my part."

"There you go." Her expression relaxed. "And, um, 'I believe it when you say you miss me, because there aren't too many butch women out there as smart and funny as I am.'"

I just laughed.

"One last thing." She looked right into my eyes. "What about, 'Okay, I'll try being friends?'"

She had me. "All right, we'll give it a shot."

TWENTY

After a few pleasant conversations during the week, Allie and I agreed to have lunch before the Friday afternoon production meeting. When she came by my office to pick me up I could tell something was bothering her, and she was making an effort not to show it. I didn't ask; if she wanted to bring it up, she would. Actually, I thought her mood might have to do with Glyn—in which case I didn't want to hear about it.

We chose a local Chinese restaurant, and kept the conversation focused on work. She half-heartedly attempted to amuse me by describing the idiosyncrasies of the television critics she was prepping for the program: one wore glasses with TV-screen-shaped lenses, another proposed giving commentary in phrases suitable for ad-spot sound bites. Then the conversation dwindled to silence, and I made no effort to jump-start it. Her depression was stifling.

I studied the restaurant's intricate decor, the black-and-gold lacquer of the carved entrance way, the carved jade tree with quartz clusters of pink and orange peaches dripping from the branches near the cash register, the banquette adjacent that looked to be an antique, with a cloudy mirror set in the top. The people who had sat on that bench, lingering together after a meal, inspecting their faces in the mirror— they and their pleasures and their vanity were long gone. Instead of the aroma of ginger and garlic that had greeted us as we stepped through the door, the air suddenly held a scent of age and dust and other things humans abhor, and I felt claustrophobic.

I was ready to ask the waiter for the check, but she couldn't keep her news to herself any longer. "Well, this morning I set myself back a few years."

I waited for her to continue, hoping she had better judgment than to involve me in the sordid details of her fling with that pretty-boy cop.

"You're probably the only person I could admit this to." She drew a deep breath and released it. "Today is my mother's fiftieth birthday. For some stupid reason I called and said, 'Hi, Mama, it's Alice, I just wanted to wish you a Happy—' and before I could say 'Birthday,' she hung up on me. Why did I do it? I should've known better." She stopped talking, pinched the bridge of her nose.

I was at first selfishly relieved. Then the cruelty of the rejection smacked me in the face. 'I'm sorry' or 'How terrible' seemed inadequate—or too obvious. "I know exactly how you feel. My mom was just as big a jerk, only now she has a better excuse for it than your mom does."

Allie smiled. "You're right. Jerks, both of them."

"We got stuck with jerks. Poor us."

"I feel sorry for us."

I ran with it. "Everyone does, haven't you noticed? See that lady over there? She ordered shrimp with lobster sauce, same as you, but you got extra shrimp, because she has a fabulous mom and you got stuck with a jerk."

She giggled. "You're nuts."

"That's because I got stuck with a jerk. I can't be held responsible for my mental status."

"Watch out, you just might make me feel better."

"According to my jerk of a mom, making others feel better is what my co-dependent little role in life is all about. Thank you for helping me fulfill my life's purpose."

"Check please!"

She saved me a seat for the meeting, and it wasn't my imagination that everyone who came into the room did a double-take at the sight of us together. Even Jane telegraphed notice to Sam when she thought I wasn't looking, raising her eyebrows and shooting a glance in our direction. I ignored it; let them stare.

Afterward, I went to Jane's office for another 'talk sesh'—as she referred to the rehearsals for our portion of the show. We'd spent countless hours at it each day, and so far had had a heckuva time keeping to the business at hand. We got lost in long conversations; a talk master, she knew how to put me at ease, and I felt free to answer at length, revealing stuff I'd never told her before. Like the countless times I'd flushed pills down the toilet. Emptied bottles down the sink. How my mom charmed my teachers, but was sometimes too stoned to help me with my homework.

I think I finally made Jane understand that Julia had been good for me, our last encounter the sole exception. I confessed how, for several months after my mother died, I literally thought I was dying, too. I had chest pains, couldn't breathe. Convinced myself I was HIV positive from unprotected sex. Was sometimes so afraid of a traffic accident that driving was out of the question. I even told her how those feelings wore off suddenly, how I did reckless things like going ninety on the freeway with no seatbelt, having oral sex with a girl I hardly knew when she had her period.

Jane accepted what I told her without judging, though she made me promise not to do anything foolish in the future. In response, I made her laugh: "My only self-destructive act lately was promising to come on your show."

I could deal with waiting twenty minutes for her to finish up God-knows-what with the writers, but I wasn't prepared for this talk sesh to go off-track in record time. She was nestled in the corner of the couch, and her face seemed flushed with a private excitement that spelled trouble.

"Well, Nita, are you and Allie talking again, or do my eyes deceive me? You wouldn't be seeing each other again, would you?"

I didn't have much luck hiding how ticked this coy attitude made me. "Would that make you happy?"

"It may not have occurred to you, but I'm interested in your well-being, and I have an idea that Allie made you happy."

"No, sorry to disappoint you, we aren't seeing each other."

She sighed, then clicked her tongue. "Don't be silly, I'm not disappointed, only I worry about who you choose to spend your time with..." Her voice trailed away.

Oh, give it a rest. The next word out of her mouth'll be Julia, wanna take bets? We're supposed to be working on the show, and she's using the opportunity to lecture me.

"I mean, the reason Julia has always upset me—"

I stood. "Maybe this isn't the best time for a rehearsal." Her expression told me she'd caught my sarcasm, and didn't appreciate it.

She studied me with a phony calm, held her silence until her voice was completely controlled. And then, her tone was almost threatening. "Sit down."

I did as told, but under protest. "I fail to see what relevance Julia has to—"

"Nita, the first person you reached out to was someone unattainable to you. True connection was impossible. You chose someone like Julia Reynolds because that's who your mother taught you to choose. I wish you and Allie had lasted, for several reasons. One is, it would mean that you were moving on with your life. That's how this conversation is relevant."

All right, she was speaking the truth, even though it came as a chastisement. Before I had a chance to say anything, she took my chin in her hand. "My fear of connecting with people almost cost me Sammy, which, roughly translated, means everything."

She released me, sat back in the couch corner, and rested her head against the cushion.

Curiosity aroused, I said what I was expected to say. "What happened?"

She closed her eyes, took her time before replying. "What happened is this. When your Aunt Kathy and I roomed together at grad school, we had a third person sharing the house..." She paused, opened her eyes, took a deep breath. "Regina Mandeville—Reggie—was pursuing a doctorate in biochemistry. And me. Our affair began two weeks after she moved in. All of a sudden, I was in love like never before. I even found her jealousy flattering. The big break-ups, the bigger make-ups, I knew I was loved."

I had the proverbial unable-to-turn-away-from-a-traffic-accident feeling.

She folded her arms across her chest. "One night she shoved me into a mirror. I was cut when it broke. On the way to the emergency room, she was in tears, said it was an accident, begged me to forgive her. The next time it happened we were drunk. I woke up with a black eye and a bouquet of roses. After the next couple of times she made it up to me by taking me to Hawaii." Her voice caught. "Still think your old aunt is pretty together?"

I didn't know what to say.

She continued in a torrent of words, "Everything was quiet until Christmas. We went to a party, she convinced herself I'd been flirting with someone, and when we got home, tried to force me to go to bed with her. I woke up three days later in intensive care. Kathy had found me. My skull was fractured, and I'd been raped with the flashlight I kept by the bed."

What the fuck? She can't be serious. This can't be true!

Tears came to my eyes. She wasn't looking at me, and I was able to wipe them away before she could see them.

"I wanted the chance of a career, and I never pressed charges. Nine months later, Reggie committed suicide—after killing her new lover."

Why was she telling me this now?

She proceeded as though she could read my mind. "I didn't mean to upset you, I just wanted you to know how important choices really are. A couple of years later, when I met Sammy, I was still so intent on protecting myself I couldn't allow myself to love her, to be intimate at all. I was too scared."

Suddenly Sam's words came to mind: Before Janie met me, she had some rough times...

She clapped a loving hand on my shoulder. "Don't be afraid to reach out to the right person, Nita."

I finally made some connections. After Allie and I broke up, I went running right back to Julia, because I felt so damn comfortable being, well, marginal—in someone else's life. Sure, my mom prepped me to play second fiddle to her illness...

"But this woman, this shithead, she..." I could hardly bring myself to say the words. "Raped you, and tried to murder you. My mother"

She interrupted me. "Your mother wasn't a violent psychotic." Her tone was impassioned, but without malice. "Still, she threw her shit all over you. She violated you emotionally. She damaged you psychologically. The only difference between you and me was that you were a defenseless victim. I let myself become one."

"Are you saying that because I was a child and you were a grown woman—"

189

She shook her head. "No. I let a shithead psychotic hurt me because your mom had just signed her first recording contract, and I wasn't thinking too highly of myself. Pop Psychology 101, but it's true."

There was nothing else to do but put my arm around her and draw her close. Early on I'd learned to abhor role reversals, had it up the wazoo with playing Mommy to my own mother. But with Jane I was just an adult comforting another adult.

Someone had taught me to be strong, and it really wasn't you, Mom.

I cleared my throat. "Someone taught me to be strong, Jane, and it wasn't my mother."

Eyes sparkling, she sat up, taking notice, I thought, that our relationship was moving into a new phase. "Oh, no, it wasn't me," she said, "it was you."

TWENTY-ONE

In the long run, the talk seshes fell short of their goal. They did not shape any portion of the actual show. But my aunt didn't seem fazed, or call them a waste of time. She'd led us through so many intensely personal areas, I knew there'd be no chance of disclosing anything too confidential on the air. As I understood it, we would move on to Plan B—leave the segments relatively unstructured, let our conversation flow about coming to terms with my mom's death and the impact of her celebrity status—but I couldn't help feeling that maybe Jane had planned it that way all along.

About two weeks before showtime, boom, I was hit with an idea that she, I was sure, would think sucked more than a fox in the Humpty-Dumpty egg factory. Part of our on-air conversation, it occurred to me, should be three-way.

And who better than Julia to wax eloquent about chasing a dream when someone so close is famous?

Would she even entertain the notion of going on TV as a profes- sional failure? Would she even talk to me again? The idea seemed too promising not to give it a shot, so I did, orchestrating my attempt at reconciliation with the delivery of a dozen cream-colored roses. The card said, "I need a favor."

"Not on your sweet, short life!" Jane screeched, turning to Sam, seated beside her on the office couch. "That woman on my show! This must be my darkest hour!"

A smile played on Sam's lips; she covered it immediately with a fake-looking yawn, a stall-tactic I hoped meant she liked my suggestion, and just needed to figure out how to defuse my aunt's very predictable reaction. There was something about the way Sam caught my gaze, holding it briefly before taking my aunt's hand, that convinced me I had an ally.

Sam asked, "You haven't heard back from Julia yet? She doesn't actually know what favor you're asking?" She fingered Jane's diamond-and-platinum commitment ring.

I shook my head no. "Yesterday she accepted delivery of the flowers, maybe only because she didn't know who they were from. But then again, they haven't shown up beheaded at my front door, either. I just wanted to run the idea past you to see what you thought, before I go ahead—"

"You may not go ahead!" Jane exploded. "Under no circumstances will I permit Julia Reynolds to set one clawfoot on this lot, much less in my studio. The very idea of me interviewing her to find out in exquisite detail how she starfucked herself all the way to oblivion makes me ill."

Good crap!

"Janie, that is entirely enough." Sam tugged on her hand, barely controlling herself; there was grit in her usual sweetness. "No matter what Julia has done or what you think Julia has done, if that's the way you're going to talk, keep it to yourself."

Jane snatched her hand from Sam's. "I won't have you telling me how to talk." Her eyes flashed with the effort of keeping an even tone.

Slowly, deliberately, Sam placed her hands on her hips. "Then what about how to think? Isn't it time to let go of this silly feud with Julia?"

Even if it wasn't my place to jump on the bandwagon right then, I was frustrated enough by my aunt's attitude to at least have a try at changing it, even a little bit. And I suddenly realized that I had a personal stake in asking that Julia come on the show. She would take some focus off me, and her presence would be…a comfort. "Maybe Julia oughtn't to have been with me, but that's the reality, and as far as I can tell, I'm none the worse for it. A lot better for many reasons, I think. And Julia was really good to Mom too. Aunt Jane, you may not realize this, but there were plenty of times when Mom was in trouble and she called Julia to come and help—"

She interrupted before I had a chance to finish my thought. "Of course I know she dragged Julia into her ugly messes. Why she just didn't call me, and keep it in the family, I don't understand. I was always ready, willing, and able to offer my services!"

But that wasn't quite the reality. Anybody who wants to be recognized for their talent isn't always there for the people who can't reward them for it, namely their family. I had only intended to say that my mom was sometimes too ashamed of herself to ask for Jane's assistance, but now that this other issue had been raised, I just went ahead and told her how I felt. "Yes, you helped whenever you were called. There were times she couldn't ask you because she was embarrassed, and...there were times you were unavailable." Her eyes met mine, her face coloring. She opened her mouth to say something, but when she shut it again without uttering a sound, I kept going. "It doesn't matter now. I think that Julia can help bring a balance to the show. She was Mom's friend, but in a way she was a rival. Mom was a bigger success."

The look Jane gave me suggested I was comparing her success to my mom's as well, but I honestly hadn't meant to. There was no reason to pay homage to her insecurity by switching into automatic reassurance mode. So I just glossed over it, explaining what I needed instead. "And to be perfectly honest, I would just feel better if she were there."

Sam shot me a reassuring smile, then mustering some of her previous austerity, turned back to Jane. "Like it or not, Julia has been an important part of our niece's life. Being able to forgive Julia for her rather inexcusable little tabloid attack and put it into perspective, makes me more inclined to trust Nita's instincts here. Julia on the show will add a whole different dimension." Sam paused just long enough for Jane to give an offended sniff, and then continued, "Look, chances are, Julia will want nothing to do with it. But Nita's concept is absolutely brilliant, admit it.'

"I'll admit nothing of the kind," she huffed, folding her arms across her chest.

Sam continued, cocking her head to one side, "Do you mean to tell me, Jane Isabel Wilde, that if I got Tonia in here right now, and asked her what she thought, she wouldn't say it's good?"

Sensing the potential loss of a battle, Jane opted for a pity-play. "If I have to interview that woman, I'll roll over and die!" She sprang up and walked toward her desk.

Sam shot me a look. "Why don't you leave us alone for a few minutes, Nita? As soon as you hear from *that woman*, let me know, one way or another."

"Sure thing."

I left the room, hearing the most reasonable of all of Sam's reasonable tones. "Now, honey..."

"Don't 'now honey' me!" Then she called into the hallway, "As for you, Nita, you may no longer consider yourself my favorite niece!"

Julia's phone call that evening began in the usual begrudging après-spat fashion, though the two months' estrangement—a record for us—was hardly the result of a spat. "I'm not sure I want to talk to you."

"Why don't we call a truce?" I couldn't resist being a smartass. "You acted bad, but I found your little in-print lesson valuable. Now, as I said, I need a favor."

She exhaled slowly into the receiver. "Is this favor three thousand eight hundred twenty-one, or twenty-two?"

Obnoxiousness is a game best played with a partner. "It's the first favor of the last half of your life."

A sharp intake of breath. "Touché, darling." Then a giggle, and a sip of what was most likely Pinot Grigio. "Why don't you come over, and tell me all about it."

"I have a better idea," I said. "Something we've never done before. How about lunch, on me? Say at The Ivy, tomorrow, at one o'clock?"

Patio seating on Robertson Boulevard in the heart of Beverly Hills means a nice snootful of exhaust every time a valet takes off to park a car, but it also was one of Julia's favorite places to fawn and be fawned upon. The perfect setting to pop the big question: Will you tell an audience of millions how, in Gina Wilde's shadow, your own career shriveled and died?

It was unseasonably warm for December, but the plunging neckline of Julia's tangerine halterdress had less to do with the weather than with making sure I knew what I'd been missing. Her now strawberry-blonde hair was cut in a deftly-layered shag that framed her face. I gave her a kiss on her cheek and the obligatory low whistle.

"Not so bad yourself, handsome," the inevitable reply.

After some small talk, a couple of Perriers with a twist of lime, and a shared gorgonzola and walnut salad, I laid the show title on her, and told her I'd be appearing with Jane. I could've predicted her double-take.

"You're what?" She eyed me. "Is your aunt putting you up to this?"

Post perfume-bottle meteor shower, her concern for my well-being was suspect, but I decided to take it from where it came. "Nope," I said, sounding, I hoped, casual to the max, "my idea entirely."

"Really." With her fork she chased a wayward leaf of Romaine around her plate before stabbing it and popping it into her mouth. She chewed slowly, maddeningly, a complete overkill. "Well, you must've undergone a complete personality change in the last few months, Nita. I don't know you anymore."

She'd said what was on her mind, and, try as I might, I couldn't resist the urge to reassure her. But why not turn it to my advantage? "Oh, Jules, don't be ridiculous. Besides, I asked to see you because there's a part for you in the show."

Boy, did she look surprised. She laid down the fork, then cocked her head, skeptical. "Am I Lucy to your Ricky? What the hell would I do on your show? My one big hit, 'Phone Booth,' for the ninety-millionth time?"

Great idea, so what if it hadn't occurred to me! "Sure—if you'd like, that would be incredible."

"But that wasn't what you had in mind, was it?"

"Well, not exactly. I mean..."

As I flubbered for an answer, I could see her putting two-and-two together, and felt relieved I wouldn't have to spell it all out. Why would she want to come on? Like people always want to tell you all about their car accident, maybe she wanted a chance to talk about the disappointment her life had turned into. How surviving it meant, in some small way, real success.

"Do you mean to tell me your aunt actually consented to have me on her show? If Jane Wilde actually thought I had any guts, she'd hate them."

I giggled, then she did, too. We left it that she would think about the idea and give me a call in the morning. How Sam would bring Jane around, only the goddess knew. But as I drove away from the restaurant, I couldn't help but feel I had the situation nailed.

That night I searched through my CDs for a song I hadn't listened to for several years, though it echoed through my mind at odd, inappropriate times, bringing me close to anger or tears, "Sylvia," one of my mother's creations, about the suicide of Sylvia Plath:

> Sylvia's on my mind tonight
> With her tentative smile
> Her propensity for flight
> I listen to her cadences
> That led right to the grave
> Except she left her children
> I might have thought her brave...

I remembered how my mother admired Plath's work, reading some of the poems aloud to me when I was too young to grasp the meaning and responded only to their emotional undertow, which I now think is a very valid way to appreciate poetry. My mom read and reread *The Bell Jar*, and once, after she'd landed at Betty Ford yet again and asked for the book, I screamed at her, "Your stay would be better spent figuring out why Plath never wrote a sequel!"

Tonight I didn't find "Sylvia" upsetting. Instead of listening just to the lyrics, I heard their irony as well. This was the addict's definitive song, and "Rush" only its cheap imitation. By her death, my mother surrendered the distinction she had so smugly attempted to draw between herself and the poet. Ultimately the song only immortalized failure.

When I got into bed and turned off the light, I let my mind wander over memories of my mom, things I might mention on the program—not of her performing on stage, or being stoned—but simply as a mother.

Like the time we were away on vacation at Pebble Beach, and she bought a big bag of salted peanuts roasted in the shell on the wharf in Monterey. I remember waking in the dark of the hotel suite to a strange crackling noise. Confused, I searched for her, finding a streak of light under the bathroom door. I discovered her sitting on the counter beside the sink shelling the nuts and popping them into her mouth. Having given into her craving, she'd retreated there so she wouldn't disturb my sleep.

Or a few years later when I begged to be allowed to keep the class pet over Easter vacation, a pot-bellied pig named Diane. Mom was exhausted, just off a tour, yet agreed when she saw how much it would mean to me. During the course of the holiday, she developed an inordinate fondness for Diane, and Diane developed...a virulent porcine version of the flu, requiring an expensive emergency trip to the vet and round-the-clock care, which my mother herself provided. Much of her ministrations consisted of the heroic newspapering and un-newspapering of a guest bedroom where Diane was convalescing, and as my mother gamely cleaned up, she sang for my amusement, 'And the farmer hauled another load away!'

During my childhood, she was a tireless competitor in Monopoly, Clue, Life, and she managed to teach me how to ride a bicycle without ever having learned herself. She who loved spike heels and short skirts and make-up, recognized my aversion to such traditionally feminine trappings and let me live in Levi's for the duration of my adolescence, even encouraged me and four of my friends to go to our high school prom in tuxes.

When I first got to U.C.L.A. and was overwhelmed by all the decisions and responsibilities suddenly facing me—choosing classes, living on my own and getting my studying done along with my laundry—she told me to play it by ear, to trust myself to know what to do. How I'd showed her time and time again I did know the right thing. Whether it was entirely true of me at the age of eighteen, I believed her, and know now that her trust in me had a lot to do with my ability to make a way for myself. Looking back, there were plenty of times when she knew how to be a mother. When I went on with Jane, that was one thing I wanted the audience to know. What they would see as a 'show' was my real life.

As I settled at my desk the next morning I knew not to expect Julia's call right away. Allie's appearance at my door, a smile tugging at her lips, was unexpected, however. Damn if she wasn't a hottie in her clingy pink minidress and chunky white monk boots. "I want you back."

My eyes met hers. The expression on her face told me she was enjoying the expression on mine.

"Relax, I meant work with you again. Want to? Damon just did something that makes me want to wring his neck. At least you know what you're doing. Hey, Jane just called me to her office. Do you have any idea what she wants?"

"No."

"Not going to tell me?" She pursed her lips.

"Seriously, I haven't the slightest."

She gave me the finger and went down the hall.

Here she was flirting with me, and the fact I liked it...bothered me. Of our brief history together, there were pages especially not worth repeating. I was pretty sure I could ask Allie out tonight and end up back at her place, in her bed, in her life. But as much as I wanted it, fear still took away a good part of the pleasure—and safety—of having her.

She passed by my office again after seeing my aunt. "Well, I just learned something pretty danged amazing. You, of all people, agreed to go on the show. Why?"

I couldn't resist. "To prove I'm no pussy."

"Oh, Nita, please!" Her face went scarlet. "Did I mention how sorry I am about that? Did you know sorry is an Eskimo word for horse's ass? Did you know horse's ass is Eskimo for Allie? Did you know it isn't true that the Eskimo have so many words for snow?"

She made me laugh. "I'm doing it because I want to."

"How much of it is canned questions?"

"We've covered a gadzillion areas. I'm not sure what we'll go with yet." My stomach was beginning to churn. "It makes me nervous to think about it."

"Are you going to talk about your mom?"

"Uh-huh."

"Are you comfortable with that?"

"Yeah."

"It was your idea?"

"Yep."

She shook her head, giving a short laugh. "O-kay, end of interview. You respond like that on the air, Jane'll never speak to you again."

"We agreed not to announce this until just before final rehearsals. Why did she tell you now?"

"She just mentioned it in passing. It surprised her you hadn't told me yourself. She said she wouldn't mention me by name on the show, but I said go ahead."

That amazed me. "It doesn't bother you anymore? Why not?"

She looked thoughtful, lowering her voice. "Well, the article essentially reports a fact: we did sleep together." She snickered. "Barely, but enough for them to get right on it. Anyway, there was no real reason to get in such a snit about it."

That annoyed me. Her 'snit' helped break us up, and now she said it was beside the point? "What a prime-cut doofus I was for taking your snit seriously."

"Listen before you get pissed off—" She regarded me as if I were someone who might be worth getting used to, possibly as a lifelong intimate who, after years of intense therapy, accepted her lovers. "I realize it was stupid for me to get so resentful at the time."

I was becoming worked up, but I kept my voice low, too. "At the time, your resentment sent you over the edge. At the time, you told me I was a pussy for not dealing with my mother. At the time, breaking up seemed the thing to do."

"At the time, I wasn't thinking very clearly." Her voice went up a few notches. "What makes you assume you have a monopoly on being fucked up? Why do rich people think they own everything?"

For the first time in my adult life I felt capable of hitting someone, and it spooked me. I struggled for composure. "Even though your words hurt, I thought they were truthful. I thought your insight might help me. At least that's how I justified it. But maybe it was your lesson to learn as well."

She put her hand on my arm, and I repressed an impulse to knock it off. "Maybe, okay? But that day Jane had really upset you, to the extent you couldn't hear my deal, and that scared me."

We skirted the real issue, both knowing, I think, that this was all we could handle. "I only heard you turning on me because you were scared." I tried to be fair. "But maybe I wasn't really listening."

"And maybe I overreacted. Just now, when your aunt told me how careful she'd be not to mention my name on the show, I realized it wasn't the stupid article I cared about so much. I couldn't handle the idea of having a relationship that was...so public. Having photographers spy on us when we were kissing. What next? You don't know this, but I went back to the library after you and I were there, and I looked at some pictures of you in the papers—taken the night your mother died, the day of her funeral. Your private life's hanging out there for the world to see. This was before you and I were involved, and I asked myself, could I manage that?" She shook her head. "The one time my being gay was made known, I lost my whole family over it."

I was starting to get it. "You felt threatened by being exposed?"

She nodded. "Yes, it set me off." She bit her lip.

I shrugged. "I can understand that."

"We just couldn't hear each other that day. That's understandable, too, wouldn't you say?"

"Totally." God, I sounded like such a dweeb.

She glossed over it. "I admit I was insensitive. I panicked, and instead of asking you to help me, I pushed you away—I saw you as the reason for my panic. And then I was punished, I lost you. Does that appeal to your sense of fair play?" She paused, looking expectantly at me. "Do you know what I'm saying?"

"I-I'm not sure."

"Concentrate. What might it mean when a woman admits she acted badly and says it matters because she lost you? Are you catching on? Are you making your face blank on purpose?" Her eyes searched mine.

"Okay, okay!" I felt trapped. "If you're trying to say something nice, why does it sound harsh? If you care for me, why are you yelling at me?"

She grinned. "It's a Jewish thing, you wouldn't understand."

I had to smile, too. "That might look good on a tee shirt."

She took a step closer. "Well, this time you heard me, at least."

"Yes, I did." She let her hand trail down my cheek. I caught it in mine. "But I need to think about what you've said. Will you be good and let me?"

She nodded. "For a while. Don't take too long."

TWENTY-TWO

The pre-program conference was a capital-D disaster. If Jane hadn't been so determined to be civil, things might've gone better. Had she let even a few barbs fly Julia's way, the conversation might've flowed. Instead, in an exchange of forced pleasantries— "And how have you been, Julia, you look absolutely terrif, if Eric ever makes good on his threat to retire to Palm Springs, tell your stylist the job's his for the asking"—it stalled and died.

The whole experience reminded me of the night my mother died, when Jane, Sam, Julia, and I piled into the Jag, ending up at the Benedict Canyon house after a whispered front-seat conversation.

"Jane, Nita needs somebody tonight."

"She's got us. For god's sake, my sister is dead. Get that woman out of here!"

"You and I have each other. Nita needs somebody. Julia, can we bring you back to the house?"

Julia holed up in the guest bedroom. My aunt and I holding each other on the living room couch. What happened, what will happen, what happened happened, what happened, what will happen, what happened happened. Later, taking up sandwiches Sam forced on me and a bottle of wine I helped myself to, I found Julia asleep on the guest bed, clutching a bolster pillow to her breasts like a baby. She woke and held me, but I didn't feel like it, so she fucked me instead. We ate the sandwiches and killed the bottle, and she went out to the hallway bathroom to pee and there was an 'oh!' of surprise from my aunt as they met. Then more furious whispertalk from my aunt's room...

Grief makes strange bedfellows.

One weekend away from showtime. If my anxiety didn't cause me a heart attack, I was set to go.

For the first time in months I didn't work on Saturday, but loafed in bed watching MTV. The phone rang at noon.

"What the heck are you doing home?" It was Allie. "Are you feeling all right? I've been here for hours, trying to look busy, and Tonia's done her best to help further the illusion. How about I come by and provide some mindless diversion?"

She arrived right as I finished dressing, taking a seat at my desk while I finished drying my hair, avoiding the futon. When I came out of the bathroom, her gaze swept over my Black Watch flannel shirt and washed-only-once classic fit jeans, and I could tell she liked what she saw. Then she took her eyes from me and glanced around the room, as if to assure herself that it was the same, that I was still the same person I'd been months earlier. I wasn't. How to let her know all the ways I'd changed?

She turned back to me. "So—I've always wanted to ask. What was your mom's house like? I'll bet she didn't keep it so neat."

"Nope." I found I didn't mind admitting it to her. "It was a mess."

"You had a housekeeper?"

"She couldn't make a dent." I pictured my mother's bedroom, clothes slung over the unmade bed, guitars propped against the walls, sheet music strewn everywhere, overflowing ashtrays, soda cans and dirty glasses... In my mind, I closed the door.

She seemed at once hesitant, and yet determined to offer her next comment. "I guess that's why your place is so spotless, and why you're so organized at work. I used to think you were just a control freak, but now I understand."

"It's important to me to have things in order." I looked into her open, friendly face. "Think I'm strange?"

"I can live with it." She smiled.

She took me to Canter's, a deli in the Fairfax district. The area's entire elderly Jewish population seemed to be there barking orders at the waitresses, who called patrons 'deah' in a whole range of condescending tones as they banged down plates of artery-clogging sandwiches, and grudgingly refilled coffee cups. "Everyone seems to be crowded into here."

"Well, not everyone. It's Saturday, the Sabbath—these are only the heathens, like me."

After stuffing ourselves with bagels and lox, we took a drive, ending up at the Griffith Park observatory. We inspected the exhibits, tested our celestial I.Q., weighed ourselves on the moon and Venus and Jupiter and Mars, and then, having exhausted our appetite for astronomical amusement, went outside on the deck.

It was a cool, bright day, with sudden, shocking bursts of wind that banished all traces of smog and provided us with an excuse for close physical proximity. We stood companionably together gazing at the landmarks of the city. I could see Dodger Stadium, the highrises of downtown and Century City and Westwood, even a faint shimmer of ocean. She captured the dichotomy of the scene perfectly. "One reason I like it here, especially when it's this clear, is that after you've had your fill of town, you can turn around and see country."

The thin, oblique winter light imparted a sharpness and also a delicacy to the hills that the direct summer sun would have only overwhelmed, the view so inviting we decided to hike a trail behind the observatory. Once many years ago, I'd glimpsed a doe in a clearing there, and ever since have expected to see her again in the same spot.

As we climbed side-by-side, it occurred to me how odd that expectation was. I wasn't really searching for the same experience itself, in all its unique and delightful particulars. I was hoping to recapture the unexpected emotional delight that accompanied it.

Allie's presence in my life was kind of like that. At first, the pleasure she brought had caught me unaware. When we broke up, I realized I was unable to recapture the same joy without her, and felt only the sting of its loss. Would I be willing again to pay such a high price for happiness?

We reached the summit and sat on a rock. The sun was beginning to set, and the white facade observatory took on a rosy orange glow.

"What are you thinking about?" She studied me with concern, and, I thought, a great deal of fondness. "Don't get frazzled about the show. It'll go fine. It's me who has a legitimate cause for worry. Every femme who sees you on TV will be mailing you her panties."

I smiled. "That hadn't crossed my mind."

"Good. If there's one thing I can't stand, it's a butch who thinks about other femmes' panties."

I shook my head. "The show, dummy. I wasn't thinking about it." No sooner were the words out of my mouth then I realized I'd doomed myself to revealing what really was bothering me.

She took my hand, threaded her fingers through mine. "You're worried about being here with me." She caressed my fingers with her thumb. "About seven months ago, I met a very nice woman. I wanted to know her much better, but was afraid, because someone else had taken all I had to give and just as easily threw it away. So I took my time, and when I thought I felt comfortable trusting her, she was there. The two of us came to know each other very well. But the reality was, we weren't ready to trust each other. We did some dumb things, and she wanted to get away from me. I let her, without telling her she meant more to me than anyone had ever, and that I loved her."

I drew her close. "Thank you for telling me," I whispered, realizing it wasn't all she wanted to hear, but not feeling ready to say anything more. I held her, trying not to allow being physically intimate with her again overwhelm me.

The sun sank below the horizon, sending a real chill into the air. We walked stiff-legged to the car, and turned the heat on full blast inside. As we thawed, she asked, "Shall I take you home, or is there anywhere else you'd like to go?"

Returning to my apartment, even with her, seemed depressing. In its neatness, a reaction to the chaos of my mother's house, I'd created a lifelessness in my surroundings I couldn't face right then. "Let's go to your place," I suggested, thinking it seemed normal by comparison, with piles of newspapers read and unread, books tossed onto the shelves, a cat to play with.

When Allie opened the door to her apartment, Lana greeted us with a volley of heartrending vowel sounds, related, apparently, to a distressing hollowness of the midsection. We started toward the kitchen, and she charged ahead of us, then twirled around our legs as we stood at the counter, a choreography evidently essential to her mission. The appearance of a can of Fancy Beast Duck à l'Orange—or whatever it was Allie spoiled her with—was heralded by desperate cries. She nearly tripped over backwards as I lowered the food dish to her.

"What about you?" Allie regarded me. "Are you hungry?"

"Not yet. Will I have to put on a similar performance to signal my misery?" We headed into the living room.

"You can be subtle about what you need—I'll pick up on it." We sat on the couch, where an uneasy silence descended, as though we both realized there was more to talk about, but neither knew how to begin. But she, at the moment a little bolder than I, took care of it with a simple comment. "It feels good to have you here."

"Thanks."

"You know what I've been thinking?" She looked at me intently, and I knew she would waste no time making her point. "About us. If I had to do it all over, there's a number of details I'd handle differently."

"Like what?"

She shook her head firmly, gave a sly little smile. "There's no point in talking about it. Maybe one day you'll let me try again."

I waited a moment before saying the words I knew she wanted to hear. "What would you do if I asked you to try right now?"

She leaned over and kissed me softly, her touch both familiar and exciting. I felt just the tip of her tongue on my lips. She moved back and looked at me expectantly.

"All right, go ahead and try."

She laughed, and I took her in my arms and held her close and kissed her. I massaged her breasts, cupped their fullness, anticipating the rise of her nipples. She reached down and felt me through my jeans, knowing exactly where her hand should go.

Then I sucked the air from her mouth, locked her tongue against mine, and pushed hard against her hand.

She took it away. "Oh, no. If you want to come, you'll have to let me touch you, not your clothes."

We undressed and went to bed, and when she put her hand on me I brought mine to her. No more of this I-never-go-first rule, not this time, anyway. She was as ready as I, moaning as I spiraled through her wetness; I couldn't help wondering who would come first.

She beat me by a second or two, and then with a light staccato of my fingers I challenged her to a second round, which I won handily. With her mouth she coaxed a third from me, proving her *exhaustive* power of persuasion, and only after she let me respond in kind did she show any sign of satiety, lying limp in my arms. "My bones feel like jelly. Would you say that was a pretty good try?" She smiled.

I sat up over her. "What would you have done if I hadn't wanted you to?"

An expression I couldn't read came over her face. "Don't ask me questions that might make me cry," she said softly.

I felt tender toward her. "You're not going to cry."

Her tone became challenging—and kind of petulant. "Sure I will, name one reason I shouldn't. Dare me?"

I traced a finger from the corner of her eye down her cheek, the same down the other. Her hair was wildly disheveled; I found to my surprise I liked it wild. "I never dare a woman to do something that would upset me. And yes, I can think of a good reason why you shouldn't. Want to hear it?"

She captured my hand in hers. "It better be really good."

"The reason is…" I kissed her. "I love you, Allie."

She smiled, first with her eyes and then with her lips. "I love you too, very much." We kissed again. "You're right, honey, that's a damn good reason."

Yet her tears started all the same.

TWENTY-THREE

On the morning of the taping, I woke in darkness beside Allie a good hour before the alarm was set to go off, and lay there listening to my blood hammering. I tried to stay still so I wouldn't wake her, but she stirred, gathered me in her arms, and rubbed wide, soothing circles across my back.

"It'll be fine, you can relax," she whispered, and I must've taken her at her word, because the next thing I knew the radio blared on, startling me from the deep sleep I'd slipped back into.

I was meeting Jane at seven so we could go over last-minute details, and Allie walked me to her office. "You know where I am if you need me."

She blew me a kiss and turned to leave, but I caught her hand. Looking at Sam and Jane seated on the couch, Sam's arm around my aunt, I said loudly, to catch their attention, "Don't go. If Jane can have hers, I can have mine."

They glanced up at us. It took a moment for the impact of my comment to register. "Well, come on in, ladies," Jane invited with a big smile.

We seated ourselves across from them, and I turned to Allie. "'Ladies'—how do you like that? She's baiting me again."

Jane came directly back at me. "Don't you think you're taking a liberty for someone about to be raked over the coals?"

"Don't give it a thought, Neet," Sam interjected, "I removed the teeth from her rake while she was sleeping last night."

Jane yawned. "What you can accomplish in five minutes never fails to amaze me. Did either of you—broads—get any rest? I'm ready to fall over. Before that happens, Nita, I need a moment alone with you."

We ended up in the conference room. As usual, it had been closed off all night with the air conditioner blasting, and as I sat there shivering I remembered my ambivalent first day as an employee of *The Jane Wilde Show*. For so many reasons entering Jane's world had been the right thing to do. I was just about to open my mouth to say so, and felt miffed when she held up her hand.

"Sweetie, we have only a few minutes." She paused, momentously, I supposed, to give me enough time to raise the ol' antenna. "So let me tell you this. When you were thirteen or fourteen, Nita, you came to me and said you had something to ask. You were so serious, it frightened me. I told you, ask me anything."

"You always used to say that to me."

She regarded me with a steady gaze. "With your mom so nutso, I thought one day you might need an ally."

"I did."

"Well, after stalling around for a while, you finally came out with it. 'You're gay, right?' I said I was. 'How did you know for sure?' You don't remember any of this, do you?" She looked at me expectantly, challenging me to acknowledge that a moment so important to her— to both of us—would remain forever lost unless she took it upon herself to dredge it up again.

Just what I needed right now, a baby story with never-before-dreamed-of embarrassment potential. I shook my head no. "Spare me the rest if I made a fool of myself."

She patted my knee. "No, not at all. You were very dear."

Oh, good crap!

"I looked at that terrified face and explained it as best I could, how realizing you're gay is a process, not definite right away, and what the clues are. How whenever I was around Anita Ciolino, my junior high school history teacher, my hands would shake. And when the other girls talked about boys, I'd fantasize about Miss Ciolino taking me out. By the way, when your mom was shopping for a name for you, guess who piped up with 'I've always liked Anita?'"

That blew me away. "I was named for your high school crush?"

"You certainly were." She reached over and tousled my hair. "Anyhoo... You wanted to hear how I knew for sure. So I gave you a PG version of the truth—the first time a girl kissed me, I knew. Something that felt so natural and beautiful like nothing else had ever, just had to be right. And one day, you would be with a boy or a girl—"

"But you already knew it would be a girl, right?" I interrupted.

"Hush." I could see she was intent on proceeding with the story as scripted. "It would be a boy or a girl, and you would feel as happy as I had. If you wanted, I'd take the two of you out to a nice dinner to celebrate. You relaxed just a little and smiled. Of course, I'm still waiting to do that dinner!"

I laughed. Would she never give it a rest.

"The reason I'm telling you this now, Nita, is that I have always known who you would be—not only a lesbian, but the kind, smart young woman it's my pleasure to know. Today will be a big day for us both, but not because we'll go someplace new. It'll just be a reminder of how far along you and I have come together." She took my chin in her hand. "I'm so glad to have this day to share with you."

I hung out with Allie to help her control the green room during the morning taping; our show was on for the afternoon. The first program sped by without a glitch. The personalized scandal sheets went over well, and the TV critics nattered to Tonia's liking. Working the green room distracted me temporarily, but during the break my anxiety took off like a racehorse. After one look at me, Allie scrapped the idea of lunch, and we went on a walk through the neighborhood.

So rarely a pedestrian, I allowed myself to be distracted by visual details. The mica that glittered in the sidewalk; an empty lot's multi-color fusion of geraniums, bougainvillea and periwinkle lupine; the leaves of birds-of-paradise powdered with soot. Even the roadway trash held a kind of interest: the plastic lid of a cup of soda, a dice of red glass from a shattered reflector, a cigarette filter tip tinged pink with lipstick. All were discarded, being past human usefulness, yet endured with a permanence no person possessed.

Depressed, I turned to Allie for reassurance. The distant expression in her eyes—she was completely gone from me and our surroundings—instantly took me from my concerns. "What's wrong?"

She gave me a smiled that was fleeting as it was fake. "It can wait until after the show."

I slowed down and put my hand on her arm. "No, it can't wait."

She jammed her hands into her jacket pockets and picked up the pace again. After a quarter of a block or so, she said, "Maybe you won't like it, so I'd better not."

I disregarded the fear that shot straight up my spine to the base of my skull, and gritted my teeth. "Go for it."

The corner of her mouth turned down a bit. "You appear on TV today, and tomorrow morning while we're trying to grab a bagel, there'll be cameras all over us."

I took a deep breath and let it out slowly, during which time I managed to stifle an impulse to ask her why she had waited until now to voice this concern. Instead I said, "Tonight we'll pick up enough bagels for the whole week, and by the weekend some other singer's gay daughter will shove me out of the spotlight onto my ass."

She giggled, then the same wistfulness settled over her again.

"What?" I said.

"You're the only one who knows I called my mother on her birthday." She bit her lip. "You made me understand why I did, but that doesn't change the fact I still can't accept reality. Now you're going on TV to talk about your reality. Where does that leave me?"

I suddenly felt as if we were crunching barefoot through broken glass. No matter what I said we would walk away hurt. I was about to do something that meant I was healing. Was her calling home really a 'relapse?' Maybe in a weird way it meant she was healing too. Maybe she wasn't denying reality, but making absolutely certain she understood its boundaries. "One thing we have in common is grief. We're going to go around with it for a long time..." I hesitated, wanting the whole truth. "Forever."

She briefly closed her eyes, then opened them wide as though trying to pull herself out of sleep, and nodded.

Encouraged, I kept going. "When we first met, your strength helped me see past the grief to the other side. Right now let me be the strong one. You'll come back to a better place in time to be strong for me when I need it again."

She tossed her head. "So there's no difference if you do this on TV, and I do it behind the scenes?"

I took a chance. "Sure there is." She wheeled around fast enough. Yep, I had her. "I get a rehearsal. You had to get it right the first time."

She rolled her eyes, then took my hand. We headed back to the studio.

I changed into a pair of navy slacks, striped button-down shirt, and Bandolino wingtips; Allie pronounced me a "classic, elegant butch." The illusion was shattered when the hairstylist and make-up artist summoned me to a royal primp-fest, combing and spraying and powdering me into appropriate camera-fodder.

Allie walked me back to the green room, hesitating just outside the door, tugging on my arm.

"What?"

She looked sheepish. "Well, this is nothing compared to what you're facing, but the thought of meeting Julia Reynolds is making me kind of queasy."

I repressed my impulse to tell her not to be silly, realizing why she'd made herself scarce when Julia had come in for prepping the previous week. "Relax, she's got nothing on you."

Julia, subtly soft-butch in black denim and cowboy boots, put her magazine down as we came in. The two shook hands, then it was up to me to start the small talk. Luckily, Julia rose to the occasion, and pretty soon they were comparing fashion merits of the latest gayboy designers. Instead of tuning out on the naturally boring conversation, I found myself observing intently, focusing on the differences between these two.

Julia's conversational tendency, of course, was towards drama and hyperbole; Allie's style was understated humor. Julia assented with an "I see," Allie chattered, "Right-right-right." Both had beautiful hands. Julia's cranberry-red nail polish made the best of her salon tan, Allie's french tips lent her a subtle sophistication. Ironic—my past and my future joined in this superficial interaction...and the sense of peace it brought me.

The stage manager summoned Julia, and I gave her a quick hug and told her to break a leg. I sat back down, and put an arm around Allie, to watch the monitor as my aunt gave Julia her introduction. The stage went black, and when the lights came on, Julia launched into "Phone Booth" like the audience was a sea of agents just waiting to reinvigorate her career, a throng of suitors dying to ask her for her

211

hand. She connected with the audience in a way my mother never had. My mother led them by the balls. Julia had them convinced they were leading her. Her way was ultimately the more controlling, because she tricked people into thinking they were in control. She was awesome, camping with the audience, dancing like a prelude to sex, completely kickass. About halfway into it, I stole a glance at Allie. She grabbed my hand. "She's great!"

"I'm glad you like her," I said.

She said, sotto voce, "I didn't say I liked her, I said she was great."

After the song ended, the audience went berserk. Jane waited before jumping on stage to congratulate her, giving the 'has been' her moment in the spotlight, then they went straight to commercial. After the break, the two settled into club chairs on the set, and the interview began after accolades from my aunt.

"Julia, you were one of Gina's closest friends. If you could share a word or two about the personal challenges you faced pursuing your own career—"

"Knowing I'd never be as famous as your sister?" Interrupting the host, not the best beginning. Carlos, the director, scrambled to accommodate the camera change. "It taught me an unforgettable lesson. In a sense, long before my career died, I reconciled myself to its loss."

I was used to Julia's candor, but it left my aunt with a momentary case of slackjaw. She recovered quickly, following Julia's lead. "Personally, Gina's fame was hard to take. I was the older sister, I was expected to succeed first."

"I expected to succeed big," Julia said brusquely, leaning back in her seat, crossing her legs confidently, slipping right into the role of tell-all guest. "Being up-close-and-personal with Gina taught me two things—that I really didn't have what it takes, and that Gina-type success wasn't going to happen for me. Which realization hit me first?" She shrugged. "It was a chicken-egg situation."

A quick camera pan of the audience revealed that everyone was riveted on her.

Julia continued, "I consoled myself by thinking that I was somehow a better person, that if success meant turning into—well, a mess—then I had too much self-preservation to allow that to happen." She leaned closer to my aunt, and the camera narrowed focus. "But Jane, I can't honestly say that was true. All those nights I sat by her when she was passed out from God-knows-what, still I was thinking—why can't this be me? When she'd wake up the next morning, she'd look at me with a kind of pity. As messed up as she might have been, she knew I thought she was better off."

The next shot was of Jane, pursing her lips as though she had just run into a long-lost friend on the street but, having forgotten her name, couldn't call out to her. She said slowly, "I saw that same look."

The look that said—Don't hate me because you'll never be me.

Who wants to be you anyway?

Jane did. Julia did. But I—

"I also said that I thought too much of myself to go where Gina went," Jane was saying, "but I'm not sure anymore that I know where she went or why. Her talent existed before the addiction. After awhile the two got all tangled up."

"After awhile there was symbiosis," Julia remarked. The studio lighting accentuated her cheekbones, making her face a gaunt, wise mask that said 'Survivor.'

Is this what endurance is?—trying to make sense of the things that kill other people? Do we try to figure it out because their deaths will somehow hurt less, or because we're afraid to be killed by the same things?

I tuned back in to hear Jane say, "It took so much effort, though, not to show how much I minded never being in the running."

There was a moment of silence, and the camera pulled back so that both women were onscreen.

"You mean you never showed Gina," Julia said, not so much as a confirmation of what my aunt had admitted, but to lead her to a new recognition.

"Yes, others have known how much it hurt me." Jane met Julia's gaze.

I waited for her to acknowledge that Julia was one of those others before realizing that it would never come—not on the air, not privately. Jane was ashamed of having acted so badly, and here Julia had the upper hand. Of the two, Julia understood how wounding jealousy could be. Her career had failed, while Jane's had taken off. Yet she remained the target of Jane's animosity. And still she was always gracious.

All of a sudden it hit me how much shit Jane took out on Julia, the history of it. Like when I was in junior high, and Julia stayed at the house for a few days while my mother was off recuperating from her latest drug binge. Everything went fine, and my mom came home okay. I don't know where Jane or Sam were, but when my aunt got wind of the whole deal, she hightailed it over and spent an hour screeching at us at the top of her lungs. Not about how my mother was a hopeless drug case. But about how she could possibly have had the poor judgment to allow Julia to stay with me. About how I was to page Jane immediately if Julia ever showed up at my school again.

Another time, when my mom was too trashed to drive me home from a friend's sweet sixteen, Julia played chauffeur. And Jane had gone off totally about why she hadn't been called. Not to mention how my mother had fucked up her responsibility to me.

Okay, the Jane-Julia animosity was not caused by my affair with Julia—that was just fuel for an already roaring fire. Julia was a convenient recipient for all the resentment Jane was too proud to reveal to her younger sister whose genius had stolen for a second, irrevocable time all the attention, approval, and love that had been Jane's birthright.

"...And that's a whole other issue..." my aunt seemed to be paddling to safer waters, "whether our private lives can make up for career disappointments."

Julia snorted. "Well, someone has to send the sons and daughters of Beverly Hills therapists to Harvard."

I tried to hang on to the momentary deflection of the intensity by turning to Allie to make a face. But I couldn't divert her, caught up as she was in their conversation, though she couldn't have been hearing it the same. She assailed me with a reassuring glance. Screw it. "Smile at me again and that's it between us."

She stuck out her tongue. I turned back to the monitor.

"...But the bottom line is," Julia pontificated as the camera came in for a close-up, "if that's the ultimate price one must pay for fame, I'm glad—for selfish reasons—to have enjoyed a taste of failure. Gina's welcome to her success." She spoke bitterly, then realizing that perhaps she had gone too far, reached over and took Jane's arm. "I'm sorry, I don't mean..."

Jane patted her hand—rather frantically, I thought—causing Julia to release her grip. I could tell that Jane was controlling herself not to recoil at Julia's touch. My aunt reassured her, "I know you don't. I've said the same thing to myself."

I've said it too.

"You've said it too," Allie remarked, startling me. I turned to her, her face kind, open, concerned.

"Hey, don't look at me. I'm not the one who wants to make it big in the biz," I teased.

When the stage manager summoned me, Allie smoothed my hair, gave me a kiss, and promised me "a quiet evening at home." The designation of her place as 'home' pleased me; however, as I approached the studio, all comforting thoughts were overcome by the presence of two hundred people, three cameras, and a bazillion white-hot lights. I remained off-stage while Jane introduced the segment, then walked out to join her and Julia.

The audience applauded, and Jane embraced me before we took our seats. "Thank you for agreeing to be on the show today. Nita works here as a production assistant, but it's her first time on this side of the camera."

I couldn't help blurting, "And hopefully the last!" The audience tittered. To my surprise, I enjoyed the response.

"Despite your reluctance, why did you decide to come on?"

"Because, appearances to the contrary, you're a much better arm wrestler than I am." This got me a real laugh, and Julia snickered. I realized I had a terrible streak of ham that could easily get out of control. Checking it fast, I added, "I wanted to because you got a lot of flak from the first series that you didn't deserve. Although, to be honest, when you first proposed the idea of the shows on Mom, I wasn't exactly thrilled."

"And why was that?"

I couldn't resist. "Because I thought you would get a lot of flak you didn't deserve." Another laugh—another snicker from Julia—but I didn't want to come off as too much of a smartass. I began to realize the incredible seductiveness of being a 'guest'—no wonder the existence of registries for people who make a career of appearing on the circuit. "You told me people would misunderstand, yet you believed in the idea, and

I've come to see you were right."

Jane took it from there. "My goal was to find out what really happened to your mom, and to express outrage at the way the tabloids were treating her memory. How well do you think I accomplished this?"

It was a question we'd rehearsed, but only now, in the context of the live interview, did I truly consider my answer. "You took care of the stupid rumors. The coroner upheld the police ruling of suicide, yet he acknowledged he couldn't be one hundred per cent positive. You found that hard to take, and I did too." It didn't seem wise to admit on the air that this part of her mission hadn't been reached.

But Jane had no such qualms. "So what you're saying is, I didn't meet that goal?"

She must have had good reason to press me for the truth, so I searched for an honest answer. "You came as close as possible. But realizing I'd never know for sure took some getting used to."

"Will you tell us how have you coped with that?"

As I hesitated, searching for the right words, Julia jumped in, buying me some time. "Incredibly well." The vehemence of her comment surprised me.

But now it was my turn, entering uncertain terrain, trying to explain how I felt without sounding as though I were equivocating. The sight of people leaning forward in their seats didn't make it easier. "If you spend your time concentrating on the answer only, you forget there's a use for not having one. Not every issue can be resolved. For me, the important thing is to learn to live without knowing—and I mean that in a general sense, as well." As soon as the words were out, I recognized how true they had become for me.

Jane responded, "It seems you are learning to live without that certainty, and without her, wouldn't you agree?"

"Yes, but I can't say I needed to lose my mother. I enjoyed her. When she wasn't high, she could be a lot of fun. Wasn't she, Julia?"

"And sometimes even when she was high," she confessed.

Jane redirected the focus to me. "Tell us about the Gina who perhaps only you knew."

I turned to the audience, addressing them directly, something, amazingly, I found easy to do. "I might disappoint you if I tried. She was what you read about. Every cliché about the tortured artist who made life hard for herself. That and…the same good memories you might have about your own mother. Reading to you all night when you had a fever. Buying you the kind of toys she wanted as a kid. Letting you know it didn't matter if you weren't precisely the daughter she bargained for. She was understanding, even if her tolerance was that of an addict who realizes the hell she puts others through because of her own limitations." I was suddenly aware of having spoken too confidentially, breaking the resolve I'd sworn to keep.

Jane leaned forward. "If you can accept someone like your mom despite her limitations, you're ahead of the game."

I felt apprehensive, but kept going. "I lived with it. Whether I accepted it is a whole other show."

Carlos gave the signal for a commercial break. When we came back it would be just my aunt and me. Jane finished the segment by thanking Julia for appearing on the show. "You brought the house down."

Julia beamed. "Wish I could stay longer, but Julia's not getting any younger, and she can't afford to miss a single session…with her personal trainer." She sent me a smirk. The applause as she left the stage was deafening.

After it died down, Jane whispered, "You're doing great."

Her encouragement didn't stop me from being disappointed by her seeming lack of insight. Had she really no clue how uncomfortable I felt, or was she so accustomed to everyone spilling their guts before a nation of viewers she couldn't see it? Once more I was confronted with the profound difference between us. Essentially I was a private person, but a key part of her character was defined by her interaction with the public. The stage was her element, and I was just—a guest. Her personality was driven by a need to both please and control, an impulse I'd never understand. At the core I worried someday it might drive a wedge between us.

Then I remembered something Allie said when we met: We have no choice about what makes us happy. The few laughs I'd won from the audience were enough to make me appreciate the kick Jane got being in front of a camera. I could take it or leave it, but she couldn't live any other way. Judging her negatively for that—and expecting her to share my perspective—was unfair.

"I'm glad you like the way it's going. I'm still nervous," I told her.

Lauren, the makeup artist, came over with her palette of powder and gave Jane a quick once-over. When she approached me, I glared. She chuckled. "Never mind, you're fine."

I looked backstage, trying to catch Allie's attention. When our eyes met, she smiled and gave me a thumbs-up.

The taping resumed, and Jane directed me to my previous thought. "Before we went to commercial, you were talking about the importance of accepting people's limitations."

"I was saying I didn't accept my mother's limitations because she had so many abilities. The way she could move people with her music, her stage presence—she moved me like that in our daily life. She made many of my days special. I appreciated having her in my life. She deserved better than the treatment she got in the tabloids."

"Yes, she did," Jane agreed softly.

I faced her squarely. "What I'm trying to say is, my mother's talent made her life swing way out of balance. Maybe most people are lucky enough to know when they're in danger of going too far, and have the discipline to pull back, but my mother couldn't. She couldn't stop herself from crossing the line...and, in the end, she never came back."

There was silence in the studio, and to fill it, I guess, I just kept going. "I'm always going to be compared to my mother. To people who don't know me, I'll never be talented enough, or sexy enough, or—straight enough. That's fine. Let the tabloids pick her bones." Jane looked kind of shocked, but I didn't stop or apologize. "Maybe it isn't right, but in a sense it's natural. People feed off those who can't defend themselves. We justify our own limitations, and learn when to curb excesses, by fixating on those who can't. That's life. Your show brought that to my attention, to everybody's. Thanks. And if anyone thinks I've been scripted today, they can go to hell."

After a beat, I heard applause. The sound was unexpected; I'd almost forgotten the audience's presence. Jane reached over, hugged me, then motioned Carlos to cut the cameras.

After the show wrapped, Allie and I joined Jane, Sam, and Tonia at the conference table. They complimented me far beyond embarrassment, regarding me with such affection I thought now might be a good time to ask for a raise, the keys to my aunt's Jag, and later, alone with Allie, one of those incredible talk-and-torture sex sessions.

Jane wanted to take us to dinner, but luckily Sam's good sense intervened. "Hon, what in your wildest dreams might make you imagine these two would appreciate spending the evening in any company other than their own?" She turned to us. "Clearly she's not in her right mind."

We got up to go, and I gave Jane a hug. "We will do that dinner, I promise."

"I'll hold you to it." She smiled. "You know, today I didn't mind being upstaged."

I couldn't help myself. "It's because we're family—and family ties can really mess up your mind. Next time I talk to you, you better have your Hollywood priorities straight."

She released me. "Ain't nothing straight about your old aunt. Now take your girlfriend and get the heck out of here."

Allie and I went directly to the car, and as she pulled off the lot, she praised me again. "You did well today, Nita. You made me proud."

"Thanks." I rested a hand on her thigh.

"I can hardly wait to see the reviews tomorrow, after we air. I know they'll be terrific. You'll get mail galore. But I'm warning you, I'm going to personally answer each piece, and let all those women know they're wasting their time."

I smiled. We approached the street where we'd often retreated for 'discussions' inappropriate to the workplace.

"Park," I said.

She shut off the engine and turned to me. Our kiss banished all memory of those disagreements. Then she took me home.

MORE BOOKS FROM NEW VICTORIA PUBLISHERS
PO BOX 27, NORWICH, VERMONT 05055
OR CALL 1-800 326-5297   EMAIL newvic@aol.com
Home page   http://www.opendoor.com/NewVic/

FLIGHT FROM CHADOR Sigrid Brunel $10.95

Anouk Turabi, an Egyptian woman pilot receives an urgent plea to rescue a woman from a forced marriage in Yemen. Anouk and lover, American photographer Karen sneak into Yemen, disguised as man and wife, but rigid Islamic laws test their love in this death-defying thriller.
About Brunel's writing: *"Strongly evocative prose and an undercurrent of eroticism."*
"This author skillfully blends intrigue, romance…

MURDER AT THE MARINA Carlene Miller $11.95

Reporter Lexy Hyatt's stay on a friend's boat turns sinister when a body is found floating in the lake. Lexy investigates, hoping to clear her new-found community, till she discovers that a friend is hiding the murder weapon
What reviewers said about the first in the series *Killing at The Cat*:
"…A superb mystery that is smoothly crafted and plays fair with the reader."

CALLALOO & Other Lesbian Love Tales   La Shonda K. Barnett $10.95

When stepping into these snapshots of lesbian lives you join this promising new author in her celebration of the ways we nourish ourselves and the women we love. LaShonda K. Barnett is an exciting young black lesbian voice.

RAFFERTY STREET   Lee Lynch $10.95

Memorable characters from her previous novels populate this glimpse into Morton River Valley and the ongoing class struggles among its citizens.
"A novel reflecting a spectrum of current events, Rafferty Street captures the emotional upheaval faced by a workingclass dyke and the strength engendered from her steadfast friends." -Terri de la Pena

SOLITAIRE AND BRAHMS   Sarah Dreher $12.95

From the author of the Stoner Mctavish series, a gritty, painstaking look at the struggle for lesbian identity before Stonewall. Shelby Camden wonders why her impending marriage seem to constrict her to the point of depression and drink. Then she meets the independent Fran Jarvis, with whom she finds she can share her innermost thoughts.

DREAMS OF A WOMAN WHO LOVED SEX Tee A Corinne $13.95

Before Susie Bright and Annie Sprinkle there was Tee Corinne, celebrating the beauty and the joy of women's sexuality. Illustrated withher stunningly sensual photographs.
"Here is lyrical confirmation,… that sex is wonderful and right." —Ann Bannon

SKIN TO SKIN Martha Miller $12.95

Nineteen stories sharing the intimate, evocative, romantic moments of women's lives.
"Martha Miller is one of my favorite erotic writers." —Susie Bright

BACKSTAGE PASS, Interviews with Women in Music Laura Post $16.95

Ani DiFranco, Alix Dobkin, Joan Osborne and more, An intimate glimpse into the personal and political lives of these rock, folk and jazz musicians.

LADY GOD Lesa Luders $9.95

Landy flees the mountains where she grew up. Claire befriends her helping Landy to untangle her sexuality, still bound up in an incestuous relationship with her mother.

ICED Judith Alguire $10.95

An action-packed novel of women's professional ice hockey. Alison jumps at the chance to coach the Toronto Teddies. It gets complicated when she falls in love with one of her players.

DOG TAGS Alexis Jude $9.95

Two female soldiers in Korea struggling to create a loving relationship in the face of harassment and homophobia.

WINDSWEPT Magdalena Zschokke $10.95

Women's sailing adventures. Mara, Olivia and Zoë come to an understanding of themselves and their goal of an all-women crew.

MYSTERIES BY SARAH DREHER

"The touchstone of Dreher's writing is her wit and her compassion for her characters. I don't think I have ever read better or funnier dialogue anywhere." —Visibilities

SHAMAN'S MOON The seventh Stoner McTavish Mystery is here at last.
A Lambda Literary Award winner *"A beguiling blend of fantasy, mystery and humor. (The series) works because she draws her characters so freshly and convincingly."*
—San Francisco Chronicle $12.95

STONER McTAVISH $9.95

The first in the series introduces us to travel agent Stoner McTavish. On a trip to the Tetons, Stoner rescues dream lover, Gwen from danger and almost certain death.

SOMETHING SHADY $8.95

Stoner finds herself an inmate, trapped in the clutches of the evil psychiatrist Dr. Milicent Tunes. Can Gwen and Aunt Hermione charge to the rescue before it's too late?

GRAY MAGIC $9.95

Stoner finds herself an unwitting combatant in a struggle between the Hopi spirits of Good and Evil.

A CAPTIVE IN TIME $10.95

Stoner mysteriously finds herself in Colorado Territory, time 1871.

OTHERWORLD $10.95

On vacation at Disney World. In a case of mistaken identity, Marylou is kidnapped and held hostage in an underground tunnel.

BAD COMPANY $10.95

Stoner and Gwen investigate accidents and sabotage that threaten a women's theater company in Maine.

SEND FOR FREE CATALOG

NEW VICTORIA PO BOX 27 NORWICH, VT 05055
CALL 1-800 326 5297   email newvic@aol.com